W9-BAL-611

TIME SPUN OUT AND NEITHER OF THEM MOVED.

Or stopped smiling.

Maybe it was the late hour, maybe it was the sense of intimacy created by standing in the darkened shop, or the connection Sean felt they shared, lives being abruptly changed, or simply a childhood of separate but shared memories of growing up in the same town, surrounded by the same things, the same people. Whatever it was, he found himself shifting a step closer. She didn't move away. And all he could think as he dipped his head toward hers was: Why had it taken half of his life to finally work up the nerve to kiss Holly Bennett?

from "Lock, Stock, and Jingle Bells"

BOOK YOUR PLACE ON OUR WEBSITE AND MAKE THE READING CONNECTION!

We've created a customized website just for our very special readers, where you can get the inside scoop on everything that's going on with Zebra, Pinnacle and Kensington books.

When you come online, you'll have the exciting opportunity to:

- View covers of upcoming books

- Read sample chapters

- Learn about our future publishing schedule (listed by publication month *and author*)

- Find out when your favorite authors will be visiting a city near you

- Search for and order backlist books from our online catalog

- Check out author bios and background information

- Send e-mail to your favorite authors

- Meet the Kensington staff online

- Join us in weekly chats with authors, readers and other guests

- Get writing guidelines

- AND MUCH MORE!

**Visit our website at
http://www.kensingtonbooks.com**

Kissing Santa Claus

Donna Kauffman
Jill Shalvis
HelenKay Dimon

BRAVA

KENSINGTON PUBLISHING CORP.

http://www.kensingtonbooks.com

BRAVA BOOKS are published by

Kensington Publishing Corp.
119 West 40th Street
New York, NY 10018

Compilation copyright © 2009 by Kensington Publishing Corp.
"Lock, Stock, and Jingle Bells" copyright © 2009 by Donna
Kauffman
"Bah, Handsome!" copyright © 2009 by Jill Shalvis
"It's Hotter at Christmas" copyright © 2009 by HelenKay Dimon

All rights reserved. No part of this book may be reproduced in any
form or by any means without the prior written consent of the
Publisher, excepting brief quotes used in reviews.

If you purchased this book without a cover you should be aware
that this book is stolen property. It was reported as "unsold and de-
stroyed" to the Publisher and neither the Author nor the Publisher
has received any payment for this "stripped book."

All Kensington titles, imprints, and distributed lines are available at
special quantity discounts for bulk purchases for sales promotion,
premiums, fund-raising, educational, or institutional use.

Special book excerpts or customized printings can also be created
to fit specific needs. For details, write or phone the office of the
Kensington Special Sales Manager: Attn. Special Sales Department.
Kensington Publishing Corp., 119 West 40th Street, New York, NY
10018. Phone: 1-800-221-2647.

Brava and the B logo Reg. U.S. Pat. & TM Off.

ISBN-13: 978-0-7582-3885-6
ISBN-10: 0-7582-3885-1

First Brava Books Trade Paperback Printing: October 2009
First Brava Books Mass-Market Paperback Printing: October 2010

10 9 8 7 6 5 4 3 2 1

Printed in the United States of America

Contents

Lock, Stock, and Jingle Bells

Donna Kauffman

For Laura . . .
because she gets it

1

Holly Berry Bennett hated Christmas. It was all her parents' fault, really. She was born ten days early, on Christmas Eve—ruining every birthday forever—and christened with a name that other children would mock well beyond adolescence. Her father, a family accountant, had been more excited by the really nice write-off she'd provided than anything else, and, when confronted with her schoolyard-provoked tears, had cluelessly chuckled that it could have been worse; they could have named her Mistletoe.

Her mother, on the other hand, would only have been more thrilled had her only child waited at least three more hours and been born on Christmas Day proper. Her mother loved Christmas more than anything, and would celebrate it 365 days a year if she could. And, by launching Santa's Workshop, a crafts, antiques, and collectibles store dedicated to all things Christmas, Beverly Bennett did.

Or had.

Holly stared out the window of the jumbo 757 as it lifted off . . . leaving Heathrow, her little London flat, and the entire life she'd built for herself in England all behind her. So, okay, maybe that life hadn't exactly turned out to be all she'd hoped for. But it was her life, dammit.

Now she was heading back to the States, back home. To her mother's life.

She fingered the set of keys that weighed heavily in her jacket pocket. Keys to her old life . . . keys to the life she'd fled all the way across an entire ocean to get away from. Keys to her past . . . and now, not a little terrifyingly, her future. Her immediate one, at least.

She tipped her head back and closed her eyes, but all she saw was what awaited her. Santa's Workshop. Owned and operated by . . . Holly Bennett.

Heaven help them all.

What had her mother been thinking? Or drinking? When Holly had made her annual trip home for Thanksgiving, the very last thing she'd expected to receive along with her mother's perfectly roasted turkey and oyster stuffing was the shock of her life . . . and the keys to the family store.

Her parents had calmly informed her that they had a buyer for the family home—the one they'd moved into almost fifty years ago as newlyweds, the very one she'd grown up in, and had been fairly certain both her parents would live out their days in—and had already purchased lakefront property in a senior community in Florida. Which they'd giddily announced they'd already begun moving into to start their brand-new, retired life.

Holly had simply stared—gaped, really—half tempted to rush her mother to the nearest hospital for a full neurological workup. None of it had made sense. It still didn't. This wasn't how things were supposed to work out. Her dad would be running his accounting business out of the detached garage-turned-office and her mother would run Santa's Workshop, until they were both too frail and old to do so—and even then, she'd pictured quite the battle. Her parents were now in their early seventies. She'd figured she had at least another decade, possibly more knowing them, before that battle would begin in earnest. Until then, she'd stay safely tucked away in London.

At eighteen she'd gone sailing off to college. Literally. To Oxford, in England. No following in her parents' footsteps. She wanted to be a painter, with her work displayed in the most interesting galleries from the West End to Milan, from SoHo to San Francisco.

She'd ended up in advertising. Which was not exactly the same thing, but was at least creative and occasionally called on her skills with pen and brush. However, her career enabled her to keep a roof over her head and still dabble on the occasional canvas when she could find the time. Italy, Spain, Portugal. Germany, Switzerland, Austria. All had provided stunning backdrops to her occasional artist forays. She'd worn out several rail passes and filled many canvases. It kept her sane in the demanding world of advertising . . . which she didn't love. But it paid the rent. And kept her far away from home and hearth.

It wasn't that she didn't love her parents; she did. They meant well. And while they might not have had the first clue how to raise their unexpected late-in-life child—she'd grown up in a house that was more a museum than an actual home a person could live in (Holly, don't touch that! Don't sit there! Leave the figurines alone!)—they were definitely made for each other. And the three of them had long since settled into a comfortable pattern of happy coexistence. They bugged her about not waiting too long to get married and start a family, she bugged them about not waiting too long to retire and get a life . . . each fairly certain their admonitions were going in one ear and out the other, and everyone was content. Right up until the day they took her advice.

It had been two weeks since she found out and she still couldn't wrap her head around it. Any part of it. She couldn't imagine her father spending time on a golf course and not umbilically attached to his calculators and computers and endless shelves of bound volumes on the most recent tax legislation. And her mother . . . how in the world was she going to embrace life in a place that never even had a frost, a place where Santa was often seen sporting board shorts and buddied up with flamingos?

And yet . . . Holly had never heard them sounding happier. They truly were giddy with it. Both of them had been lifelong workaholics, dedicated to vocations they dearly loved as much as they dearly loved each other . . . and, in their own absentminded way, their daughter, who had largely raised herself, with the help of this housekeeper or that and the occasional babysitter. But now? Now they were two of the most relaxed, happy, laid-back strangers she'd ever met. How could she be mad at that? Hadn't she been telling them they needed that very thing for years?

She'd just never seriously entertained the idea that they'd actually do it. Nor had it ever crossed her mind that her mother would leave Holly the family business. Why? Why would she do that? Holly knew what her mother had said. She couldn't bear to sell it to a stranger, and the few employees she had were all retirees who weren't interested in taking on the full-time burden. And she couldn't possibly sit there and sell off her precious, beloved pieces, one by one. She simply couldn't bear it.

So, she'd bequeathed it—a little early—lock, stock, and jingle bells, to her only daughter. Holly had always figured that, at some future point, when her mother passed on, she'd be faced with the burden of dismantling the shop and doing with it whatever one did with such a thing. Never once in her wildest dreams—or darkest nightmares—had she contemplated it would be dumped in her lap while her mother was still alive and kicking . . . and would know exactly what was being done with it.

And, to make it even better, Christmas was in ten days. Which meant her thirtieth birthday was in nine. Double goody.

If she planned to keep the shop, it couldn't stay closed, which her mother had reminded her during her most recent phone call. Her mother, who had been packing for the three-week Mediterranean cruise she and Holly's father were taking. In December. During High Season. High, having to be the operative word, Holly was certain. Her mother hadn't even sounded twitchy when she discussed the store. She and her father had been far too busy, running off to play cards, going out to the theater, visiting Sea World. Sea World. With friends. They had dozens of them now, apparently. They'd had their home in Frostproof—a name they both found hysterically funny—for all of three months now. It was like they'd run away to summer camp for seniors. Permanently.

One thing was very certain. They weren't coming back.

Holly stared at the thickening layer of clouds, still fingering the keys in her pocket. She had taken the remainder of her annual holiday time and the rest of her sick leave to come back and sort things out. Which meant she had a whole two weeks and three days to figure out what in the hell she was going to do with the new life that had been dumped on her.

It didn't seem like near enough.

2

Sean Gallagher loved Christmas. It brought back some of his very best memories. Leaving Willow Creek, Virginia, and going on holiday to his grandparents' farm in Cork, Ireland, spending time with the tumble and chaos of his very large, very extended family, with more cousins than even he could keep track of. He loved the rich, centuries-old family traditions that had gone along with it, from the food, to the decorations, to the music, and to the storytelling. He always wanted to stay longer, had always left happier, eager for summer to come, when he got to go back again for school break. But even those long, languid summers couldn't compete with the twelve days he got to spend each year during the Christmas season.

His grandparents were gone now. His parents were, too. But the rest of that very extended, chaotic family still existed and thrived, and had been in large part the reason why he'd regained his focus and perspective after such a devastating and sudden loss. The Gallagher clan thrived in both Willow Creek and County Cork, but as he'd taken over running the family restaurant after his parents' death, it was a rare occasion now when he was able to go over and see the Ireland-based side of the clan. And definitely not at Christmas.

Sean unlocked the front door to the restaurant, then positioned the large, oak-framed chalkboard at an angle so his customers would see the day's specials upon entering through the heavily carved doors with the stained glass, mullioned windows, both hand-crafted by some of his Corkborn cousins. He turned to head back to the kitchen, knowing the day was going to be a busy one, but paused when he saw a car pull up in front of Beverly Bennett's store across the street. It was an airport taxi. He continued watching.

Everyone in Willow Creek had been stunned when Bev and Stan Bennett had up and retired. He still couldn't quite believe it. When he'd gone over to give her and Stan his best wishes, and ask what she intended to do with the place, she'd stunned him again when she assured him that Holly was coming home from England to run it. However, in the ensuing weeks, Sean hadn't seen any sign of that. The store had remained locked up and dark, through what was easily the busiest time of the winter season for their little Civil War town. In fact, it had gotten to the point where the only car he'd expected to see pulling up in front of the brightly painted row house shop was one with a Realtor inside.

But it wasn't a Realtor who climbed out of the black and white cab.

It was Holly Bennett.

He'd known the Bennetts his entire life, but, for the past seven years as fellow business owners, they'd developed a true friendship based on mutual respect and support. Still . . . Sean couldn't deny that hearing that their only daughter might come back to town had been welcome news.

He'd had a crush on little Holly Bennett for as long as he could remember. Not actively the past dozen or so years since she'd been gone. She only came home on Thanksgiving, and that was crunch time for him business-wise. So, other than a passing wave, he hadn't really ever been given the opportunity to see if there might still be an ember or two left over from the flames he'd always wanted to fan back in their high school days, but had never worked up the nerve to try.

So, despite knowing the hubbub and controlled chaos that awaited him back in the kitchens, and his cluttered office as well, he took the time to indulge himself in watching her climb out of the cab. She really hadn't changed much from high school. Sure she was more polished, presumably more mature, her features and her fashion sense a bit more refined. But her dark brown hair still swung around her shoulders like a shiny, silky curtain, and even in her smartly belted, British tweed coat, she was still a slight little thing who looked like she might blow over in a stiff wind. He knew better. She might be nothing like her gregarious, outgoing, fireplug of a mother, but he knew from growing up in the same small town as she that she not only had her father's reed-thin frame, but his reserved, rock-steady strength as well.

It hadn't surprised him a bit when, as a barely turned eighteen-year-old, she'd moved a continent away to continue her education. Or that she'd stayed to build a life for herself in such a metropolitan, worldly city as London. He had no doubt she could handle whatever life threw at her. She'd been preternaturally poised as far back as he could remember.

He watched as the cab pulled away, leaving her with a single piece of luggage and what looked like a computer bag slung over her shoulder. She didn't immediately go inside. Instead she stood, curbside, and stared up at the store that had become part of her family decades before either Sean or Holly had come into the world. Sean knew the whole story by now. Bev had grown up in Willow Creek and had started dating Stan while completing her business degree at the University of Virginia in Charlottesville.

Stan had been a few years older, born in Charlottesville, but had inherited a family home in Willow Creek and was establishing his own accounting business there. They'd been planning their wedding by the time she graduated and took over the dusty little antique book shop in town from Old Lady Haversham. Both Bev and Stan had poured everything into their respective businesses, and took the same kind of pride and joy in watching them grow and flourish as most folks did with their children. Holly had come along much later. In fact, though Sean was a few years older than Holly, his parents had been several decades younger than hers.

Like Holly, Sean had gone away for college, too, only he'd just gone as far as the Culinary Institute in New York. He loved his family dearly, but while his mother and father had built the family restaurant in Willow Creek using cooking skills they'd learned at the elbows of Sean's grandparents, great-aunts and -uncles, on both sides of the ocean, he'd wanted classical training. He'd envisioned opening his own place in the nation's capital, attracting the locals, the politicians, and the out-of-towners. There were Michelin stars in his future, he'd been sure of it. And though he'd missed being in the middle of the boisterous Gallagher clan, he'd only been a train ride away, and the visits back and forth had been frequent in both directions. His parents and the rest of the family had supported his dreams and he loved them all the more for that.

And then, in one night, everything changed. His life, his dreams, his foundation, his strength. Instead of moving to D.C. and beginning the climb toward opening his own place, his parents' death had brought the brand-new culinary graduate back to Willow Creek instead. But while he still missed them both, every day, he'd never regretted the new path fate had set him on. As it turned out, he loved running Gallagher's, loved having family and lifelong friends surrounding him. He wondered if he'd ever have been so truly fulfilled with his old dreams, but was too busy, too content and focused on the here and now to really give it much thought.

Staring at Holly, he remembered what it had been like, coming back. Only he'd come back into the warm embrace of extended family, sharing their grief over a devastating loss. She was coming home to an early inheritance, her parents happily alive and kicking up their heels in the Mediterranean right about now. So . . . no grief, no tragedy to overcome. But, perhaps, a similar weight of sudden obligation on her slender shoulders. Did she resent it? Was she happy to be back?

He couldn't fathom what it would be like to come home to, well, no home, actually—he knew the house was newly occupied by a young couple with toddlers—and no family waiting with open arms. Only a darkened shop welcomed her back. She'd always been quiet, smart, focused. He remembered how he'd catch her watching his boisterous, crazy family with a combination of terror and wonder in her oh-so-serious deep brown eyes, and wonder what she was thinking. Her family was the opposite of his: small, neat, tidy. But friendly. He'd always found Mrs. Bennett's holiday world somewhat amazing and the woman herself nothing short of a wonder. He enjoyed the friendship they'd developed, and had often spent time chatting with her at her shop when he'd bring her dinner on the nights she checked in this late shipment or that. He'd enjoyed Mr. Bennett, too, and could see where Holly got her seriousness and quiet demeanor from. He wasn't much of a talker, but he was dedicated to his wife and their business, and Sean respected both. He still couldn't really process that they were off playing golf and cruising the high seas. It was almost impossible to picture it.

He watched Holly and thought maybe there was a grieving of an entirely different sort taking place there. The fact that she'd had the taxi drop her off at the shop with a single suitcase indicated a certain level of ambivalence. But what did he know? And why did he care?

"Sean! There you are. You've got O'Hara on the phone, barking mad about the fish order, and the damn grinder is acting up again. What the bloody hell are you doing?"

Sean waved a hand back at his cousin Mickey. "You know how to fix the grinder, and tell O'Hara that if he hadn't tried to pawn off that load of crap scallops on me, I wouldn't have canceled my order and gone to Halloran's instead. His loss."

"Sean—"

"Handle it, Mick." And, without really giving it any actual thought, he strolled straight across the street.

3

"Hey, let me help you with that."

At the sound of the deep voice, Holly spun around. Sean Gallagher. The living, breathing embodiment of every single one of her high school fantasies. Feverish fantasies, they'd been, too. Of course, popular Sean, football and basketball star Sean, cheerleader-of-the-week girlfriend Sean, had never once paid her the slightest bit of attention. When they were in school, anyway. Of course she'd seen him almost every day of her life outside of school, given their parents ran businesses across the street from one another.

He'd nod on occasion, even wave to her when he was alone. But most often he was surrounded by a half dozen teammates and friends, or two to three times that in Gallagher's, and Holly hadn't the first clue what to do with a person like that. Especially when that person featured very prominently in every daydream and night fantasy she'd ever had. So, like the awkward geek that she'd been back then, she'd stare back at him, likely with a deer in headlights look, then duck into the shop and hide. All the while bitterly chastising herself for not being more forward and confident in herself when given such perfect openings.

Thankfully, her mother had never had a clue. One of the few times Bev Bennett's total absorption in running the shop had worked in Holly's favor. The instant Holly had popped into the store after school, or debate team practice, or art club, her mother would sigh in relief at the extra pair of hands and put her straight to work. On those days where Sean had privately favored her with that big smile of his, she was thankful for both the haven and the distraction. Today, neither were readily available. The store was locked up and there was no bustle of customers to demand attention.

Just big, broad-shouldered, blue-eyed, dark-haired, brightly smiling Sean Gallagher.

Who, at thirty-two, was only about a million times hotter than he'd been at eighteen. She was afraid the same could and would never be said of her. No amount of London polish would turn the small town mouse into a big city swan. She clutched the handle of her suitcase like it was her only lifeline to safety. "I—that's okay," she stuttered as he drew closer. "I've got it."

Her less-than-commanding self-confidence didn't exactly stop him in his tracks.

"Those boots look great, but I'm guessing they're not much on traction," he said quite genially, as if they were longtime friends who'd simply bumped into each other. "I'm sure you weren't expecting to come home to slush and ice. Here." He reached her side and gently, but quite decidedly, took hold of her suitcase handle. He propped his elbow out in an offer of personal support as well.

Clearly he had no clue whatsoever that he was a far greater threat to her equilibrium than any ice storm or three-inch boot heels could ever hope to be. The thought that, after all these years, he was not only standing right in front of her, talking to her, and smiling that devastatingly gorgeous smile at her, but wanted her to put her hands on him? Okay, just one hand. But still: It made her feel utterly ridiculous to still be so affected by him this many years later, when, obviously, the reverse had always been, and forever would be, true. Which . . . duh.

So, with everything else she was struggling to deal with at that moment, including a maelstrom of emotions ranging from confusing, heart-tugging homesickness to abject terror that she wouldn't be able to run away from it ever again, the additional hormonal surge of seeing Sean Gallagher up close and personal was simply one too many things to tackle.

"Thank you, but I'll be fine," she said, striving to sound a little more in charge of herself, made harder by the fact that, even in heels, she still had to look up what felt like a mile or so, to where he towered over her.

"Holly Bennett," he said, making her name sound almost . . . reverent.

Clearly she was hallucinating that last part. Leftover dregs of her teenage fantasies. Serious jet lag. Whatever. She was exhausted and stressed out and he was just standing there, all casually godlike. Anyone would have a hard time thinking straight. "Yes," she said, somewhat stupidly, in response, but not knowing, really, what else to say to that.

"It's me, Sean," he said, then added, "Gallagher."

As if she might not be aware.

"I—right. It's—uh, yes. Yes, I know who you are. And—well, it's a pleasure. Sean. To see you. Again." She stuck her hand out. It was that or start digging a hole straight to China. And there she was, with no shovel.

He grinned and took her hand, but rather than give it a polite, casual little shake, he held on to it. In fact, went so far as to cover it with his other hand, apparently completely unaware what that did to her already overloaded hormonal circuits, considering he just stood there, smiling down at her with something that looked like a mix of delight and affection plastered all over his handsome face.

It was that affection part that totally froze her up. Reverting her back to sixteen, when all she could do was stare. God only knew what expression was on her face. All she knew was that his hands were big and warm . . . and her body was swiftly following suit on the latter part.

She'd like to think a dozen years living independently in London, in the fast-paced world of advertising, would have long pushed her past her shyness and the paralyzing fear that always came with speaking in front of groups. Sometimes groups of one. Especially when they looked and sounded like Sean Gallagher. And, back in London, she most definitely had. She wouldn't have made a very successful art director if she hadn't. And she had been. Successful. But that was business. This . . . she didn't know what this was. All she knew was she was a long way from London, and her smart, confident, savvy London self hadn't apparently made the trans-Atlantic flight along with her.

Standing there, staring, she still felt exactly like the awkward sophomore she'd once been, looking at all of his senior perfection and feeling her tongue tie into knots. Right along with her stomach.

"I miss your folks," he said as they continued to stand there, and stare. "But I got a postcard and note from your mom from their cruise ship. Sounds like retirement is agreeing with them."

"Yes, yes it is," she said, finally coming out of her pheromone stupor and slipping her hand from his. "Well, I shouldn't keep you. I'd—I'd better get inside and—" She glanced at the store and faltered. She had no idea what she was going to do when she got inside, so she just plastered a smile on her face and grabbed the handle of her suitcase before he could again. "Good to see you."

"I heard you were coming back to take over the store," he said as she bumped her suitcase up the curb and fumbled with the keys.

"I—" She didn't know yet what she'd come back to do, or not do, but she wasn't going to tell him that. "Right." Finally, blessedly, she turned the lock and the dead bolt and swung the door open.

"I'm glad you're back in town, Holly Bennett."

She glanced back at him, standing there, hands shoved in his pockets, chef apron tied perfectly around his hips, somehow looking all the more manly for it. He also looked like he was freezing.

"Me, too," she said inanely, for the lack of any real reply of substance. Or honesty.

Just then someone stuck their head out of the front door of the restaurant. Where Sean's hair was a dark, thick mop of waves, this head was closely shorn and red. But the easy grin and dancing eyes proclaimed him yet another Gallagher. And, if that wasn't enough, the thick brogue was final proof.

"Sean, me boy, we're sinkin' in here, doncha know. And O'Hara's called back twice now. I think you can get quite a deal on the mahi mahi and the scallops both if you play it right. You can flirt about later." He sent a small salute and a wink toward Holly. "Unless I finish me chores first."

"Right, Mick," Sean called back, never once taking his own twinkling eyes off of Holly. "My cousin," he told her, by way of explanation. "Come from Cork to spend the holidays. And make my life even more impossible, that one," he finished, doing a fine imitation of a brogue himself.

"I'll let you get back to it," Holly said, feeling just as she had all those years ago, watching his unruly, boisterous clan tumble and wrestle about. Part envious of what it must be like, to always know you had the bosom and embrace of a big family to sink into anytime . . . and part petrified of what it would be like to never have a moment or thought completely and entirely to yourself. She tore her gaze away and dragged her bag through the door.

"Welcome home," Sean called out, sketching a salute of his own before jogging back across the street and through the door his cousin was still holding for him.

"Home," Holly echoed as she closed the door behind her. She turned to look at the shadowed room, lined with crammed full shelves and dotted with the odd, eclectic antique furnishings. It was a place she knew like the back of her own hand . . . every aisle, every shelf, every tile of the floor. And which, at that moment, seemed completely alien to her now that she was totally in charge of them. Owned them, in fact. It was cold. And dusty. And dank smelling. Things her mother's place had never been.

Except it wasn't her mother's place any longer.

She tucked her hands under folded arms, trying to ward off a chill that had little to do with the heat being turned down and the electricity switched off.

Home.

All that was left of it, anyway. Holly started to tremble a little as she allowed her gaze to travel the depth and breadth of the place. Her place. Now that she was standing here, the real enormity of the decision her mother had left her to make hit her full force. It made her want to call her mother right then and there and angrily demand to know how in the hell she could do something like this to her. Or jump back in the taxi, race back to the airport, and flee once again to London, where she'd send word to Florida that, thanks, but no thanks, then simply get on with her life.

But the taxi was gone. And so were her parents. At least until after the new year. She glanced across the street, to the yellow glow that emanated through the windows and door of Gallagher's. Warm and inviting. With people talking, working, knowing, and understanding their purpose.

She looked back at the interior of the shop, her shop . . . and wished like hell she had even an inkling of what that felt like. Because, standing there, finally ensconced once again in the cheerful, fairy-tale world of Christmas her mother had so lovingly built and tended to, Holly felt no rush of longing, no ache of homesickness that made her want to cling to the familiarity of the past. She hadn't realized until just then that, somewhere in her mind, perhaps she'd been hoping—praying—that that would be what happened.

Instead, the reality was that she felt even less connected to this place than she ever had before.

"Bah, humbug, dammit," she muttered, giving in to the feelings that had plagued her since her mother had handed her the keys with that knowing smile and face full of hope. She dragged her bag farther inside and locked the door behind her. "Merry freaking Christmas."

4

Sean was distracted all day. Night, too. He found himself putting in far more front-of-house appearances than usual. Not because there were service issues, or because he wanted to spend more time chatting up new customers, although he managed to deflect a few of the former, and make sure the passing-through-towners were having an enjoyable meal. No, he found any excuse to be in the front of the restaurant because that was where he could look across the street. To where Holly Bennett was currently residing. Like some kind of lovesick teenager, mooning over the girl who got away. Which . . . well, it was certainly a lot easier for her to get away when the guy never, exactly, did anything about getting her.

It was closing in on one in the morning when he was finally ready to lock up and leave. Only, instead of heading out into the small rear lot reserved for him and his employees, climbing into his truck, and heading home . . . he headed out the front door, boxed meal in hand, and went across the street to Santa's Workshop. The lights in the front of the store were off, but there was a golden glow seeping out from somewhere in the rear of the store, which he happened to know was where Bev's office was. Or, he supposed that would be Holly's office, now. So he was doing the neighborly thing . . . bringing over a hot meal for the new kid in town, freshly off a long flight from the U.K. Neighborly. Friendly. That was Sean Gallagher, all right.

"You are so full of shit," he muttered as he tapped lightly on the glass pane of the front door. When no one appeared from the back, he knocked a bit harder. He didn't want to startle her, but how else was he going to play Good Samaritan unless she knew he was standing outside her door, at one o'clock in the morning, freezing his ass off . . . being neighborly.

He was just about to turn away when he saw her poke her head around the corner leading to the back of the store. He waved and lifted the box in his hand so she could see it.

She didn't exactly come running to unlock the door, but she didn't wave him off, either. It was a start. He laughed silently at himself. How pathetic was this? He could hear his assorted cousins and relatives now. *You've a full life, Sean Gallagher, but when it comes to the fairer sex, you're a sad, sorry man. Women throwing themselves at you all but nightly, yet you subject yourself to this.*

Of course, said women usually came into Gallagher's in packs, and had imbibed perhaps more than what was strictly recommended, then simply behaved accordingly. Not exactly the sort of behavior to get his attention, at least not in a positive way. His cousins—the female ones—told him women needed the extra courage of a drink or two because he was "too intimidating" to approach. Good looking, successful, single, usually topped their list of reasons why, along with workaholic, no life, unwilling to commit to anything other than running the restaurant. The male side of the family mostly scratched their collective heads and wondered, aloud, and at great length, why he wasn't taking them all to bed. Hourly. And not necessarily one at a time.

He basically avoided the conversations regarding his bachelor status, especially after hitting thirty, rather than subject himself to their endless and highly detailed theories, and worse, their plans to "fix" the situation. Which, to his mind, didn't need fixing. Yes, most of the Gallagher clan began adding to the massive, mutant-size family tree long before his ripe old age of thirty-two. But most of them didn't carry the burdens he did, either, even if he did so willingly. He considered his life to be a full and content one. It just also happened to be one that wasn't all that conducive to conducting a long-term relationship.

Which was the other sad, sorry truth of why he was standing outside Holly's door in the middle of the night, a box of food in one hand and a hopeful smile on his face. The wee hours were pretty much his only free time. He watched as she unlocked the door, noting that her smile had been brief and not entirely welcoming. In fact, she looked quite tired and perhaps a bit more weary around the eyes—which weren't currently making any direct contact with his—than simply a long flight followed by a long day and now night, might warrant. He'd thought a personally cooked meal might be welcome, but now he wondered if perhaps she was more in need of a warm shoulder.

"Hey," he said when she pushed the door open. "I was closing up and saw your light was still on back there. I used to bring your mom a meal on occasion when she was doing the books or working on orders late. I thought you might appreciate one as well. I know it's been a long day for you."

She did look at him then, and before she could mask

the weariness with a polite smile, her expression said it all. Long day didn't begin to cover it, apparently. "I—that's very nice of you. You really didn't need to. I ordered down at Jimmy's earlier, for a sub."

He could have told her it had been over eight hours ago when he'd seen Jimmy's little brother pulling up in front of Santa's Workshop with the carryout sign stuck to the roof of his pickup truck, but then he'd have to explain why he'd been noticing things like that. "It's shepherd's pie," he told her. "You can always reheat it tomorrow. It's always better the second day anyway. There's a salad in there, too. And some rolls."

She took the bag from him. "You really didn't have to go to all that trouble."

"It's no trouble. I do it for a living, remember?" He was trying to alleviate the tension a little, put her at ease, but it appeared she was well beyond standing around making polite small talk. Not that he could blame her. "Is everything okay?" he heard himself ask, then immediately wanted to kick himself for doing so. Clearly she was not okay, and just as clearly, she didn't appreciate being not okay in front of him. Still, it wasn't in him to just turn and walk away.

She frowned briefly, seemingly surprised by the question, then her expression smoothed again. "It's been a long day; there's a lot to do." She lifted the bag. "Thank you for this; it was very thoughtful."

"If there's anything else I can do to help—"

"You've already gone above and beyond the call of duty here."

"Like I said, it's what I do, and I saw the light on." He tried a smile. "I also make a good listener. Family my size, you learn early. It can't be easy, leaving England, coming back to your hometown, taking over the business."

She held the bag a little closer to her chest, like a shield, but didn't say anything.

"If it helps, I know a little something about that."

She dipped her chin, and he found himself reaching out to tip it back up again. "Hey, I didn't say that to make you feel bad. But I do know about having plans derailed and a life you never thought you'd end up with being dumped in your lap."

She stared into his eyes and for the first time he felt he was really looking at Holly Bennett.

"You probably think I'm being a bit of a spoiled brat," she said. "I mean, you came home because of an unspeakable tragedy, while my parents just retired. Which, at their age—"

"Yes, but most parents don't retire and head off to a new life and dump their old life on their only child."

She tilted her head slightly. "I thought you and my parents were friends."

"We are. I love your folks. But that doesn't mean I automatically vouch for all their decisions."

"Did you regret coming back to run your family restaurant? You seem—"

"Happy? I am. Very. And I didn't necessarily expect to be. Turned out that all my training has benefited me just as much, if not more, in taking over Gallagher's as it would have if I'd gone off on my own in D.C. like I planned. But I was lucky. I was already heading in a direction very similar to my folks, and their folks before them. It was more a detour down the same path than a whole new journey."

"If you had come back and hadn't been happy . . . would you have stayed anyway?"

"I don't know. I have the benefit of coming from a very large family. So, it's possible I'd have trained one of them, or a handful of them, to take over, and I'd have gone back to my original plan of opening a more upscale establishment. They'd have only been a few hours apart, so it's possible I could have run one and overseen the management of the other."

"Why didn't you go ahead and do that anyway? Have your cake and all that?"

He smiled easily. "Because I am happy here. I learned why it was that generations of Gallaghers have cooked and run restaurants, here and in Ireland. It suits me . . . perhaps more than that other world ever would have. And I still have the training. It's affected the menu here and there. I get to play a little with things that interest me. So I think I am having my cake."

She nodded, then fell silent again, apparently lost in thought.

"You know," he said at length, "you didn't follow in your parents' footsteps, in terms of being a shopkeeper, or even in the antiques business, right? Your mom said you are an artist."

"I'm in advertising."

Sean knew that, but he also knew that, according to her mom, anyway, it was just what paid the bills. Art was her passion. "No one is going to fault you if you decide this isn't for you. Your mom—"

"Says she'd be fine with whatever my decision is."

"Well, then . . . ?"

Holly sighed lightly. "That's what she says. But it's not how I feel. Now that I'm here. I know what this meant to her. If she was truly okay with dismantling it, she'd have done so."

"There's a difference between being okay with it no longer being here . . . and quite another to be the one in charge of taking a beloved possession apart, piece by piece. Maybe she simply didn't have it in her and knew that you being not so emotionally attached might find that easier. I'm not trying to overstep here, but . . . it's your legacy to do with as you please, right? Maybe you should just think of it that way. It could be something you find you enjoy . . . or the sale of it could provide you with the nest egg to pursue your own dreams. Don't you think your parents would be happy with either outcome?"

She held his gaze for the longest time. "What I think is that I wish I could have this conversation as easily with them as I'm having it with you."

He smiled. "I know they're your parents, and nobody knows them better than you do. But if you want an outside friend's opinion—"

"I think I already have it." She smiled then. "And it's appreciated. More than you know."

"Anytime."

Time spun out and neither of them moved. Or stopped smiling.

Maybe it was the late hour, maybe it was the sense of intimacy created by standing in the darkened shop, or the connection he felt they shared, lives being abruptly changed, or simply a childhood of separate but shared memories of growing up in the same town, surrounded by the same things, the same people. Whatever it was, he found himself shifting a step closer. She didn't move away. And all he could think as he slowly dipped his head toward hers was: Why had it taken half of his life to finally work up the nerve to kiss Holly Bennett?

But just before his mouth could brush hers, she took a small step back. "Sean, I—thank you. For the food. I should probably—" She was looking anywhere but at him.

He touched her jaw, turned her face back to his. "It's okay. I understand. Long day. I shouldn't have complicated it further."

She surprised him then, when her lips quirked a little, before she looked away again.

"What?" he prompted, ducking his head to catch her gaze again.

She paused, then took a breath and said, "There was a time when I'd have died and gone to heaven, just thinking there might have been a moment like . . ." She gestured between them.

It was such an unexpected comment, Sean didn't immediately have a response. His body wasn't nearly as slow on the uptake, however, and moved forward of its own volition. "Wait," he said, reaching out, touching her arm. "What did you—what?"

He was close enough, even in the shadowed light, to see the color steal into her cheeks, but perhaps it was his own uncustomary clumsiness that gave her the wherewithal to reply. "When we were teenagers, I . . . I guess you could say I had a crush on you."

"No way."

Now she laughed. "Are you kidding? Even you aren't that humble. You know darn well you were the most popular guy in school. If it was female and had a pulse—"

"I'm not being disingenuous. But . . . you?"

Her eyes widened and she took a big step back. "Wow. Okay, so I know I was dorky and would never give a cheerleader a run for her money, but—"

Belatedly he realized how that had come out. "No, no, that's not what I—Holly." He closed the gap between them, then took the box from her hands and set it on the counter. "I watched you every day for . . . well, it felt like forever. You never looked like you'd give me the time of day. You were so poised, so sure of yourself, so . . . different from the other girls."

She snorted. "Right. They could all get a date."

He turned her face to his again. "Because teenage boys are idiots. Myself included. You have no idea how many times I wanted to say hello to you, but—"

"You can't be serious."

"Dead serious. And, you're right, I didn't have a problem getting dates, but most girls came on to me."

"Poor popular guy, you," she said dryly.

"What I'm trying to say is, you're right, I didn't have to work all that hard at getting the attention of the opposite sex. Except for you."

"I have a hard time—an impossible one, actually—believing for one instant that you spent even a second of your time thinking about nerdy little Holly Bennett."

"You weren't a nerd. You were beautiful. Then, and now. Your hair was always so shiny and you had the prettiest brown eyes. You confused the hell out of me. You always looked so serious, and so . . . focused. Like you knew exactly where you were going."

"Yeah, that was the horn-rim glasses. I was just as clueless as everyone else, trust me."

"You certainly didn't come off that way."

"So, what, you're saying you were too intimidated to approach me? It wasn't like there was a crowd clamoring there. And even if there was, you'd have parted that sea with nothing more than a smile. You could have anyone you wanted. You can't honestly want me to believe you didn't think you had a chance with me."

"I can, because it's the truth. You have to realize, that—and I'm not complaining, but this is just fact—I was very popular, which meant a lot of people, my peers, teachers, coaches, my family, everyone looked up to me as some kind of icon or role model, and it was a lot of pressure, trying to live up to that. I knew what I was good at, but—"

"You were good at everything."

"I was good at taking advantage of sure things. I knew I could play sports. I knew I'd get a yes if I asked out a girl who was all but throwing herself at me. I knew the teachers liked me and that if I showed interest in class, they'd reward me." He tilted her face up to his. "What I didn't know, and was too chicken to find out, was if the one person who seemed completely unaffected by me would return my interest . . . or turn me down flat."

"So, was I just some kind of challenge, then? Get the one girl who isn't chasing after me?"

"If it was just a game, or a contest, I wouldn't have hesitated. I was a very competitive kid."

"So . . . I don't get it."

"I didn't want to risk the rejection. Not with you. It would have mattered."

She held his gaze for a long moment. "You really mean that, don't you?"

"Is it really that impossible to believe? But yes, I couldn't be more serious. I watched you, wanted you, for a very long time. After school, or on weekends, when I was at the restaurant and you were working over here, I did try to catch your eye. Sort of gauge the interest."

"You were always surrounded by a million friends, and your whole family—"

"So . . . you did notice?"

"I'd have to be dead not to notice you. And . . . yeah. I noticed that you'd be nice, wave, smile. But I thought that was just you being you. You were popular for a reason. People liked you because you were friendly, charming, outgoing. All the things I wasn't. So . . . I watched from a distance. If you think your ego was all tied up in not being publicly humiliated, multiply that by, oh, a million, and maybe you could get what it would have taken for me to ever presume to try and get your attention."

"You had it without even trying." He chuckled then. "I can't believe we spent that whole year—"

"Years," Holly muttered, then looked away when he ducked his head to catch her eye.

"Years?"

"You're talking about your senior year, when I was a sophomore. But I noticed you way before that. I mean, we more or less grew up across the street from one another."

"Oh, I noticed you before then, too."

A brief smile crossed her face, and maybe there was a little blush again. She didn't say anything else, though.

"So . . ." he said at length, suddenly feeling every bit the nervous teenager he'd been. At least where Holly Bennett was concerned.

"So . . ." she said. "Thank you, again, for the dinner. And for, well, making me feel retroactively less of a nerdy dorky teenager. It shouldn't matter, so many years later, but—"

"Holly."

She paused in her nervous chatter and looked up at him. He saw her throat work and was close enough to see her pupils expand. "Yes?"

"I'm not eighteen anymore. And I don't give a damn about what people think. I still don't like rejection." He grinned. "But I'm not afraid to risk it."

"What—what are you saying?"

"I'm saying that some attractions don't fade with time. In fact . . ." He reached up, pushed that silky fall of hair off her cheek. "Sometimes, they just get more intriguing. Especially when you're old enough to know where intriguing attractions can lead."

She didn't just swallow hard. She gulped. "I, uh—I don't know if I'm staying. I mean, I just came to—"

"Aren't you curious?"

"Curious? About—"

"About following up on that mutual attraction. Unless—unless, you're otherwise—"

She shook her head. More of a jerky move, really. "No, I'm not otherwise anything. Except otherwise unsure if this—um, pursuing this conversation any further is a good idea. I mean, maybe it's just as well to leave the teenage fantasy as just that? Why risk ruining a sweet memory?"

"Now who's afraid?" he gently teased, his fingers still in her hair.

"Bwak, bwak," she said.

He could feel the slight tremor beneath his fingertips as he traced them along her jaw, then slid them beneath her hair and tilted her head back with the slightest of pressure. "So," he said, slowly leaning closer, "you really don't want to know?"

"Is that all it is?" she asked, her voice husky and soft. "Curiosity?"

"It's as good a place to start as any."

"Some people—" She had to pause, clear her throat, which made his lips twitch. "Some people get to know each other first, before—"

"We're hardly strangers."

She shifted back a little. "We're pretty much exactly strangers."

"Okay . . . so what do you want to know? I know what I want to know."

She actually rolled her eyes, which choked a little laugh out of him.

"I didn't mean that. Well, not exactly that. Yet, anyway."

Her mouth dropped open at that, and it was really almost just too much to take.

"It's just a kiss . . . a hello."

"And if it's just . . . pleasant?"

"Then a hello is just a hello. We're friends, Holly. Or, at least I'd like us to be. It doesn't have to be more than that."

"Awkward, though."

"We're the only ones who'd know. And the friendship stands."

"I can't believe I'm standing here, in the middle of the night, bargaining over a kiss. With you."

He grinned, but she stepped back. And took the box of food, hugging it, almost too tightly from the sound of crinkling cardboard.

"Why don't we move straight to the friendship part," she said.

He lifted his hands. "Okay." Then he shook his head. "Turns out it doesn't feel any better fourteen years later. The rejection thing," he clarified.

"I don't know what I'm going to be doing a day from now, much less a week, or a month. My life is . . . complicated. In ways it hasn't been in a very long time. I can't handle further complications. Not right now."

"It might have just been pleasant," he said, teasing her, wishing he wasn't so disappointed but respecting her wishes.

Now that smile came back, and it did things to him, surprisingly intense things, which made him wonder if perhaps she hadn't made the wise move.

"It might have been pleasant for you," she said, "but I can pretty much guarantee it would have ranked a lot higher on my scale."

Now it was his turn to stand there and stare.

"I really need to—you know." She gestured her head, toward the back of the building.

"Um, yeah. Right." He turned and walked back to the front door. "Don't forget to lock up behind me."

"I won't," she said, staying where she was.

He supposed so they didn't risk being in each other's personal space again. He paused at the door, though, then looked back at her. "I think you're right. When we kiss, it's going to be a hell of a lot more than pleasant."

5

Holly heard the tapping on the door downstairs and immediately stopped shoving the large packing crate toward the dormer window and away from her makeshift bed. *Sean?*

She knew it was foolish, the little skip her heart took, the extra zip in her pulse. Even if it was him, there was no point in getting all schoolgirl-crushy about it. She'd spent far more time thinking about their almost kiss in the wee hours last night than she should have, especially considering the laundry list of things she absolutely had to be thinking about. It was more than a little mind-blowing to know, to even think, that Sean Gallagher had been attracted to her. Ever. But they were adults now, and she had some very adult responsibilities to attend to. Ones that left no room for reliving childhood fantasies. Much less contemplate trying to turn fantasy into reality.

She used her reflection in the pane of glass in the china cabinet that was shoved up against the wall behind the door to push at her hair and check her teeth. Realizing she was primping, she stuck her tongue out at herself and tried to get her head in the place it needed to be as she walked downstairs. The fantasy was pretty damn good if her dreams last night had been any indication, and he'd been right about time only enhancing the details of those fantasies, but the dream world was the realm in which all thoughts of Sean Gallagher were destined to remain.

She pasted a professional, friends-only smile on her face, prayed it was even in the ballpark of looking believable, and turned the corner at the base of the stairs into the main part of the shop . . . only to have the smile fade and her shoulders involuntarily slump a little when she spied who it was at the door. And who it wasn't.

She wasn't ready for this conversation, but she'd known word would get out she was back and she'd have visitors before too long. She'd just hoped that too long would have been a little bit longer before this particular visitor popped up.

She gave a nod to Mrs. Gillespie as she unlocked the door. Arlene Gillespie had worked part-time for her mother for more years than Holly had been alive. She was a tiny wisp of a thing, even smaller than Holly, not the type to indulge in chitchat, though she knew her antiques and could give you, in great detail, the provenance of each piece in the store's entire and ever-changing inventory without ever having to refer to a single catalog. Holly was certain she'd been a librarian in a former life.

Her expression was much as Holly had always remembered it to be, neither smiling nor frowning, but merely intent. She opened the door and stepped back to invite her in. "Mrs. Gillespie, how nice to see you." That was another quirk of hers. Everyone, even her peers, had always called her Mrs. Gillespie. It was only because her mother had signed her paychecks that Holly even knew her first name.

"So, you've finally come back," Mrs. Gillespie said without preamble.

Holly closed the door behind her and did her best not to roll her eyes as Mrs. Gillespie unwrapped the long knit scarf that was swallowing her neck whole and unbuttoned her olive green overcoat. She left her hat on, but did take her gloves off. Which meant this was not going to be a brief visit. Lovely.

"How have you been?" Holly asked.

"My bursitis doesn't appreciate the cold weather, but, otherwise, I can't complain." She laid her gloves and handbag on the counter and gave the store a keen once-over before turning back to face Holly. "When will you be re-opening? This close to the holidays, you've already forfeited most of your seasonal profits."

Holly held her gaze, most likely like a deer in head-lights. Something about the way Mrs. Gillespie focused on a person made it next to impossible to prevaricate. "I—I'm not sure I will be." There, she'd said it. Put the words right out there.

Mrs. Gillespie surprised her by nodding. "You never did have a head for this. You're more the dreamer."

"Dreamer?" Holly was honestly surprised by the description. Eight years spent surviving in the very cut-throat world of advertising had hardly made a dreamer out of her. She'd always thought her mother was more the dreamer, living in a fantasy world of sleigh bells and Santa Clauses.

"Running off to Europe, head in the clouds, wanting to become a famous painter." She turned her attention back to the store. "What would you call it?"

"I work in advertising."

Mrs. Gillespie didn't seem to give any more credence to that comment than Sean had the night before. Holly continued. "I don't know what my mother has told you, but painting is not—"

"What keeps food on your table, I'm aware." She

turned back to Holly. "Your mother found a way to make her passion pay for itself. She has a good eye for both whimsy and collectibles, and the business education to know how to turn a profit at it." She cocked her head slightly and clasped her hands in front of her coat. "What will you do with all she's built here?"

Holly was at a bit of a loss as to how to respond to that. On the one hand, Mrs. Gillespie didn't seem the slightest bit surprised that Holly might not attempt to continue on in her mother's footsteps, and although not entirely easy to read, she wasn't thinking there was disapproval there, either. "I don't know yet." Which was absolute honest truth. She'd spent the day and a half since arriving looking over the books, checking the inventory, the title to the building, which her mother had owned for some time now, and the taxes on the building, all of which her father had neatly categorized, summarized, and filed in tidy folders and binders in her mother's office. And she still wasn't certain what her best course of action would be. Or how long it would take before she could flee back to London.

And fleeing was exactly how it felt. Just as it had over a decade earlier.

"A shame you couldn't have found a way to return sooner. Might have lost what window you had to sell the thing off, lock, stock—"

"And jingle bells," Holly murmured, knowing it was true. She waited for Mrs. Gillespie to continue with the lecture, but her interest had once again returned to the store.

Holly was drawn out of her thoughts as she watched the older woman continue to sweep her gaze, quite steadily and deliberately through each area of the store, without taking so much as a step or even unclasping her hands. Holly frowned a little, wondering what was going through the woman's mind, certain she'd hear about it momentarily unless she did something to move this visit forward to its conclusion. "Can I get you anything? I have tea brewing in the back, or—"

"This isn't a social call," she informed her, not breaking her steady regard of the store, which was now on the far corner.

Holly hid the dry smile that threatened, certain Mrs. Gillespie would not be pleased by Holly's amusement with her eccentricities. Then another thought occurred to her. While none of the women who'd worked for her mother had done so full-time, or drew any significant income from it, it was an income. And perhaps, Mrs. Gillespie was here trying to determine if she was going to be getting her old job back, but too proud to ask. Holly supposed she'd already answered that question, so now all that was left was to allow her to save face and leave of her own accord, in whatever manner she wished to contrive. Holly would follow her lead.

So, no one was more surprised than Holly when Mrs. Gillespie abruptly turned to her and said, "Have you come up with a figure?"

"A figure?"

"An asking price," she clarified, her expression still flat and unreadable.

"An asking price for—oh, you mean—" Holly stuttered to a halt, really caught off guard this time, then frowned and said, "Were—are you . . . interested? In buying the place?"

"No."

Holly frowned. "Okay. I'm not following, then. Do you know of someone who is?"

"I'd like to set up a meeting with you," she responded. "To discuss possibilities. Unless, of course, you already have outside interest, or alternate plans."

"No, I—I hadn't—" She felt like an idiot, and she really needed not to be. Mrs. Gillespie was a shrewd woman, and Holly was fairly certain the woman would take full advantage of Holly's lack of business sense if it stood to gain her anything. It was simply the smart thing to do. And Mrs. Gillespie was nothing if not smart. "I'd be happy to talk with you, once I have had time to better acclimate myself."

"How long a process will that be?"

Holly's mind was racing now, and she had to work hard to corral it until she was alone with time to really think all this through. But all she could think at that moment, standing there, was that, of all people on the planet, who'd have thought that Mrs. Gillespie could turn out to be her savior. "Can I ask . . . when my mother announced she was retiring, why didn't you approach her directly if you were interested in making some sort of offer or deal on the place? The timing would have been much better, seasonally, and—"

"She was quite clear about wanting to bequeath it to you. It was your inheritance. It wasn't up for discussion."

"I don't know that she really thought any of you would want the place. It's a lot of work and—"

"My dear, I've helped to run the place since long before you were in diapers in a playpen back in your mother's office. I'm quite well aware, certainly more so than you are, as to what it takes to run the place."

Holly didn't want to state the obvious, but Mrs. Gillespie was even older than her mother, in her late seventies, at the very least. It was one thing to work fifteen or twenty hours a week for someone else. Did she really want to tackle running a store at her age? "I'm certain you do, I was just . . ." She had no idea how to phrase it without insulting the woman. And given she could very likely be the answer to all of Holly's fervent prayers, that was the last thing she wanted to do at the moment.

"There is another reason I've waited."

"Oh?"

"This place, the contents, were your mother's passion. Clearly she was of no mind to see it sold off, bit by bit. I don't know that she held out any true hope you'd take it over, but she just wanted to leave it as it was, so that her memories of the place remain intact. I respect that."

"Okay." Holly wished her mother had made Holly feel that sure about things, but hearing it from Mrs. Gillespie actually gave her a great deal more confidence in her growing certainty of where she was going to go with her inheritance. Mrs. Gillespie was right about one thing. Holly might not have found a way to pursue her own dreams, but she did know that this wasn't her path.

"I waited because, while I admire your mother, both her business acumen, and her eye for a good piece, I don't hold with her fondness for the Christmas holiday."

Holly knew the surprise was clear on her face. "But, you've worked here for—"

"I love antiques. I love the history, the workmanship . . ." She drifted off, as if suddenly overtaken by her own passion. It was only a momentary blip, but an important one.

Holly's first real glimpse, she thought, of the woman behind the ever-present clasped hands and oh-so-serious expression.

"Back in the day, had your mother taken even so much as a few weeks longer to make an offer on Mrs. Haversham's place, I would have been the one making the offer."

Holly's mouth dropped open. "You wanted to run a shop? Did my mother—"

"She knew. We discussed a partnership, but her vision for the store's content was wildly divergent from my own."

"So, you settled for, what, working here? Why?"

"The town was far too small then for more than one decent antiques store. It's because of me that we branched out as much as we did, with some of the larger pieces. I talked your mother into using those to display her collectibles and we both found a bit of a balance, I suppose. We were both newlyweds back then, but I began my family straight off, and working at all back then was simply . . . well, let's just say our arrangement was a good fit. Your mother and father saw eye-to-eye with their dreams. My husband, God rest his soul, did not. So, I accepted the way of it, and we made it work."

Holly was absolutely dumbstruck. First off, she couldn't even picture Mrs. Gillespie as a young newlywed, much less a young mother. Holly knew she had two grown children, both of whom had children close to Holly's age, and had lived out of state for most of Holly's life. "Later, when times changed, and the town became more of a tourist destination, with the history and the battlefields . . . did you ever consider opening a shop then?" There weren't any other antiques stores directly on Main Street, but within ten to twenty miles, there were a few collectible and antiques establishments, as was fairly common now, in the more rural, picturesque Virginia countryside.

"The die was cast, as they say, and I accepted the way of it. I had other pursuits, and Mr. Gillespie and I did our fair share of traveling."

"I'm sorry," Holly said, "about his passing." She had heard through her mother that Mr. Gillespie had passed away from a heart condition several years back.

Mrs. Gillespie straightened her shoulders, her posture becoming even more rigid, if that were possible. "Thank you," she said, clearly uncomfortable with any display of actual emotion. "When can we schedule a meeting?"

"What, exactly, are we discussing? You said you weren't interested in buying—"

"I'm not. What I'd like to discuss with you is a lease arrangement. You do own this building, do you not?" When Holly nodded, she continued. "Clearly, at my age, purchasing the place would make no sense. Both of my children have done quite well for themselves, and while I could afford something of a late-in-life folly, as they call it, they don't need to be saddled with it after I'm gone."

Unlike what Holly's mother had done to her, she might as well have said. She didn't have to.

"I thought perhaps we could discuss a purchase price of the pieces I'd like to keep, and I can help you arrange to sell the rest, for a brokering fee, of course, which I will use to invest in new stock." She stood there, hands clasped, hat perfectly perched on her smooth gray bun, gaze focused steadily on Holly. Unflinching.

Holly marshaled all of her advertising client toughness and held the gaze just as unflinchingly. "I'm definitely willing to consider it. If you could give me a day or two, we'll sit down and talk details."

This didn't meet with immediate approval, if the slight downturn of her pursed lips was any indication, but, after a moment, she nodded. "Very well then. I'll wait for your call." She gathered her gloves and scarf and buttoned her coat. Once she was bundled, Holly saw her to the door, where she paused and looked back at Holly once again. "There are other buildings with leased space available. I want this space, this building, as I know all of its quirks. And I know you. But don't keep me waiting. I'm not getting any younger. And I've waited long enough to pursue my passion." With that, she stepped through the door and walked off down the street.

Holly stood there, partly dumbstruck, partly amused . . .

mostly stunned. Could the solution be so simple? She stepped back into the store, her mind already swimming with all the things that could unsimplify it. Did she want to be a landlord? Would living in London make that impossible? How long would it take to sell off the unwanted inventory . . . and how in the hell would she come up with the appropriate lease agreement?

She was just closing the door when she heard someone shout her name. She looked up to see Sean trotting across the street, a broad smile on his handsome face . . . and a Gallagher's take-out box in his hand.

Her heart did that slow, melting slippy-slidey thing and her pulse rate tripled.

"Hey," he said, all big and room-swallowing as he slipped inside the door. She closed it behind him, blocking out the winter chill . . . and blocking in something that was definitely providing a lot of heat.

"Hey, yourself," she said, trying to make the mental switch from business to . . . well, there was no denying the surprise was a pleasurable one.

"I brought lunch, but that was mostly an excuse."

"Excuse?" She locked the door, then turned and looked up at him just as he set the box on the closest shelf and took a step closer to her.

"I've been thinking about this all day. Night, too, if I'm being honest."

"Thinking about what?"

"This." He slid a warm palm along her cheek, sunk his fingers into her hair, and tipped her face up to his. "I know your future plans aren't certain," he said, his voice a deep rumble that sent a series of the most tantalizing shivers down her spine. "But I already lived with the regret of not pursuing you once. I don't want to make that mistake again." And then he kissed her.

And her knees buckled, and she grabbed hold of him. And kissed him back.

Oh, wonderful. More things that weren't going to be simple.

This was either the best idea he'd ever had, or one of his worst mistakes in the making. At the moment, with her fingertips sliding up the back of his neck and her sweet body pressing fully against his, it was feeling like his most brilliant decision ever.

He scooped her up, lifting her off her feet and bringing her face up more evenly with his own so he could take the kiss even deeper. He moved them farther into the store, backwalking her until they reached the front counter by the register. He slid her onto the smooth glass surface, then pulled her back toward him, hands on her hips as he moved between her legs, urging her to open to him as he slid his hands up her spine, then lost them again in that silky waterfall of hair. Why on earth had he waited so long to do this?

She was making these tiny little guttural noises in the back of her throat that were doing insane things to his body. Namely making him so rock hard it was almost painful to stand, but then she was tucking her feet around the back of his thighs, pulling him closer. And now he was the one groaning as she snuggled herself perfectly around him. It was sensation overload, on every level.

Their kissing was escalating as rapidly as his pulse rate and he knew it was only a matter of time—seconds at the rate they were going—before clothes were going to get yanked off and things were going to happen that he—oh, he desperately wanted them to happen. Perhaps more, in that moment, than he'd ever wanted anything to happen. Ever. But this—this was not what he'd had in mind when he'd crossed the street. Kiss her, maybe seduce her a little, enough to get her to agree to at least think about giving the two of them a chance to find out what might be. Rationally. Flirtatiously, but rationally.

He hadn't counted on one taste of her leading to this kind of volcanic eruption of need and want. And an eruption was just what he was risking here if he let this go on an instant longer.

Heart pounding, breathing labored, he forced himself to tear his mouth away from hers. "Holly—" was all he could manage.

"Yes," she said breathlessly, her fingers curling into his shoulders as she instinctively pulled him closer again.

"I—we—wait," he said before she could claim his mouth again. Claim him. In fact, he already felt it. How easily she could slip right in, under his defenses, which were remarkably nonexistent at that moment. Was it because he knew her? Because she was so familiar to him, having been around his whole life, that he wasn't wary, wasn't overthinking? Or was it because she hadn't pursued him, and was quite possibly leaving? Thereby making that "how to make a relationship work" problem he typically had a nonissue?

He wasn't a coward, and he always put his partners' needs in front of his own. Just as he was always up front regarding who he was and how his life operated. And, with Holly, all of those things were magnified tenfold by her life and what it might entail.

So, why was it, staring into her big, brown eyes, that rather than tell her all the reasons why this might have been the big mistake he'd feared it would be . . . he just felt this ridiculous sensation of hope skyrocketing through him. Holly equaled hope. It was that simple. And that crazy.

"I want you," he said.

Her face bloomed with the most delightful shade of pink, but her gaze stayed on his. "I—I think I was getting that."

"But I didn't—I mean, this isn't what—"

The bright twinkle in her eyes instantly shuttered and she tried to shift back out of his arms, the pink in her cheeks now looking to be more from embarrassment than the blush of a woman flattered by his attention.

"No, no, wait." He pulled her in close, reluctant to let her put any more space between them, both because having her there felt all kinds of right and because he was afraid she'd start building walls if he gave her half a chance. They were down now, as were his . . . and he was determined to keep them that way.

"What I was trying to say was, I want you, but not on the counter of your mother's store. Trust me, another thirty seconds, and—" He broke off as his body surged with approval for that idea. He dipped his chin, took a steadying breath, then looked back at her. And suddenly, whatever he said next took on amazing levels of importance. Crazy as it sounded, crazier as it felt, it was like he was potentially making or breaking his entire future in that one, singular moment. "Holly, I want a chance. That's what I came here to tell you. I can't explain it, and maybe you think I'm crazy, but I—"

"I don't think you're crazy," she said, her voice quieter now, but the look in her eyes said a whole lot more was going on that her tone was not belying.

"I just didn't want to move so fast that we mistook one thing for another. I want you, but I want you deliberately, with very specific intent, and I want that first time to be in a place where we can both explore and figure out what . . . what this is. What it could be. Do you understand?"

She looked at him for a long time, and he'd never felt so at a disadvantage, like there simply weren't words available that would put the chaos and irrationality of all the things going on inside his head into some sort of sane, logical order. Because this wasn't sane. He'd wanted a kiss, a chance, a conversation, perhaps. But one taste, one touch, one of those tiny little noises she'd made and it was like . . . wow, he couldn't even describe it to himself.

"Yes, I do. And I want to," she said, at length. "But . . . I don't know, Sean. I—the timing, it's—"

"It's now," he said, never more sure of anything. It was stunning, really, the certainty he felt. Stunning and crazy-town crazy. And then he was blurting it all out, which was probably the stupidest thing he could ever do. But this was his one shot, his one chance, and he wasn't blowing it this time.

"I know it sounds crazy, and it should because it is, but I'm banking that maybe, if you're really just honest with yourself, you'll agree it's the same with you. That kiss . . . that was real and honest, and it wasn't just a hello-get-to-know-you kiss, was it," he stated, not even making it a question, because in his mind, it wasn't. "It was something else, like a waited-a-lifetime-for-that-kiss kiss, you know? And maybe I've always known that it would be that way with us." He was babbling now, and he didn't care, couldn't stop. "Maybe that's why, as a teenager, I couldn't approach you. I wasn't even close to ready at that point in my life to tackle something so important, so potentially life altering. And on some level, maybe I knew that. Maybe I always knew it would be big. Extraordinary. Or maybe things really just do happen when they're supposed to."

She wasn't looking at him like he was crazy, so that was one good thing, but her expression was shuttering, and he panicked, a little.

"No, no, don't do that. Don't shut me out. I know this is way over the top, but it's like . . . you'll run back to London if I don't say something to make you stay and give me a chance, and so I'm just saying everything that's popping into my head, and I know it's too much and I know—"

She shut him off with a kiss.

He grabbed her face and kissed her back, but there wasn't a promise there, in hers, not yet. And she pulled back before they could fall off that cliff again. "Sean . . ." She paused and took a moment to collect herself, and he wanted to see her eyes so he could gauge what she was thinking, but he let her have the time to compose herself, her thoughts, and waited, which was perhaps the longest few seconds of his life. She looked up again, and there wasn't regret, so his heart stayed hopeful. "I'm interested, too. I am."

"But?" And his heart paused. Clutched, really. Because Holly Bennett wasn't a second chance, change-her-mind kind of woman.

"But . . . I don't know. I don't know you. I don't know where my life is taking me. I think I might have a solution for the store, but it's not one that will keep me here."

How did a man stand there and explain to a woman who was perfectly right when she said she didn't really know him, that he was the only one in the universe she truly needed to know, because he was hers. Meant for, had to be, once in a lifetime hers.

Because . . . that was crazy. And he wasn't.

"Do you believe in fate?" he asked, wanting logic, linear thought, and progression, but knowing there wasn't any.

"I don't know what I believe in."

"Your job, in London. Do you miss it? Is it something you could see yourself doing here?"

She didn't answer him right away. But no warmth had entered her eyes, no natural affection or fondness, when he'd mentioned it. Which he knew wasn't the case when he thought of Gallagher's. He loved his place in the world. But did he have the right to ask her to consider abdicating hers to give him a chance? And what did he really have to offer her? She didn't want the shop, she wanted . . . he hadn't a clue. Maybe she didn't, either. But his life he did know, and it was a crazy one with crazy hours, filled with crazier people, most of them blood relations, so . . . what on earth made him think she'd willingly sign on to that? Even if London wasn't calling her passionately . . . at least it was a known quantity, a safe, reasonable alternative. She hadn't come back here because she wanted to be here . . . she'd come back because she was forced into it.

So, it would seem, the very last thing he should be doing was forcing her to do that all over again, just to be with him.

"I'm good at it," she said at length. "I don't know that I'd want to start all over again doing it here, though."

Good at it. Not that she loved it, or was passionate about it, but good at it. "Is that enough for you? Doing something because you're good at it?"

She lifted a shoulder. "It's what it is. I don't hate it.

And . . . it's always there while I figure things out. I don't have another back up plan."

Me, he wanted to shout. *Let me be your back up plan*.

"This other alternative solution for the store . . . how long do you think you'll be here, sorting that out, if it works?"

"I don't know. I took my annual leave to come here. I have through the new year. Then I have to go back."

"Would you be willing to sort through this—us—while you're here? See where it might go?"

Had he not been looking closely, he might have missed that leap of want, that instinctive reaction of delight, at his suggestion. He latched on to that. Holly might not want to admit her secret desires, or that she could reach for a new star . . . even to herself. But she wanted to.

"I don't want to lead you on," she said. "Or myself. Just because we're both interested—"

"Should be reason enough for any two people to explore what might be. It's not something that happens every day, Holly. Or ever, for some people. Just give it a chance, me a chance. Speaking for me, I'd rather risk the hurt, the ultimate rejection, than never trying at all. At least then I'd know we'd made the effort . . . and that it wasn't meant to be."

She didn't say anything, and he wanted, badly, to press the advantage he knew he had. Their physical attraction, that chemistry, was natural and explosive, and one little kiss right now would probably be enough to tilt her decision in his favor.

But so much of this was out-of-the-ordinary nutty, he really wanted any decision she made to come without the cloud of pheromones and desire, but with a clear mind and an open heart.

"I think we're asking for trouble, Sean."

"And I think we're asking for the moon. But we might as well reach. You can't get what you don't go after."

She smiled briefly then and shook her head. "Are you always so certain about things?"

"Sometimes. But when I am, I most definitely am." He cocked his head. "I thought you were always certain about things."

"I thought so, too," she said. "But nothing seems to be staying the same. And things I thought I knew, like with my parents, aren't what I thought at all. So . . . maybe for the first time, I'm feeling like I'm not certain of anything." She looked at him. "And I don't know if I can tackle another uncertainty right now."

He tipped up her chin and looked into her eyes. "But now is when I'm here. And you're here. And we get the chance. Tackling uncertainties . . . that's how you get the answers."

He kissed her, but this time it was slow and thoughtful, and with the absolute intent of letting her know it wasn't the wild, out-of-control lust that had him saying these things. Or feeling these things.

Her eyes were a little glassy and unfocused when he lifted his head. He covered her hand with his own and slid hers to cover her heart. "Feel that?" he said, quietly. "That's what mine's doing right now. I just want the chance to have more of that. With you."

He left her hand there, on her heart, and stepped back. Her feet slid down from where they'd been tucked around his legs, so her heels tapped the front of the counter. Where she sat, looking a bit lost, a bit dumbstruck, and a lot confused.

"You know where to find me." He turned, unlocked the door, and walked out. He heard the ringing of sleigh bells as the door swung shut behind him. The walk back across the street was the longest one he'd ever taken. And he prayed like hell that wasn't the last time he'd ever see her. *Come and get me, Holly Bennett.*

He pushed the door open to Gallagher's and walked into the burst of people chatting, silverware clanking on dishes, laughter, the sound of the coffee grinder going, and the general chaos that was the soundtrack to his life. And it was his life, and life-giving to him.

He turned around then and looked back across the street. At the quiet, darkened little shop and its lone occupant, sitting in total silence. And he felt his heart squeeze, then drop. What on earth would ever compel a solitary, quiet woman such as Holly Bennett to step into his cacophonous world? Much less give him a chance?

Nothing was the answer that came to mind. Absolutely nothing.

Who was he kidding, anyway?

But for the rest of that day, all that night, and for the endless two days that followed, every time the tinkling bell rang on the front of the door, signaling another customer entering, his pulse would spike, his heart would lift, and his spirit would find a sliver of hope . . . and each time that hope would be dashed when it wasn't Holly crossing the threshold.

So, on the dawn of the fourth day, he realized he had a decision to make. Sit back and take her silence as a final answer . . . or continue his quest?

7

Holly wiped the long sleeve of her tee across her forehead and blew the hair that had slid—again—out its ponytail off of her face. She looked at the clipboard containing a printed list of the entire inventory of the store, and back again at the little secretary desk crammed into the corner of the storage room she'd been using as her living quarters. It simply wasn't on the list.

She'd discovered that while her father had kept the books for the store in meticulous fashion, her mother had a bit more, let's say, creative approach to cataloging the store's contents. There was no doubt she had a good eye for product and good business sense, Santa's Workshop was solidly in the black and had been for years, decades even, despite economic fluctuations. But when it came to cataloging every last figurine and antique cabinet, her mother's idea of grouping and organizing the objects were entirely different from Holly's, or, she was pretty certain, anyone else's, either.

She'd tried checking things off the list as she went through each area of the room, then, when she couldn't figure which category certain things fell into, she'd played scavenger hunt and tried tracking down the listed pieces one category at a time . . . but when that still left pages of unmatched items, she'd been forced to call in reinforcements.

Mrs. Gillespie had just left after coming back a second day to help her sort through it all, and this was what was left. A single, antique oak secretary desk. Mrs. Gillespie had assured her that her mother didn't have any personal stock in the store, nor had she ever used it to store anything from home. If it was here, it was for sale. But there was no tag, no item number sticker, nothing.

Still, if this was all that was left unsorted, fine by her. She'd been prepared for much worse. And Mrs. Gillespie's help had brought the added benefit of giving her the opportunity to sticker every piece in the store that she wanted to discuss purchasing. She'd also given Holly information on several different methods she could use to off-load the rest of the inventory. They hadn't discussed, as yet, leasing terms, as Holly hadn't yet decided if she wanted to tackle the role of landlord. She had talked to an estate lawyer about her options there, as well, and was mulling over the surprising number there were to contemplate. Every time she thought she'd answered one question, five more popped up that required more discussion.

At the moment, the lone piece of remaining unclassified inventory was the least of her worries. She tossed the clipboard on the red crushed-velvet divan she'd been using as a bed and turned her thoughts to the most nagging issue of the moment. And that was hunger.

She looked through the second-floor dormer window across the street to Gallagher's and tried, unsuccessfully for what felt like the millionth time, not to think about all those things Sean Gallagher had said to her. In some ways, it was like a surreal dream, a movie sequence that had happened to someone else, an actress playing the role of mousy ingénue faced with the surprising, unrealistic pursuit of the impossibly handsome leading man. An out of body experience, for certain, because things like that never happened to the body of Holly Bennett.

And, oh, the effect he'd had on her body. There was still an automatic, instinctive swoon response each and every time she really allowed herself to relive those moments. Those incredible, intoxicating, possibly-if-she-dared-let-it life-changing moments. But . . . who did that? Who leaped like that? Well, besides someone like Sean Gallagher, for whom leaping really couldn't be all that scary. After all, how many hard landings could he have had?

Not that Holly had led some kind of sheltered or failure of a life. She was bright, smart, good at her job, and she'd dated. Plenty. There had even been men with dashing accents and fashionable wardrobes. She'd dumped and been dumped . . . but truth was, she'd never once really had her heart broken. So who was she to talk about hard landings?

She sighed and leaned back against the little desk and fanned her face for an entirely different reason. And admitted that never once, in her entire dating life, had she ever been kissed like that. And that the real reason she hadn't walked across that street, and straight through that restaurant and right into Sean Gallagher's kitchen and kissed him back in that same devastatingly slow and marvelous way he'd so perfectly claimed her mouth the other day, at precisely twelve fifteen—she'd noticed the Santa's belly clock over the door he'd walked out of—wasn't because she was afraid of men, or of dating, or of taking chances.

It was because, this time, she was afraid she could get her heart broken. Quite thoroughly shattered, in fact. All those things he'd said, each and every word had resonated inside of her, screaming one word: truth. She knew it, felt it, as surely as he did. Shocking and stunning as that was to even contemplate.

But the odds weren't in her favor. He didn't travel in her world and she most definitely didn't travel in his. She had no idea what to do with a huge, boisterous family full of people who would likely scrutinize, judge, and hold her up to who knew what kind of impossible standards when it came to their beloved and cherished Sean. Yes, clients did that with her on a routine basis, but she knew her worth in the world of advertising.

She had no idea of her worth as it pertained to holding on to someone like Sean Gallagher.

And so, chicken that she apparently was, she'd shamefully stayed hidden in her haven of an inheritance and focused on answering the questions that had finite, rock solid answers instead. That she could deal with, and had to deal with, anyway. Sean and all that he represented and potentially promised was simply too huge, and seemed too . . . fantastical fairy-tale to seriously contemplate.

Her stomach growled. Loudly. It was well into the afternoon and she hadn't eaten since the bagel she'd gotten from Margie's, the little coffee and pastry shop two blocks down, earlier this morning. She could call the deli again, get another cold cut sub. She looked out the window. Or she could cross the street and order something more filling. And muster up the courage to tell Sean that she'd decided to lease the shop space to Mrs. Gillespie and would be heading back to London. Which wasn't exactly true. Yet. But still, she wasn't staying, that much she knew. So, it was for the best to go over there, make peace, not leave things in limbo, remain friends. Surely they could be adults about this.

Right. Who was she kidding? She wanted him so badly she could taste it. And it was ridiculous how badly she wanted to taste him. Again. And again. If she marched into his office, there was a far bigger chance she'd kick the door shut and beg him to take her right there, right then, right on his desk, than realistically discuss any rational thought of how to retain something as simple as a basic friends-only friendship. She'd certainly fantasized about the former. The begging part, the demanding part. Not so much with the rational let's-be-friends part. In fact, she'd never realized how many places there could be to have spontaneous, erotic, hot as hell sex in a restaurant until she'd closed her eyes at night.

Jimmy's Deli it was, she decided, slipping off the secretary, then tripping over the end of a rolled-up rug she'd shoved there earlier while checking things off lists. This sent her wheeling back against the little rolltop desk, which rocked hard back against the wall and caused a heretofor unseen spring loaded hidden compartment door to pop open in the recesses of the rear of the nook-and-cranny desktop. She bent down and peered into the shadowed interior of a newly revealed hidey-hole. "Huh. Cool."

But, before she could investigate further, the sleigh bells rang over the door downstairs and she cursed under her breath. She'd forgotten to go down and lock up after Mrs. Gillespie had left. Customers, both old and new, had come by over the past few days and tried the door or pressed their noses against the glass. When she could, Holly just ducked them, leaving them to see the closed sign and realize the store wasn't open despite there being lights on inside. However, on occasion, she'd been sighted, and was forced to wave, or make brief, mostly awkward conversation about when the shop would re-open. But she'd never left the door unlocked so they could just stroll in.

"Lovely," she muttered, and grabbed the clipboard off the divan before heading out into the hall toward the stairs leading down to the shop floor . . . only to run smack into Sean, who was on his way up.

And he looked . . . determined.

"Holly, we need to talk."

He was empty-handed this time—figured—but she was momentarily too discombobulated to put him off with the excuse that she was headed out for lunch, so she ended up blurting exactly what was on her mind, instead. "I—uh, was just thinking the same thing. In fact, I planned to come over to talk to you later." Which wasn't a lie, exactly, since she had been thinking about it but hadn't pinned down exactly how much later that later would be.

His previously set expression lightened somewhat and his eyes crinkled a bit in that way she was already coming to like. A lot.

"You were?"

It was that hopeful note in his voice that did her in. "Yes, well," she hurried to say, to explain, before anybody got their hopes up, especially her. "I just thought you should know, I'll be leasing out the store. So . . . I'm not going to be staying. And I wanted—well, I didn't want to leave things, you know . . ." She ran out of steam at that point, mostly because the twinkle blinked out and his shoulders fell a little, and both of those things not only made her feel horrible . . . but also a bit terrified, like a fool who was about to make the biggest mistake of her life.

"Oh." He stood there, looking a little sucker-punched and she realized he might have been storming the castle, all intent on making a speech or . . . or some last big gesture to get her to decide things in his favor, and she'd just robbed him of his big, planned-for moment.

"Is . . . that what you came over to talk about?" she

stuttered, feeling badly for how this was going, but having no clue how to make it any better.

Well, other than to throw herself at him, drag him to the floor, and have several hours of wild, uncontrollable, lust-slaking sex with him.

But that would be wrong.

Wouldn't it?

"Holly . . . I—" He just broke off, then raked his hand through his hair, and they stood there just past the top of the stairs staring at one another.

She had no idea what was going through his mind at the moment, but going through her mind was that it would all get better and a lot less awkward once he left. Then they'd either pretend they'd never had any interaction and wave or nod casually at each other if they, by chance, crossed paths between now and when she left . . . or studiously avoid making any kind of contact whatsoever. Even that would be less awkward than this.

So why was it that the thought of him walking away, of never, not once, seeing him again, not like this, not where anything was possible and she could say or do anything she wanted, if she just allowed herself the courage to . . . well, want. Something. Anything.

Anyone.

"You're not selling the place?" he said, at very long length, apparently not ready to escape into their distant, casually waving future any more than she was.

"I— I don't think so. I've had an offer, to lease it out, but it won't be the same store. Antiques, but sans the Christmas part."

He looked over his shoulder, down the stairs. "Aw, that's a shame. I like the Christmas part."

"You're kidding."

He looked back at her, and the smile was back, though

the eyes were still not crinkling. In fact, he looked . . . well, hurt. "No, I'm not. I love Christmas. I love all that it represents."

"Gross commercialization and an excuse for unrestrained instant gratification?"

"Says the advertising guru. No, I was speaking more metaphorically than commercially. I like that sense of wonder and hope, that miracles can and do happen. I mean, I don't believe in pinning all your dreams on a single day of the year or having wild expectations that no one can fulfill. I'm just talking about . . ." He shrugged. "I used to go to Ireland every year for the holiday, to visit my family there, and so, for me, it was always a time of singing, laughter, great food, warmth and fun, and just . . . love. So, I guess it's just that part that attracts me. And what's downstairs, it's . . . well, it's either a symbol of it or a reminder of it. Whimsical or spiritual. I like it all. Can't help it."

"You know what's ironic?" she said, and for the first time, put into words everything she'd always felt about that day.

"No, what would that be?"

"That my parents—well, my mother, but my father doted on her, so for him, too—loved, obviously, that season, so much so that they embraced the ideal of it and incorporated it into their way of thinking, all year-round. And though it was a pure and honest affection, they also made a business out of it, so, though not grossly commercialized, it was still defined by more than just a love for whimsy and the spiritual connection of it all. It was a hectic time of year, always, when sales were brisk and my mother was exhausted. I lived in a home that was a tribute to that holiday the way Graceland is a tribute to Elvis. We had tours, singing, parties . . . all to celebrate this amazingly, supposedly fun wonderland of a season. For me? I'd have killed to just have had my mother and father on Christmas Eve, or morning, or both, all to myself, to just celebrate in peace and quiet and just . . . be." She looked him in the eye. "I love what you describe and can see why it brings you joy, both at the memory and the reality. But for me? I never had any of that, despite, supposedly, living in the center of everything it symbolized my whole life. I ended up hating it. All of it."

To his credit, he didn't bat an eye, and more important, he didn't look at her like she was emotionally bankrupt, or the poor cinder girl who needed a hug. Which is mostly why she'd never, past adolescence anyway, confided her feelings on the subject to anyone.

"When you lived in London . . . you didn't try and create your own version of what you wanted it to be? With new friends, cohorts, compatriots?"

She shook her head. "I came back for Thanksgiving, which we did celebrate as a family, usually one of the last times either of my parents were coherent before plunging into the chaos of the big sales season and end of year tax season for my dad. So, there were good memories tied to that day, at least comparatively speaking. At Christmastime, I'd take the rest of my vacation leave and . . ."

"What, go lie on a beach somewhere and work on your tan? I could understand that."

She was tempted to just nod and say yes. It would have been easy enough. But she felt, considering it all, that he deserved all of the truth. "No, I'd get a rail pass and travel around Europe with a sketch pad, pencils, and paint. Different destinations, different years. But that's what always brought me comfort, growing up in this world of Santa on steroids, so I clung to that. I reveled in it, to be honest. I wasn't hiding, I was celebrating the thing I loved most. So, maybe that is my Christmas spirit."

"Why don't you pursue that? Your art. Clearly it's your

passion." His lips quirked a little then, and a tiny bit of that twinkle surfaced again in his eyes. "Or are you not good enough?" A bit of the brogue snuck into his voice, and she couldn't help it, she smiled, too.

"I don't know. I just know I enjoy expressing myself that way. But I don't know that it would be a wise move, to try and figure out how to earn a living at it. Easier said than done. I can wield a pen and brush more effectively in the advertising world. Still art, still creative, but with a more clearly defined career path."

"And paint, then, simply as a hobby?"

She folded her arms over her clipboard. "Seems like a wise, healthy way to approach matters, yes."

"Hmm." He folded his arms, too. And leaned against the wall. "Are you happy with that arrangement? Does it feed your soul? Are you fulfilled?"

"I—I think it just is what it is."

"You said you were leasing this building, but not all the contents. What are you going to do with it? With all the things down there?"

"Sell them. And before you ask, yes, my mother knows. Or will, as soon as she gets back from cruising the Mediterranean." But she'd given her blessing. Even Mrs. Gillespie seemed to think her mother had thought it inevitable. "I hope to have it all done before she gets back, just present it as a fait accompli. Even though she knows it's likely coming, it will probably be easier on her that way."

"I think you're right, but that's not why I was asking. What will you do with the profits? I know, none of my business, but . . . I'm asking anyway."

"I—" She broke off. She really hadn't even thought about that part. "I don't know. I mean, there are a lot of things I have to figure out if I'm going to remain owner of the building in deed and so it will probably go toward . . .

handling all of that. Which I won't be able to do from overseas, so I'll have to hire someone. Or retain . . . someone. I'm still looking into all of that."

"Why not invest it in you? Why not take your inheritance and do with it what, in spirit, your mother was giving it to you to do. To carry on, perhaps not with her dream, but with your own?"

Holly stood there, clutching the clipboard as if it were the only connection left to rationality and reality and . . . anything that wasn't this crazy life raft that Sean was tossing to her. Like she was out to sea. And needed rescuing. She didn't. She was fine. She'd go back to London, back to her safe job, and her traveling, and her painting for herself, and be perfectly, one hundred percent fine. Dammit.

She turned on her heel and walked back into the storage room-turned-sleeping quarters, hating the sudden knot in her gut. And the lump in her throat. And the zip in her pulse. It didn't bear thinking about. Not really. Fantasy. That's what that was. How dare he just casually toss that out there. Because now she wouldn't be able to pretend she had no alternatives. But even if she wanted to consider it . . . what would she really do with the money to make it happen?

"Holly?"

She swung around. "What?"

"I didn't mean to upset you." He walked into the room. "Why not do it? Haven't you ever dreamed of it?"

"Of what? Of making some kind of living as a painter? As an artist? Maybe when I was nine. But then I grew up. And I found a way to provide myself with a career that would allow me to travel to the most beautiful places in the world and paint them to my heart's content. I thought that was a pretty fair deal."

He walked right up to her, then took the clipboard

from her arms and tilted her face up to his. "And is it? Is your heart content with that?"

"It has to be."

He smiled then, and she felt herself begin to tremble. "Why?"

"Sean—" The word came out more a whisper, a plea.

"You don't give yourself enough credit. You have parents who are both self-made, successful, and happy in their chosen professions. Why have you settled for less?"

"My parents are proud of me, they—"

"I'm not talking about impressing them, I'm talking about fulfilling the promise they gave you."

She would have snorted had it been possible to make a sound. But he was far too close, so deep inside her personal space she was losing track of where she ended and he began and all of her previously so well established boundaries . . . he didn't respect any of them. In fact, he didn't even seem to recognize boundaries existed. And maybe they didn't for men like him. "My parents barely knew how to be parents."

"That might be true. My parents spent their lives sweating in that restaurant and allowing their only son to be raised by a large extended family. But they loved me, that I never questioned. And I know you didn't, either. My parents gave me all kinds of gifts that might not have had a thing to do with sitting with me while I struggled with my homework, or being there when I was freaking out because it felt like the entire world was expecting me to bring home a county championship. But I learned so many other things. Didn't you?"

"I—yes, I suppose I did."

"Then why aren't you taking advantage of it? Reaching, like they did, for what you want?"

"I don't know."

He pulled her closer, slid his hand beneath her hair,

pulled her face closer to his, until she was on the tippiest of her toes. "Reach for what you want," he said, his lips brushing hers. "I came over here today because I'm reaching for mine." He smiled, and the twinkle was back in full force as he brushed his mouth over hers. "Come on, Holly. Reach with me." He kissed her then, and it was intoxicatingly slow, and wonderful and perfect, the way his mouth fit over hers, the way he coaxed her tongue into his mouth, the way he gave, then took, then gave again, until her head was spinning and her body felt like it would simply float straight up to the ceiling if he wasn't holding her down.

"Sean," she whispered when he lifted his head. "You're braver than I am."

"Says the girl who took off across an entire ocean, to a foreign land—"

"England is hardly—"

"Shh, let me spin my tale of Holly's Great Adventure. You've had one, you know. Most eighteen-year-olds, especially ones reared in small towns, would freak at the thought of moving out of state. Even I stuck close. Not you, racing off to Oxford, settling in London. You reached."

"I ran."

He lifted his head then and let her slide down his body so her feet were once again flat on the floor. Funny, but when he looked at her the way he was now, she still felt like she was floating.

"And now?" He pushed her hair from her face, stroked her cheek with his thumb, searched her eyes. "Are you running again?"

"I—don't know. Maybe. My life is there."

"You had a life here, once."

"I did. But it's not one I want to come back to."

"Good, because that particular version is no longer here. But there is a foundation here, a place you know, that you loved, that loves you. With people you've known your whole life. Who would support you, because you're a Willow Creek girl. You've had family around you your whole life, if you'd just opened your eyes and looked. They don't have to be bound by blood or a shared gene pool, you know."

"I do. Know that." But did she? Had she ever really taken the time to think about it that way? She'd spent most of her time wishing her life was different and plotting a way to put it behind her, start over.

"Don't beat yourself up about it. You didn't exactly have anyone pointing the way. Nobody blamed you for taking off, you know. They all thought you were quite the smart, sharp one, so worldly and bold. They were all proud of you, still are. But they'd love to have you back."

"They—it's been a long, long time, Sean. They don't even know me. Not the adult me."

"One thing I learned about this town is that you're always known to the ones who knew you when."

"Maybe that's true for the Gallaghers. Everyone loves your family and you are a good percentage of the town all on your own."

He laughed. "We both have a place here. Your mom and dad were both loved, respected, and you gain a lot, automatically, just from that."

"Doesn't seem right," she said, more to herself than him, "given I didn't appreciate it all that much."

"That's the other part of small towns . . . you're always one of us. Flaws and all."

Now she laughed. "Says the flawless guy."

His eyebrows raised in true surprise. "Hardly. Step across the street and any number of my cousins or aunts will happily list for you all of my faults in colorful detail. On second thought, I'm trying to get you to give me a shot here, so forget I mentioned that."

Her laughter faded but the smile remained. He made it almost impossible not to. He was charming, and sexy as hell, and the way he kissed her . . . there was no comparison she could draw, because it was incomparable.

He backed up and sank down onto the divan, pulling her down into his lap. "Just . . . think about the things I've said. At least give it some consideration. All of it. Not just the me part." He grinned. "Well, maybe put a little emphasis on that. See? Not flawless. But I find myself feeling really greedy where you're concerned. Like so much time has passed already, and I can't stand the thought of losing any more of it. It's too precious. That's another thing my parents taught me."

"Oh, Sean— "

"I didn't say that for the sympathy vote. But it is something I carry with me. It's why I do most everything I do. No regrets, that's my motto. And it's a good one. Maybe you should think about it in those terms." He shifted and laid her back on the divan, lowering his head toward hers.

She should have pushed at his chest, let him know that he was taking things too far, assuming too much, but when her hands came up they ended up clutching his shirt . . . and pulling him closer, not pushing him away. "I don't want regrets, either," she said, her voice dropping to a trembling whisper as he shifted his weight so he could lean more fully over her. "I just don't know which one that would be."

"Maybe this will help you decide."

She tasted sweet and warm and perfect, and Sean was pretty sure he could kiss her for hours. Days. The rest of his life. There was little that was lush about her small frame, and he'd have to be careful not to crush his weight down on her, much as he wanted to feel her under him. However, what she lacked in curves she more than made up for with that mouth, those lips. They were full and soft and so inviting he thought he might lose himself there forever. And when she kissed him back? Every part of him responded. She kissed him like she did everything else, with such direct, focused intensity. And she fit him, her mouth to his, there was no fumbling, no trying to find just that right angle.

And her mouth was only the start. The idea that there was so much more to explore, to discover where else they fit together, made it hard to think, hard to focus. He wanted it all, all of her, right now.

Patience, patience... When creating a new dish, working to get it just right took endless amounts of patience, but that never bothered Sean; he never wavered. In fact, the journey of discovery often taught him more than the actual dish itself. Trial, error, attempt after attempt until all the flavors were there, layered just right, to burst on the taste buds in the exact way he wanted them to.

Holly Bennett was like an exquisitely prepared dish . . . so many layers, so many flavors . . . he wanted to savor it all. Inch by inch, taste by taste. For that, he had endless patience. He moved from her mouth down to her chin, then along her jaw, before stopping to spend time along that soft, tender part of the neck just below her ear. She gasped when he nipped along the side of her neck, then moaned and arched beneath him as he leaned over her, working his way along her shoulder, pushing aside the loose collar of her tee. "More," he murmured, when he went as far as the opening would allow. He slid his hands down her waist, and lifted his chest just enough to push up the tee. She didn't stop him and he didn't wait for further approval. Holly was a thinker, a planner, an analyzer. But right now, he wanted her to go on feelings, instincts, and reach . . .

He wanted—badly—to stretch out next to her, but the divan was too narrow, so he shifted to the floor, to his knees, as she stretched out fully. Seeing her pale skin being bared against the red crushed velvet was almost more than he could stand. He was already so hard he wasn't sure he could be any more aroused, but felt himself twitch, and harden further as he slipped the tee over her head, leaving her bared to him in nothing more than the tiniest of pale blue silk bras. He needed more hands, and another mouth, so he could be tasting all that delicious, creamy skin while tugging off her jeans and finding out if what was beneath matched what was on top.

He dipped his head and ran the tip of his tongue around her navel, then slowly tracked up the center of her torso. She twisted a little, pushing her body toward his mouth, moaning as she arched her back. Her eyes were closed, her hands in fists beside her head. Good, he thought, lose yourself in me, let yourself go . . . let me take you.

When he reached the scraps of silk that covered her breasts, her nipples were thrusting hard against the soft fabric, tempting him to take them into his mouth . . . taste, touch, tug, lick. So he did. Her hips were moving now, pumping up, and he slid a flat palm down her belly, flipped open the button to her jeans, and continued sliding his fingers past the waistband, the zipper inching down as he toyed along the edge of her silk panties, all the while still teasing her nipples with his tongue.

"Sean—"

"Shhh," he said, moving up, over her body, biting her chin, nipping her bottom lip before taking her mouth again, this time with the intent of claiming her as fully as he could in a kiss . . . while his fingers slid under the silk panel . . . and down between her thighs. She arched sharply against his fingers as he slid them over her, then grabbed his shoulders, digging in her nails as he slid his tongue and fingers inside her at the same time. He felt the long, deep groan vibrate through her as she moved against his hand and greedily took his tongue into her mouth. It was as close as he'd ever gotten to coming before getting his pants off.

The way she responded to him drove him harder. He continued stroking her, fingers and tongue, and felt her pump faster, suck harder on his tongue, moving with him until both motions had a definite rhythm. He felt her gathering, knew she was climbing, and he wanted, with a need that bordered on desperation, to yank off his pants and be fully inside of her when she hit that peak. But then she was there, and her fingers were in his hair, tugging, pulling, raking his scalp as she arched again and again, making incredibly earthy noises in the back of her throat that did things to him he couldn't describe.

He'd never wanted like this, needed like this . . . it was fun and thrilling and sexy as all hell, her sprawled on this crushed velvet divan, the pale afternoon light across her body, his hands on her, in her, his mouth, how she tasted, the scent of her . . . all of these things, these images, swam through his mind like a tumbled kaleidoscope, each one a tiny snap shot of a moment he'd remember for a very long time.

And to think he'd just come over here with the intent of making her listen to his very well thought out arguments on why she should give him—them—at least a shot.

She was shuddering—aftershocks—and he slid his hand back to her stomach and changed the tenor of the kiss. Softer now, not so aggressive, but unwilling to leave her entirely. He had no idea where she'd go in her head when this was over, but he wanted it to be forward, no re-treating. And he hadn't the first clue how to make sure that happened.

Her fingers slackened, but she kept toying with his hair as he continued kissing her—lazy, slow kisses now, searching, tasting, reveling. There was something almost more intimate in them now, than before, when they'd both been charged up. He'd always enjoyed kissing, but purely for the physical pleasure it brought. This was . . . different. This was communication, it was connection . . . and it was so much more than purely physical.

Finally, she pushed a bit at him, moved her mouth just enough so that it shifted from his own. "Sean . . ."

He lifted his head enough to look into her eyes and felt his body punch right back into full tilt gear with what he saw there. Dreamy, unfocused, so rich, like the finest dark chocolate.

"I can't believe I . . ." She looked away, briefly, but he tipped her chin back so their gazes connected again. "I don't . . . that's not—me."

"Oh, I think it was wonderfully, beautifully, perfectly you." She started to talk, but he brushed his fingertip over her lips. "I don't think less of you, if that's what you're wondering. It's just as out of character for me." He pressed his fingertip on her lips, then stroked them. "Thank you for trusting me. With you. And for just going with it. I—I know that's probably outside your comfort zone. It meant a lot. To me. That you did." He leaned in and brushed his mouth over hers. "It makes me hunger, Holly. I want more. I want you." He lifted his head and looked down into her eyes. "I want more of this, but I want more than this. You do know that, right?"

The smallest of smiles played around the corners of her kiss-softened mouth, and he swore he'd never seen anything so beguiling. "I think you've been pretty up front about that."

"I push. Fair warning. When I want something, I push hard."

"Pushing hard isn't always a bad thing." Pink instantly bloomed in her cheeks and she choked a laugh as she quickly turned her head away. "I can't believe I said that out loud."

He nudged her gaze back to his, smiling himself now. "Holly uncensored. I like it. A lot. You can say anything to me, you know."

"I've already said more to you than . . . than anyone." She took a moment, never breaking their gaze, then seemed to gather herself, and he immediately went on guard. "Sean—"

"Holly, don't think it through right now. Just . . . can we keep going with the flow? See what happens next? Just . . . let it unfold, however it does? I know that's not

how you prefer to do things, but this once, give it a shot."
He grinned. "It's worked out pretty well so far."

She studied him. "You know me surprisingly well."

"You have no poker face. I can see the wheels turn."

She flashed another brief smile. "Good to know."

"I have to get back across the street. Prep for the dinner rush."

"Oh, okay." She immediately started to wriggle out from under the way he leaned over her body. "I—I have a million things to do, too. My—where's my shirt?"

He hated the sudden awkwardness. "Right here." He grabbed it off the high back of the divan, but held it out of her reach when she put her hand out. "Allow me." He was determined to keep her used to him being in her personal space. He wanted her to be comfortable with him putting his hands on her, with him being intimate with her, both casually . . . and very intently. He could only hope and pray that, at some point, she'd feel the same about him. But it had to start somewhere. He took her hand in his and tugged her up.

"Sean, I can—"

"I know, but I want to. You get to every day. I get to now." He shook the T-shirt right side out, then bunched it up and pulled it over her head.

She spluttered a laugh as she blew and puffed the hair out of her face. "Bed head, so attractive. New and improved, with more static cling."

Sean chuckled as she worked her arms through the sleeves, but he was the one who pulled the soft cotton down around her waist, then pinned it with his hands, keeping her rooted to the spot. "You do wonders for static," he said, kneeling on the floor between her thighs. He lifted up to kiss her mouth, then her nose. "In fact, you're the best looking electric shock recipient I've ever seen."

She moved her hands up, then her eyes went wide as

she realized her long strands of hair were in a static halo around her head.

"Very zero-G, really," he teased.

She tried to smooth it down, but that just made it worse. "I need some water, it's the only way to—"

He leaned in and kissed her, then smoothed his palms down over her hair, and magically, when he lifted his mouth, her hair was smooth and back to normal.

"How did you do that?"

He rose and tugged her to her feet, then slipped his fingers through hers so their palms met. "I've got a little body heat thing going at the moment. Can't imagine why."

She smiled, blushed a tiny bit, then said, "I'm sorry you're . . ." She rolled her eyes a little and he was torn between laughing and carrying her off somewhere where he could have her all to himself until the end of time.

"I'll live, truly."

"I know, but . . . I'm generally not so selfish."

He smiled and pulled their joined hands up between them. "Good to know."

"Sean—"

She was looking all serious again. Time for him to cut and run while the glow still lingered. "I'll bring dinner over later. If it's not too crazed in the kitchen, I'll bring enough for two." He leaned in and kissed her, hard and fast this time. At least he'd meant it to be. But somehow his mouth just wouldn't leave hers, and then her hands were on his shoulders, and his were in her hair, and she was tilting her head to one side to give him better access . . . and he was a goner for another good five minutes.

When he finally lifted his head, they were both a little unfocused and breathing a bit erratically. "Seriously," he said, "what you do to me. I'll be back. Seven thirty, eight."

And he left her there, dazed and a bit disheveled—both of which he was directly responsible for—and somehow stumbled down the stairs and across the street without giving in to the very strong urge to stay right were he was, until they were both dazed and disheveled some more. A whole lot more, in fact.

As he pushed through the doors to the kitchen, he was immediately enveloped in steam and the rich scent of beef and roasting potatoes and decided that not only was he going to be free for dinner, but—"Mickey!" he shouted.

His cousin stuck his head around from the other side of the kitchen where the sinks were. His pale Irish skin was flushed from the steam of scouring pans. "Yeah, boss man?"

"You want to close tonight?"

His expression was a mixture of delight and abject terror. Which meant he was ready. "Just me?"

Sean nodded. "You think you're ready to be the boss man for a few hours?"

Mickey grinned. "I was born ready, boy-o."

"Good, because tonight's the night."

Sean grinned as he moved into his office and closed the door behind him. If he was very, very lucky, tonight would, indeed, be the night.

Holly moved to the window and watched Sean cross the street. She could hardly believe what had just happened, what she'd let happen—encouraged to happen, if she was honest with herself. She should be feeling remorse, or worry, or . . . something. Something other than the huge urge to do a little dance around the room then wander back to the window, and stare, longingly, at the door to Gallagher's, reliving every single moment, every word, every breath, every . . . "Wow," she said, lifting the hair off her still-heated nape. "That was—he is—" She leaned against the desk again and laughed at herself. "Yeah. Wow, sums it right up." She spent a moment or two marveling over the kind of stupid silly giddy feelings she had. Had she ever in her life felt like that? That was an easy one. "Never."

She tried to control the rush of emotion so she could think. She had so much thinking to do. More now than before. Important decisions to make, bigger ones, now. Potentially life altering. And yet, she kept staring out the window. "What am I going to do with you, Sean Gallagher?"

She thought about him over there, inside the restaurant, with all those other Gallaghers milling about . . . Gallaghers she'd be personally meeting, mingling with, adjusting to, if she wanted to have Sean in her life. She gave a little shudder. A room full of professional clients clamoring for her were one thing. The tightly knit bosom of Sean's family was quite another. "Okay, so I'm not ready to think about that part yet."

She stood, making the desk wobble, which reminded her about the hidden compartment she'd found just before Sean had arrived. It was amazing that she was able to recall anything that happened before he got here. The last hour of her life had truly changed everything. It was like, from now on, her life would be compartmentalized as happening Before Sean and After Sean. Or, perhaps, Without Sean and With Sean.

She bent down to get a better look in the desk, her mind still spinning on how just a few days and one person could so drastically change her perspective on everything. Spying something tucked away inside the little cubby hole was finally enough to jerk her thoughts back to the present. "Huh. What do you know." She reached her hand inside and slipped out a slender, bound volume. A book? Maybe it would help to explain where the piece came from, or why it wasn't listed in inventory.

She walked over to the divan and sat down as she carefully opened the cover. It was clearly old, very old judging by the faded silk fabric cover and hand-stitched binding. There was no title on the cover, and she realized why as soon as she opened it. It wasn't a published book. It was someone's journal. Or diary. A slender piece of ribbon, which might have been pink once, but had yellowed badly with time, was tucked between the pages, marking a spot about two thirds of the way into the book. But, instead of going to that spot, she started at the beginning.

Holly carefully turned the once glossy cover page over and stared at an unlined page filled with row after neatly written row, all done with what appeared to be an old-fashioned ink pen. The handwritten lines filled up that first page, leaving little white space, and all the others that followed it were the same, until the aged slip of ribbon, which marked the final entry. The ink was a faded brown now, and as she carefully leafed through the pages, there were spots that were almost faded entirely away.

She went back to the beginning and skimmed, looking for a full date, but there were none she could find. Days of the week, and sometimes months, were noted, but no years. None marked inside the cover, either, or anywhere that she could discover. No name of the owner, either. A shame, she thought. She might not have been the antiques hound that her mother or Mrs. Gillespie was, but she hadn't spent a life growing up around them without some of the knowledge of provenance and the like wearing off on her. At least a little.

At the moment, there was more to her curiosity than simply dating the book or the desk it had been stashed in. Not that one necessarily had anything to do with the other. Anyone could have hidden the volume inside the desk at any time over the intervening years. But, though she couldn't confirm with her mother at the moment, even Mrs. Gillespie had agreed that, as far as she knew, she'd never seen the little antique rolltop before. And given how it had been tucked so far back into the corner of a room used only for storage, and then behind several other large pieces that Holly had had to rearrange to make room for herself as well as do the inventory . . . who knew how long it had been back there. But, given the dust and location, it had to have been quite some time ago. A decade or more was highly probable, and possibly multiples of that. In fact, for all Holly knew, maybe the little

desk had come with the place when her mother had purchased it from Mrs. Haversham almost fifty years back.

She shifted so the natural light illuminated the journal pages better, then eventually shifted back onto the divan the way it was designed to be used. She started reading . . . and within minutes, everything else faded away and she was engrossed in the unfolding story. A story, that as she continued to read, both moved her . . . and stunned her. Because the names mentioned in the book weren't all unfamiliar to her. As the sun set, she pulled the chain on the standing lamp she'd positioned next to the divan and continued reading, without pause.

She'd had no idea how much time had passed until she heard the sleigh bells downstairs. *Dammit.* She'd never gone down and locked up behind Sean earlier. How long had she been sitting there? She glanced out the window and saw that it was fully nightfall. She heard heavy tread on the stairs and her heart began to race. But it wasn't simply a reaction to what had happened between them earlier . . . and what she hoped would happen between them tonight, if she were completely honest.

No, her heart was racing, in part, due to the book laying in her lap. Because the people talked about in this personal journal weren't just known to Holly . . . they'd be familiar to Sean as well.

He dangled the take-out box in the open doorway before stepping into view. "Hungry?"

She looked up from the journal she'd been carefully closing, and everything inside her growled. Oh yeah. She was hungry all right. Starved, in fact.

She'd thought it might be awkward, or that she, at least, would probably be awkward, seeing him again after what they'd been doing the last time he was up here. But he was all smiles and easy charm and hot, freshly prepared dinners, and it was like they did this all the time.

If you stay here in Willow Creek . . . you could do this all the time.

He pulled over a tassled, overstuffed ottoman with a very detailed Santa face embroidered on the top, then shifted her feet and sat down on the edge of the divan, next to her hip. "You know, there's something weirdly disturbing about having Santa stare at you while you eat." He put the boxes down on top of the oversized footstool, so all you could see was the velvety red hat and the snowy white beard.

"Tell me about it," Holly said, shuddering in memory of all the Santas who'd stared at her over the years, and not just at the dinner table. In some ways, it was amazing she hadn't developed a clownlike phobia about the man. "You know the part that goes 'he sees you when you're sleeping'? Yeah, that gave me nightmares for years, because he did actually watch me sleep. Every night. All year long."

Sean laughed and she loved the natural, full sound of it, like a guy who did it often and openly. It made her feel all kind of warm and fuzzy inside. Which didn't seem exactly right since she'd just Santa bashed, but she held on to the feeling anyway.

"I do love Christmas, but you're right, I can't imagine what it was like, living in winter wonderland twenty-four-seven."

"We're even," she said as he opened a box and handed her a linen napkin rolled with real silver inside. "I only had to put up with a make-believe character. I can't imagine living with the number of real people you reside with on a daily basis. At least my army was inanimate and perpetually jolly."

"Oh, I'd say the Gallaghers are a pretty perpetually jolly bunch." He winked at her. "You know, you could actually cross the street and come inside where we could sit and eat at a real table."

She inhaled the scent of beef and potatoes like a woman starved and sighed in deep satisfaction. "If this tastes half as good as it smells, you could probably lure me over there just by dangling a bowl of stew under my nose."

He grinned. "I'll keep that in mind." He popped open his own take-out box, then nodded at the book still tucked in her lap. "What's that you're reading?"

She couldn't believe she'd forgotten. "I found this in the little rolltop desk there, in a secret compartment. I'd just unearthed the desk earlier today and discovered it wasn't anywhere on the inventory list. I was hoping the book might explain where it came from and why it's here."

"And did it?"

"Well . . . not exactly. But it explains a lot of other things. And it involves both of our families."

He paused in midbite. "What?"

"And the Hamilton family, as well."

"Hamilton family. As in Hamilton Industries, Hamilton?"

Holly nodded.

Lionel Hamilton, who was in his eighties now, about nine or ten years older than her parents, was the last in a long line of Hamiltons who had either owned or run most of neighboring Randolph County. Hamilton Industries, and the Hamilton family, were responsible for keeping pretty much everyone who lived there employed for at least the past century or so, and it was through their varied businesses that the otherwise rather rural county continued to prosper. And prosper well.

"Anything juicy?" he teased.

"Oh, you might say that."

Sean's smile faded and he laid his fork down. "Really? Like what?"

"Did you know that Trudy Hamilton used to live in this very house? Well, back when the bottom part was a rare and antique bookshop and these rooms up here belonged to Old Lady Haversham, she did."

"Lionel's wife, Trudy? Didn't she pass on some time ago?"

Holly nodded. The Hamiltons were local royalty, like the Kennedys must have been to the folks of Hyannis Port and the rest of Cape Cod. The details of their very privileged lives had always been reported on in both local papers and the bigger circulations in D.C. and Richmond. "This was long before she became Mrs. Hamilton, though. Her maiden name was Haversham."

"She was related to Old Lady Haversham?"

Holly nodded again. Neither she nor Sean had ever met the older woman, as she'd long since passed on before they were born, but stories of the eccentric old woman were a well-known part of the small town lore. The black sheep of the Havershams of Charlottesville and Raleigh, a very well respected and wealthy tobacco family back in the day, all deceased now. "Trudy's fortune went to Lionel. She was the last of the family line."

"Right, there was talk about how it was actually the Haversham fortune that rescued Hamilton Industries from near bankruptcy way back when, right?"

"Right. And I think Lionel is only survived by his great-nephew, who—"

"Famously rejected the family fortune. Doesn't he live somewhere down South?"

"North Carolina, I think."

Sean picked up his silverware again. "So, what's the juicy part?"

"Well, Trudy and your grandmother were good friends. At least for the length of one spring and summer."

Sean's eyes widened. "Really? How could that be?"

"And they babysat my mother, on many occasions, that summer."

"How old were they?"

"Trudy and your grandmother were probably only a few years apart at most, if that. They were teenagers, the summer I'm talking about. Fifteen and sixteen, respectively. So . . . about sixty-five years ago. My mom would have been around seven or eight."

"Interesting, for sure. I'll have to ask my aunts if they'd ever heard any stories. I mean, having Trudy Hamilton here in our town . . . that would have been quite something."

"Well, she didn't become Trudy Hamilton for another five years, but I guess even as a wealthy Haversham, it might have made a little noise. Certainly, later on, after she married Lionel, I would have imagined there would have been 'Trudy slept here' kind of stories, but . . . who knows. Maybe it was just a lost summer. I know her family, and probably Trudy herself would have most certainly been hoping it was."

Sean looked confused. "Why?"

"She came here on a 'vacation,' " Holly said, using air quotes. "The way young girls had to go away to visit relatives for a time often did. Back in those days, anyway."

Sean took a moment, then the confusion cleared and his eyebrows rose. "She was pregnant?"

Holly nodded and lifted the volume. "This was her diary or journal, while she was staying here. Right in this room, I'm guessing. I think they sent her here because, at least according to this, Old Lady Haversham was more than a little eccentric. She was a bit loony, or at least her extended family certainly thought so. She was definitely on the outs with them, never talked to anyone, spent all her time holed up here in the bookshop. Anyway, back then, Willow Creek was even more of a small, rural town than it is now, and so the Havershams tucked Trudy away here to have her child, then she'd come back and no one would be the wiser."

"Wow, but I didn't think she had any children, ever."

"Well, she didn't. At least, not that anyone knew about. And, it gets more interesting. Your grandmother was the one who helped her get rid of the baby."

Sean looked momentarily horrified. "Get rid of, you mean she—"

"No, no, I don't mean before, I mean after the baby was born. Your family has been part of St. Francis's congregation forever, right?"

"Right, so what are you saying?"

"According to Trudy, your grandmother was with her when she gave birth. It sounds like it might have been here in the house. Anyway, I'm not sure what the plan was after the baby was born. According to Trudy, her aunt wasn't exactly on top of things."

"Did she even know Trudy was pregnant?"

"Yes, but I don't know that she really paid much attention to her. Trudy lived up here and didn't even help in the shop much. That was why she was excited to go hang out with your grandmother when she would babysit. She'd sneak out in the evenings and go to whatever family your grandmother was sitting for, and hang out with her. One of those was my grandparents' old house, sitting for my mother."

"So, after the baby was born . . . ?"

"Your grandmother took it to the church and left him with the nuns."

"It was a boy?"

"Apparently. So, I'm guessing he was adopted, or put into foster care, or whatever the system was back then."

Sean sat back. "So . . . Trudy Haversham, who went on to become Trudy Hamilton, had a child. An heir. Both to her fortune . . . and, I guess Lionel's. . . . Her child, if he's still alive, wouldn't he be the direct heir? I mean, he's older than Lionel's great-nephew, and though not direct blood of Lionel's, he would be direct in line for the Haversham fortune, right? And, if he's passed, then I'd guess that his offspring, if he had any, would be next in line. Pretty big bombshell, when you think about it."

Holly smiled briefly. "I know. Bombshell in a book. The question is, what do I do with it now?"

10

"All I know is that we don't have to decide right this second. It's been in there for decades, so another day or two won't matter." Sean took the book from her hands and carefully set it on top of the china cabinet. Then he took their empty dinner boxes and set them aside as well. Holly looked up at him questioningly when he put his hand out for her.

"Go for a ride with me?"

"What?"

He smiled. "A ride. I thought we might take a little drive, look at the Christmas lights." He took her hand and pulled her up so her body came up flush against his. "Now, don't rush to say no. I'm well aware of your feelings on the holiday, but lights are just lights. They're pretty to look at and they don't stare at you while you sleep."

Her lips quirked. "I'm not that big a scrooge, you know. Actually, I kind of like the lights part of the holiday. It's hard not to be cheery when you drive by a twinkling display."

"Great." She started to say something, but he dipped

his head and caught her mouth in a slow, sweet kiss. "I know you have a million things to do, but you've been holed up in this place for days now. An hour or two out won't kill you and might help clear your head a little."

She held his gaze for a moment, then smiled. "Well, I'm not so sure about the cleared head part. Something about being in your proximity seems to muddle that up a little."

"In a good way?"

"You were in the room earlier today, right?"

He laughed. "Yes, I believe I was."

"Alrighty then."

He kissed her again and scooped her up against his chest and spun her around.

She was laughing, too, when he put her down, but said, "What was that for?"

"For making me feel like spinning around like a kid. Turns out it's even more fun as an adult . . . when you've got another adult in your arms at the time."

"Imagine that," she said, her brown eyes shining.

That was what he wanted to see. And for a very long time. "Come on, let's get your coat and get out of here."

He'd brought his truck over and parked it in front of her shop, which made her nudge him with her elbow when they stepped outside.

"Pretty sure of yourself."

"Actually, I delegated closing to my cousin tonight, so I was done when I came over here. I knew if I had to go back through the restaurant later to get my truck I might get trapped, so I parked out here. And I didn't want Mickey to feel like I was checking up on him."

"Very thoughtful of you."

He opened the passenger side door and helped her up into the seat, then leaned in after her. "Well, it wasn't an entirely altruistic move."

"When did you come up with the Christmas lights tour idea?"

"When I realized it was either get you off of that crushed velvet sex goddess sofa you have up there, or strip you naked and make love to you on what is probably a very uncomfortable piece of furniture."

To her credit, this time there was no blushing. Good. That meant she'd been thinking about him, about them . . . and was, perhaps, getting more comfortable with letting things continue to develop.

"You're right," she said, then when he wiggled his eyebrows, she laughed and added, "that is the most uncomfortable piece of furniture ever made. At least for sleeping."

"Why are you sleeping on it, then? It's also drafty in there, you can't be comfortable. Why not stay in a motel or one of the inns."

Willow Creek was small, but there was a clean, neatly kept little motel on the edge of town, and several of the older homes had been turned into bed-and-breakfasts.

"When I got here I really was feeling pretty overwhelmed, still am, to be honest, and I guess I just didn't want to have to deal with people. It might not have been the best thing to do, to hole myself up in the shop like I did, but I really needed to sort through things, and to think, and it just seemed like the thing to do."

"Well, it's a good thing I've come to your rescue, then."

"Meaning?"

"Meaning I have a very large house—" He broke off long enough to shake his head for her to not interrupt. "—with several bedrooms, all of which have beds and only mine is occupied. Even my couch is more comfortable than that slab you've been sleeping on." He leaned down and kissed her, fast at first, then dipped in for another one, then another. "You can have pick of the house, Goldilocks. I'm the only bear in residence."

She rolled her eyes, but she was grinning. "I'm sure the next thing you'll be telling me is you're a teddy bear."

"Only if you believe that you'd sleep more soundly curled up with one."

She laughed outright at that. "Why don't we get on with our tour of lights here, before people start unplugging them for the night."

"Okay, okay." He ducked in for one last kiss, then pushed her hair back, touched her cheek, as he finally moved back. "You know, I think I had it all wrong anyway."

"Had what all wrong?"

"About which one of us was doing the rescuing." He didn't let her question him on that, but closed the door after she'd situated herself in her seat, then scooted around to his side. He had no idea how he was going to handle knowing Holly was under his roof, in a bed other than his own, and not give in to temptation. Or at least tempting temptation. He glanced over at her and found her watching him, only mixed in with that always thoughtful, always intent look . . . was what looked like affection. The kind that just comes naturally when you look at someone you honestly care about.

He was grinning as he turned on the engine. So, that would be his motivation. To do whatever it took to keep that look on her face. And not give her any reason to feel otherwise.

He was still grinning over an hour later when they finally pulled into the driveway of his home. The drive had been both relaxing and informative. They hadn't talked business, or about their burgeoning relationship. Instead he'd shared stories about his family, she'd asked about his culinary training and what most compelled him about cooking, he'd asked her about when she'd started painting, and the conversation simply continued on, flowing easily and naturally.

"This is your place?"

"Yep. Bought it a few years ago. Used to be—"

"The McElroys' place, right?"

"Right. Old Mr. Eddie's kids moved him to a senior home over near them in Charlottesville and put the house on the market. I like that it's in the older part of town, not too far from the restaurant, but not right next door." He flashed her a smile. "And not next door to any of my relatives, either."

"Most of them are over on the west side, right?"

He nodded. "Newer homes, closer to the highway, and the stores and schools." He turned off the engine. "It's quieter here, an older, more sedate neighborhood, for sure, but with all the chaos of the restaurant, I like the peace, the retreat."

She was looking at the house. He was looking at her.

"Did you ever think you'd want a family? I know you love yours, but, as you said, being surrounded by them all the time, night and day, seven days a week . . . and your parents only having you . . ."

"Only because my mom couldn't have more. She had some complications with me. She'd have had a dozen if she could have, and my dad would have loved it, too." He laughed now, as he looked at the terror that crossed her face. "I don't have any predetermined ideas on what kind of family I want. I guess I do know I want one, at least that's how I see my life going. But . . . I'm not a big future planner in that regard. I'm happy with letting it take its own course."

She glanced at him, then smiled when he reached

across and took her hand. "I think you've really done well for yourself, Sean. You're happy, you love what you do, you have a nice home here . . . surrounded by family and friends. I think your folks would be so proud and happy."

"I'd like to think so." He tugged her hand a little, and she slid across the seat to be closer to him. "You know, I meant what I said earlier."

"Which part?"

"About just wanting you to be comfortable, to have a bed, get a good night's sleep. I know how much stress you're under, and that I've been a part of that, so consider it the least I can do."

She didn't say anything right away. Instead she looked down at where their hands were still joined, then finally, back up at him. "Okay."

He smiled. It was a start. That's all he wanted. Starting meant they were moving in some direction. Together.

Then she smiled, and reached up and cupped his face in her palm, leaned forward until her mouth was a breath away from his, and said, "So . . . what would be the most that you could do?"

His heart leapt, his body beat that by double, and he completely lost his train of thought. "I—uh—"

She laughed then, and kissed him. "It's good to know I'm not the only one who feels occasionally discombobulated by this."

"No . . . not the only one," he said on a short laugh. "You know, you don't have to—"

"I know I don't. But after this afternoon, I'd be lying if I said I hadn't thought about it. A lot. Okay, nonstop. And I don't know, yet, what I'm going to do. Here, in London, so many things yet to be figured out, decided on. Normally I'd want to take my time, be sure of every little thing. I'm not normally so spontaneous, especially about this." She touched his face again. "But, like you said, now is when you're here. And I'm here. And I want . . . what I want. In fact, it's the one easy decision I've had to make. I don't want regrets. I want time with you."

He grinned. "Have I mentioned how much I love that you're such a decisive woman?"

"Remember you said that."

He was still smiling as he walked around and helped her slide from the truck. "How about a nice bottle of wine, maybe a fire in the fireplace. And we'll see where we end up later."

"I think Goldilocks never had it so good."

11

Holly leaned back against the couch from her spot on the living room floor and watched Sean add more logs to the fire. He'd done nice things with the old house. Gleaming hardwood floors, fresh paint on the walls in earthy tones, leather couch and big overstuffed chair, thick woven rugs everywhere . . . and lots of bookcases. It was warm, decidedly masculine, but cozy and inviting. Just like the owner.

"When do you have time to read?"

He poked at bit at the embers. "My hours are a little crazy and sometimes I don't get home until the wee hours. Reading helps me switch gears from all the things I have to worry about with the restaurant."

"I do the same thing, actually. There are these wonderful antiques and used bookstores in London. Picadilly, Notting Hill, Portobello Road. When I was particularly stressed out over a client or an account, I'd escape the office for an hour or so and head out to one or the other."

Finished, with the flames popping again, Sean shifted back to sit next to Holly, stretching his arm out along the seat cushions behind her. "And painting?"

"You know, I didn't do much of that in London itself. I saved that for my trips away. Not that there isn't plenty of inspiration there, but—"

"You needed to escape completely, to really indulge yourself and revel in it."

She looked at him, surprised. "Exactly. I always said I should start sketching, just give myself the pleasure, make room for it in my day-to-day life, but it wasn't really the right fit there, the right balance, with the hours I work and the pressures. You're right, I needed to block out time entirely to really enjoy it."

He stroked the back of her neck, her shoulder, and she knew it wasn't really the wine that was making her feel so warm and tended to.

"Do you miss it?" he asked. "I mean, the work, the city, browsing the shops, all of it?"

"Yes. It's what I know; it's my life. Has been for a long time now. I honestly didn't think coming back here would have any influence on how I felt about it. It's home to me now, that's just how it is. And I'm okay with that. If anything, I thought coming back would strengthen that feeling."

"Did it? You don't miss living here? Not homesick?"

She looked at him. "It's not home, really. Not anymore. My folks are gone; the house is no longer ours; the shop is dark; my life, my old life anyway, really doesn't exist."

"You want to go back to London, then?"

She held his gaze for a long time and was thankful that he said nothing else, didn't try any further to influence her thoughts. She knew, could see, the trepidation in his eyes, his face. She knew what he wanted. He was asking her, very honestly, what it was that she wanted.

"A few days ago, I would have said yes. There really wouldn't have been any other response to give. There is

nothing for me here." She covered his hand with her own.
"Or there wasn't anyway."

He wove his fingers through hers, but let her find her
words. But the hope was there again, the spark of it, and it
was amazing what it did to her. Every single time.

"I came here wondering how I was going to handle
what was my mother's entire world in a way that would
satisfy us both, and I honestly had no idea what that was
going to be. But I can't sit here and say that I'm dying
with homesickness for London, or my job there . . . I do
miss my friends. More important, I think, is that I miss
the comfort and security of knowing who I am there,
what my purpose is. I don't know who I am here anymore
and I had major doubts on knowing how to handle the decisions I had to make here."

"And now?"

"Now I'm more secure about that part. I know what I
want to do with the store. I'm confident it's the right
thing. I just have to work through the steps of figuring out
how to make it work the best way possible, that is the best
for me."

"And?"

She squeezed his hand. "And then there's you. Compli-
cating the hell out of things. On the one hand, London
offers steadiness, confidence, security. You . . . you tanta-
lize me with what ifs . . . about us, about what there
might be. You make me think, and question . . . everything really. My life, my passions, what I really want. You
make me question if playing it safe and just staying on the
path that offers me security, if not personal fulfillment, is
really what I want from my life." She looked at him, into
those eyes that were so steady, at a man who was clearly
willing to offer her the place and time to try to find answers to some of her questions. If she was only brave

enough to try. "The time I carved out for myself to come here and resolve things . . . isn't long enough for me to resolve those bigger questions. And it's scary, terrifying really, to think I'd have to literally jump from frying pan to fire, in order to give myself a chance to find out. I can't go back and sit in my flat in London and figure out if what I really want is here in Virginia. If I want to try and find a way to pursue art . . . to pursue what might be with you, I'd have to stay here. No safety net."

"I wish there was something I could say, or do, to make that easier for you."

"I know." She touched his face. "I know you really, truly mean that. But this is up to me. A true crossroads. And . . . I don't know yet." She sat her wineglass down and shifted onto her knees, touched his face. "I don't know that it's fair, and I want to be fair—"

"You're being honest. That's all I'll ever ask."

"I know enough to know that I don't want to go upstairs and sleep alone. I want to be with you. Spend time with you. Learn whatever I can in the time I have, to help me figure things out. I don't want to rush . . . and I don't want to waste a single moment. Is that making any sense? I know it's terribly selfish but it's just the truth, and I—"

He cut her off by tugging her to him and kissing her. This time it wasn't seductive, or soft, carnal, or sweet. This was a declaration, pure and simple. This was a man staking his claim. And he was claiming her.

And everything in her responded to that like the proverbial heavens were opening and the angels were singing. Kind of hard to be immune to that. Not when everything in her wanted to respond with equal passion, equal determination, to claim him as her own, too. To make it clear that she was putting the world on notice, that he was what she wanted, and damn anything or anyone who got in her way. In that moment, it was so crystal clear to her . . . if only all the moments that followed would also be so crystalline.

He shifted them around, lowering her to the floor.

"Sean, I can't promise—"

"I didn't ask for a promise. I don't know what you'll do tomorrow, or two weeks from tomorrow. What I do know is that I have you right now. And you have me. For this moment in time, I'm okay with that. I'm selfish, too, Holly. If this is what I can have, then I'm not walking away. Not willingly. You gave me a choice. I choose you."

She pulled him down on top of her and shoved every last single doubt from her mind. No place for those tonight. Later. Much later, if she was lucky. For now, she was going to give in to what she was feeling, and show him that, give him that. She smiled. "I want this. I want you."

His grin was so fierce, so . . . primal, it made her entire body quiver in response. "I know exactly where I want you, and it's not on this rug." He shifted back and scooped her up into his arms before she could react.

"Sean—"

"Come on, Goldilocks. I think you'll find this bed is just right."

The hallway, the stairs, all of it was a blur. Her heart was pounding, and it only increased when he lowered both of them into a sea of down comforters, pillows, and what had to be the most heavenly bed ever. Something of it must have shown in her expression.

"We Irish like our fine linen and feathers."

"It's a wonder you ever get out of it," she said as he sank into the soft cloud with her.

The twinkle in his eye was downright wicked. "I was just thinking that very same thing myself."

He kissed her then, and she wrapped her arms around

him and let his weight sink her fully into the bed. He kissed her with such intent, so steady, so constant, so . . . perfect. His hands on her were confident, but also almost reverent. He didn't pause, didn't question, but he made her feel cherished, indulged. She wasn't even sure how or when each piece of their clothing came off—they seemed to melt away under clever fingers—she only knew that when she felt his warm, bare skin caressing hers, covering hers, she felt like she really had found heaven. Her heaven, anyway.

He started shifting his kisses from her mouth to her chin and she knew where he was leading this, and she was all for that . . . next time. Right now she wanted all of him, right where she needed him most, and she shifted beneath him moving her hips.

"I want so much more of this," he murmured against her lips. "I feel like I'm starving, only I don't know exactly where to begin the buffet."

She laughed, then shifted her hips directly under his. "How about here . . . we'll go back for appetizers and dessert later."

He moved just enough to grab at the drawer handle of the nightstand. "I'm already protected," she said, "and . . . it's okay, if you're—"

"I'm okay, too."

She smiled up at him. "Then come here."

"Have I mentioned how I like it when you've made up your mind about something?"

She smiled at that, and he slipped his arm under her back, beneath her hips, lifting her so effortlessly, but so her shorter body matched the longer length of his, where he could tease her, nudging her, and still kiss her at the same time. He paused, just as he began to push into her. "Holly . . ."

She was gripping his shoulders, but slid one hand to

his face, touched his cheeks, his chin, ran her finger over his lips. "What?" she whispered.

His grin was slow and devastating and made her instinctively push up, taking him a tiny bit deeper inside of her. "This might just be my best Christmas ever," he said.

She surprised herself by laughing. "Me, too. Christmas and birthday, all in one." Then she wrapped one leg around his hips and lifted herself onto him, making him groan as he slid the rest of the way inside of her.

He was careful, with his larger size, her smaller frame, but they quickly found their rhythm, and laughter faded to soft moans, deep growls, and eventually, slowly, labored breathing and damp, heated skin, and climbing faster, and faster still. He tucked her up more firmly against his hips so he could sink deeper and connect her to him in a way that made him push her past that shimmering edge into the long, indescribable shudder of pleasure. Wave upon wave of it, until she felt him gather, and moved with him, tightening around him as if it were the most natural thing to do, taking him over the edge just as effortlessly and perfectly as he'd done with her.

He was careful not to collapse his weight on top of her, not that she thought she'd have minded. She couldn't breathe anyway. Aftershocks were still tremors of exquisite sensation after exquisite sensation and her mind was everywhere and nowhere, all at the same time.

Their breathing gradually slowed, and she felt him search for her hand and weave his fingers through hers, then closing his hand around hers, so much bigger, so strong, so steady. Until she felt that slight tremor . . . and realized that maybe she was a steadying force for him, too. Something about that single gesture, as they lay there spent from ridiculously perfect first-time lovemaking . . . was the most intimate part of the entire act, and what had tears gathering sweetly at the corners of her eyes.

But before she could worry about them, or how he might interpret them, he was pulling her closer, tucking her against his broad chest. And she felt both of their bodies relax as if taking a huge, unwinding sigh of contentment. They both yawned at the same time, laughed sleepily at themselves, and snuggled more closely together.

"I have to leave early. Around five," he said drowsily. "Market—have to buy produce. You can stay here. Long as you want."

Stay. How wonderful that sounded, she thought. At that moment, she never wanted to leave. Holly slipped her arm across his waist, pushing away all real-world concerns for just a bit longer. "Mmm," was all she managed before letting sleep claim her.

She ended up waking before he did. It wasn't even dawn yet. In fact, she had no idea what time it was, but the hint of light that filtered in through the slatted wooden blinds was still moonlight. She sat up, pulling the soft sheets and thick comforters around her when the chill of the air away from Sean's big, warm body pebbled her skin. Sean. She shifted so she could look at him. So big, warm, wonderful . . . sweet, amazing . . . and hers. The pure affection that coursed through her wasn't something she could deny, even if she couldn't rationally explain the depth or power of it. Sex, lust . . . maybe. But it didn't feel that way to her. Not solely, anyway. He'd touched her in far deeper, more intimate ways than anyone ever had, and most of those moments hadn't taken place in this bed, but sitting in the cab of his truck, standing by the counter of her shop, or lounging by the fire in his living room.

A smile stole across her face as she continued to watch him sleep. She had no idea how much time passed, but the urge to grab a pencil and paper, to sketch, to draw, to paint, sitting right there, in the bed, was almost overwhelming. It made her fingers twitch, the urge was so strong. She must have made some sound, because he reached out, eyes still closed, and found her and pulled her to him.

"Hey, you," he said, his voice a deep rumble. "Come here."

She moved into his arms like they had danced this particular dance many, many times. For the difference in their sizes, they'd found a comfort with each other's bodies remarkably swiftly, and their rhythm was just as easy and natural this time as it had been before. And that's where her thoughts ended, as Sean started making love to her again.

When she woke again . . . he was gone. She sat up, certain the grin on her face was quite smug and satisfied. And she was okay with that. She gathered her clothes and dressed, then sat back down on the edge of the bed again, and thought about the night they'd just spent together. And asked herself if going back to London was what she really wanted. Or just what was easiest. Safest. And if she didn't go back to London . . . then what?

She found a note from Sean and keys to his other vehicle, which was his parents' old car, on the kitchen counter. It all felt so . . . natural, so easy. Could it be so easy? Well, the relationship with Sean part seemed like it would be . . . but what in the hell was she supposed to do with the rest of her life if she moved back here?

Her thoughts weren't any clearer by the time she got back to the shop, and while the meeting later that morning with the estate lawyer did answer a great many of her questions about handling the shop lease, she felt like her head might explode with all the things she still had on her mind. That was when she found the diary and remembered the bombshell discovery of the day before.

And, without thinking too long or hard about it, she grabbed Sean's keys, grabbed the diary, and took off toward St. Francis. She realized it for the procrastination maneuver it was, but who knew? Maybe getting a few answers about someone else's life would put her own into better perspective.

12

It was funny how quickly Sean had come to think about Holly in the course of his everyday life. She hadn't even been back a week, but it already felt like she'd always been in the back of his mind, even as the organized pandemonium that was his life swirled around him, both jarring and comforting. Sometimes, the greater the uproar or hubbub, the more he thought about her . . . and it surprised him how much easier just thinking about her smile, or the way she arched into him when he kissed that spot just above her collarbone, made the insanity of the world that was running a restaurant that much easier to sort through and maintain.

Just as he caught himself in yet another highly detailed daydream, and thought about trying her cell again, there was a tap at his office door. Without waiting, Mick stuck his head in.

Sean looked up. "You know, it's customary, after the knock, to wait for—"

"Pretty lady to see you, boy-o. I thought you might want to cut down on the formalities."

And, as if his constant thinking and daydreaming had

conjured her up, Holly walked into his office. It shouldn't have been such a profound moment, but it was. Her, there, in his space for once. Surrounded by his life, the sounds, scents, and general mayhem of it. Like this perfect little island of serenity in the midst of turmoil. Only, once the haze wore off and Mick closed the door behind her, did he see that she wasn't, exactly, looking all that peaceful.

"What's wrong?"

She didn't even take the time to notice his office, which was probably just as well. He knew where everything was, amidst the piles and stacks, but that was the extent of his organizational skills. "Can I—" She motioned to a stack of files and order forms on the only chair facing his desk. He was already shoving back his chair, prepared to leap over his desk if need be, to make room for her, but she carefully shifted the pile to the floor and took a seat. Then immediately sprang up and began pacing.

Sean frowned. "Holly? What's going on?" He stood and came around the desk more calmly this time, then finally stepped in front of her, effectively cutting off her path.

She paused, then abruptly said, "I had a lot on my mind. When I left your place. I woke up happier and more confused than ever. And I—didn't know where to go next, what to figure out first. Oh, and thanks for the car. I hadn't thought about it, and I had a meeting with the lawyer, so it was really great of you to do that, and—"

"Did something happen at the meeting? Did you figure out about the lease?"

"I did and no, that wasn't it. Actually, I think that's going to be easier than I thought. And Mrs. Gillespie is helping me with setting up having a few buyers come in, and an auction house appraiser to look at the stock she doesn't want. I—I think it's going to be okay."

He tipped up her chin. She was talking a mile a minute. "Something rattled you, was it—" He really hesitated bringing up the night they'd spent together. It had meant everything to him, and he knew he was possibly setting himself up, allowing himself to hope like he was, but he couldn't seem to stem it. He wanted her. He wanted a chance to see what they could have together, and no amount of rational deliberation or commonsense talks he'd had with himself today was going to change that, apparently. "What's going on?" he finally asked.

"I—even with the solutions for the shop issues, I . . . I had so much on my mind. Mostly about you, about my life in London, my job, what my life here would even be like if I tried . . . I just—I needed out. Away. I needed to focus on something else. This morning I watched you sleeping, and I felt this need, this overwhelming urge to sketch, to draw, to create and I know it's all this uncertainty and that's how I vent."

"So . . . did you?" The idea of her watching him while he slept, much less drawing him, should have been disconcerting, and he supposed it was. But mostly it was an incredible turn-on.

She shook her head, clearly still distracted by whatever was really on her mind. "I didn't have the supplies, at your place or the store. But that was probably a good thing . . . or maybe not. I really don't know. If I'd spent time working things out with paper and charcoal, or some watercolors, then I probably wouldn't have grabbed the diary instead." She held his gaze again now, only more directly this time. "And gone to St. Francis with it."

He had no idea what he'd been expecting, seeing her so atypically rattled, but that hadn't even occurred to him.

"This is about the diary?" Enormous relief coursed through him. She was thinking about staying here, about moving her life here; those were the tidbits he'd gleaned from her burst of chatter; that's what stuck in his head. That she'd woken up happy.

"Sean, it's about more than the diary. It concerns you. Your family."

"What?" He tried to clear his head, pay attention to what she was saying. "How? I mean, I know you said my grandmother was the one who helped get the baby to the nuns, but what else could that have to do with my family, especially now?"

"That's just it, I don't think they gave the baby to the nuns."

Sean frowned. "What in the hell else would they have done?"

She put her hand over his arm. "They found a home for him. I'm pretty sure that home was with your family."

Sean felt himself sway slightly. "They what?"

"I talked to the priest and showed him the diary, and I spoke to the mother superior. They weren't personally there at the time, of course, but they've both been there since shortly afterward."

"I can't believe they'd have told you anything."

"I just let them read the diary and I knew, from the looks they shared, that they knew . . . something. I asked them in more detail about the adoption policies back then, just in general you know, and all they would tell me is that the way things were back then, they just tried to find a loving home, where and when they could. And . . . I don't know how I pieced it together, but I thought about your grandmother being the one to bring the baby to them, and how huge your family is, and so I just supposed, out loud, that it could be someone like the Gallaghers and their faces gave it away.

"I reminded them that there were no Havershams left, and that only Lionel and his great-nephew were left on the Hamilton side . . . and that if one of the Gallaghers was an actual blood relation, didn't they deserve to know?"

"What did they say?"

"Nothing. That was all . . . but Sean, wasn't that enough? One of your relatives is Trudy Hamilton's son!"

Sean leaned his weight back against his desk, sending a pile of paper cascading but ignoring the mess it made. "I guess it's possible, but . . . which one? I mean, my dad was the last of thirteen kids. My grandmother was almost as old when she had him as your mom was when she had you. And though my dad only had me, the rest of his brothers and sisters . . ." He waved an absent hand to the restaurant beyond the door to his office. "Well, you know how that went."

"Don't you think it's important to find out?"

"Why, because they might have claim to Hamilton's money? I don't know that anyone in my family would risk the damage such news could do just for the sake of a possible inheritance."

"What damage could it do?"

"Think about it . . . you said yourself that it was Trudy's money that helped bail out Hamilton Industries. If she had an heir that predated, or possibly precluded Lionel . . . I'm just saying, having all that come out, I don't know what good it would do."

"If it was you? I mean, if you weren't a Gallagher by blood . . . wouldn't you want to know your history?"

"Anyone in Willow Creek with the name Gallagher is family. Born into it, married into it, even divorced from it in some cases. Once a Gallagher, always a Gallagher. Nothing would change that. Putting this out there would only lead to possible divisiveness within the family. Why do that?"

"I'd want to know," Holly said quietly. "It wouldn't change how I felt about my parents; they raised me—they loved me. But I'd want to know." She handed him the book. "This really belongs to you. One of you, anyway."

And, with that, she turned and walked out the door. He thought about calling her back, but the entire exchange had caught him so off guard, he simply sat there, book clutched in his hands, wondering what in the hell had just happened. And what he was supposed to do about it.

13

So much for clarity. All her little jaunt that day had done was roil up even more confusing emotions. She shouldn't have just shoved the book in his hand and bolted, but she'd panicked a little. It wasn't that she truly cared what Sean decided to do with the diary, but their entire exchange, his talking about his family with such pride and fierce loyalty, had only served to make her feel that much more an oddball in contrast. Her life was so vastly different from his. Had she really thought she'd so seamlessly fit in? Yes, it was easy when she was with Sean, but that was only so many hours of each day. What about all the rest of them?

The bells on the shop door jingled out front, making her heart lurch. She wasn't ready to see him again, talk to him again, but it wasn't Sean. It was one of the appraisers. Mrs. Gillespie was really on the ball with this thing. Holly greeted him and was soon swallowed back up in the ongoing, and for the first time, blessed distraction of dismantling her mother's old life.

It wasn't until much, much later, that she had another chance to think about her own.

Sitting in the office, she finally closed the folder on the growing stack of papers she was accumulating as the final closing of the shop was all coming together. She rubbed her eyes, then the back of her neck, as she thought about what her mother would say when she returned from her trip to find that Holly had sold off the stock . . . and leased the store to Mrs. Gillespie. Maybe she should have found someone completely out of her mother's orbit to take over the space, or just put it up for sale. "Lock, stock, and creepy Santa Clauses," she muttered.

But she was helping make someone else's dream come true, and ownership of the building was an asset for her. It was something solid, a move toward building some kind of future for herself—at least investment-wise—beyond renting a flat and working in a field that was more security blanket than passionate goal. She picked up the envelope that Mrs. Gillespie had dropped off earlier. The woman might be old and eccentric, but now that she had her own passionate goal clearly within her grasp, she certainly wasn't wasting any time. Holly smiled briefly, remembering Mrs. Gillespie's response to her when she'd made a similar comment as she'd been handed the legal-size package.

"I'm seventy-eight years old; time isn't exactly a commodity I can afford to waste." She'd folded her hands in front of her once Holly had the envelope in her hands, and added, "It's not at any age, if you truly understand the value of life." Then she'd walked out and left Holly to deal with the appraiser.

She thought about going for some dinner before opening up the packet and seeing exactly what her new tenant was proposing. Apparently unwilling to wait for Holly to come up with a price, she'd gone ahead and put together a proposal. Which, as far as Holly was concerned, was a relief. She'd run it by her lawyer and the accountant he'd recommended she retain and see if they thought it was a viable offer, and barring any wild requests or lowball rent arrangements, she was certain they'd have a deal.

And then what?

Her thoughts shifted to Sean. She wasn't even sure what to do this evening, much less the rest of her life. After her little theatrical exhibition in his office, he'd left her to her own business, presumably to regain some semblance of sanity. Which, to be honest, she appreciated. It had been both an emotionally charged and an emotionally draining week. She just hoped he understood that. And was fairly certain he did. In fact, that was the thing about Sean that drew her the most. He was understanding, willing to talk things out, a good communicator, and not afraid to tell her when he thought his ideas might have more merit.

So, did she go over there, talk with him? He was probably in the midst of the dinner rush at the moment, so probably not the best time. Was she supposed to just show up back at his house tonight? She felt like they should talk again first, reconnect, before she just strolled into his house. Goldilocks, indeed.

Deciding that looking at the proposal was less complicated, she slid out the documents and slid the cover letter to the side to glance over the basic setup of her proposed lease agreement. The payment structure actually seemed fair, though she'd still vet it with her lawyer and accountant, but . . . she peered closer. What was that part about . . . "commission for works sold will be kept separate and apart from any and all tenant–owner contractual obligations for the . . . what?" Frowning, Holly flipped through the rest, then finally went back to the cover letter. "What the hell is she talking about, commission on works done? Done by what? Or who?"

Then she picked up the cover letter and started reading . . .

and realized it wasn't simply a form letter, but a descriptive part of the proposal. She read through the whole thing, slowly sinking back in her chair . . . as Mrs. Gillespie presented to Holly what her future in Virginia could actually be. All mapped out and wrapped in a very wonderful bow. "Huh," she said, unable to articulate her stunned surprise any more clearly. It was all . . . a lot to think about, but already, she felt her pulse thrumming with excitement. Could she really do this? Did she dare?

She was so lost in thought, in trying to quell the burgeoning hope before thinking the whole thing through with a more rational, practical eye, that she apparently didn't hear the sleigh bells ring on the shop door. So she about jumped out of her skin at the knock that came on her door. She really had to get better about locking the damn shop door.

"Hey, there . . . hungry?"

She looked up to find Sean filling her doorway. And everything inside of her bloomed to life. That was the effect he'd always had on her, even as a little girl. Why was she fighting so hard to figure out why things wouldn't work between them, instead of fighting to find any way possible to keep him around forever? Well, thanks to Mrs. Gillespie, of all people, now she just might have the remaining answers she needed to do just that.

"Starved," she said. She tossed the letter aside, excited to discuss everything with him, get his take, realizing how much she'd already come to value his opinion. It was comforting, and the sense of real security she needed, the first building block of a foundation to a new life that was so vital. . . . Oh, my God, she thought, she was really going to do this. But first things first. She pushed her chair back and stood, coming around the desk as he entered with delicious smelling take out boxes.

"Beef stew again, but—"

"It smells like heaven, and I probably should feel horrible for taking you away from your busiest time at the restaurant, but—"

"You know," he said, putting the boxes down on the chair and leaning against her desk so he could pull her into his arms. "I'm starting to discover that I've trained my people better than I realized. As it turns out, the world doesn't come to an end after all if I step out for a few minutes, or hours." He grinned and it was cutely self-deprecating. "In fact, I've been informed that there is a general appreciation for me getting a new life and not micro-managing theirs for a change."

"Anything I can do to help with that?" she asked, smiling back.

"As a matter of fact . . ." He pulled her in closer and kissed her.

He smelled of warmth, and kitchen cooking, and everything she'd ever wanted. After a life of feeling like she didn't fit in, from childhood on up, and always being that square peg . . . she finally felt like she was fitting in. Right where she was supposed to be. And when she kissed him, she poured all of that into it, everything she was feeling—her excitement about the possible new chance for her future, to reach her own goals, goals she'd never allowed herself to even contemplate.

When he finally came up for air, his gaze was more than a little unfocused. "Wow," was all he said. "I . . . wow."

She laughed a little, then grew more serious. "Sean, I'm sorry about the way I acted with the diary. I just—"

"No, don't apologize. Sometimes, coming from such a large family, from such a broad foundation of love and support, I forget that other people don't have that, and I felt kind of selfish in being more concerned with preserving that than really thinking that what might be best for that one person is worth a little disturbance. I should trust in the strength of the very foundation I do have."

"What are you saying?"

"I'm saying that I think we need to find out who Trudy Haversham-Hamilton gave birth to . . . and if he's a Gallagher. In fact, I've already put things in motion."

Her mouth dropped open. "You have? Already? But I just gave you the diary—"

"You started the path, and I'm going to finish it. I contacted the great-nephew—"

"You contacted a Hamilton first? Sean, do you think that was wise? They're the ones who stand to lose—"

"I did some digging, on Lionel's only remaining heir, Trevor Hamilton. He lives in North Carolina and has built what amounts to a private social services firm designed to help those in need, especially young entrepreneurs. His wife, Emma, used to work for Lionel. They've been married about three years now and, from what I could dig up, she'd started a pet-sitting service down there but moved on and branched out into building her own rescue service and permanent sanctuary for animals who can't be placed in homes. Everything, apparently from hamsters to horses. It's really quite the operation."

"They sound like an amazing couple."

"I thought so, too. Trevor has built his business from the ground up. No Hamilton money. And given what he and his wife have devoted their lives to, I really don't see where they'd be the grasping, greedy ones, wanting to screw a potential blood relative out of what was rightly theirs. So, I thought I'd start there."

Holly smiled. "I think you did amazingly well in only a few hours."

He smiled back. "I have to keep up with you, don't I?"

"So . . . what happens next?"

"Trevor was planning on coming up to see his great-uncle for the holidays anyway. Apparently Lionel has been in ill health for some time now. So I set up a meeting with him. His wife will be with him. And we'll talk about what is the best step to take." He shrugged. "Then, I guess I'll start working from this end, to figure out if it's really true, if someone in my family is really related, then put them in contact and . . . let the rest work itself out however it happens."

She reached up on her tip-toes and kissed him. "Thank you." She smiled. "For reaching."

He grinned. "Holly, I know sometimes I seem like I know everything, like having my background makes things easy for me. It's different, and it's wonderful, but I'm just as apt to make mistakes as anyone. I don't want to make a mistake with you. And I don't want my possible single- and sometimes narrow-mindedness when it comes to my clan, to prevent someone I love from finding out what might truly be meant for them. And that includes me."

Holly stared into his eyes and knew this was a man she could spend the rest of her life falling in love with. "Sean Gallagher . . . how in the world did I get so lucky?"

He laughed. "I'm really glad you see it that way."

"I really, really see it that way."

He was still smiling but looked more closely into her eyes. That was another thing she was coming to love about him. He didn't miss much. Which could prove to be a problem, she supposed, when she'd rather remain more enigmatic about something . . . but she wouldn't trade it.

"What else is going on behind those beautiful browns?" he asked. "You look . . ."

"Happy? Excited? A bit terrified?"

"Uh . . . yeah, actually. Is it about the shop?"

She nodded. "And you. And me. And my future." She looked directly into his eyes. "Here in Virginia."

He went still. She swore, in fact, that she felt his heart stop. The hope that sprang to his eyes, no matter how much he might be trying to restrain it, was all she needed to see. This was as huge, as important, to him, as it was to her.

"Virginia?" he asked.

She nodded. "Mrs. Gillespie dropped her lease proposal off with me today. She wants to lease the first and second floors of the building, but she wants me to retain the third floor. And use it as an art studio. Then sell my paintings and artwork on commission through her antique and collectibles store."

Sean's eyes went wide. "That's . . . brilliant, actually."

"I know, right?" Holly jumped up and down a little, unable, any longer, to keep her excitement under control. "It's terrifying as hell . . . and yes, brilliant. And . . . I really think I'm going to do it! It feels really, really right."

Sean laughed and stood up and spun her around. She was starting to like that about him. A lot.

"Do you have a little more time," she asked, "before you need to go back?"

"I brought dinner for two; I thought I'd eat with you. Then yes, I do have to go back, but Holly, we're going to celebrate, in style, I promise. I just have to—"

"Take me for a ride? Right now? We can eat our stew in the truck."

He tilted his head, but his eyes were dancing. "Okay. Where are we going?"

"Christmas lights."

"You want to do the tour again?"

She shook her head. "I want to go buy some."

His grin was slow and devastatingly sexy. "Really."

"Yes, really. I was thinking on the bushes and the trees on either side of the front stoop."

His forehead wrinkled. "The shop doesn't have—" Then his expression cleared. "You mean . . . ?"

"You're the Christmas spirit guy. I'm thinking your place could use a little holiday twinkle. And maybe a little practice in holiday spirit wouldn't kill me."

His expression softened and he let her slide down his body until she was sheltered in his arms. "I think maybe we need a lifetime of practice." He leaned his head in and kissed her. "Merry Christmas, Holly Berry. Welcome home."

She smiled against his mouth and thought she'd finally figured out what was so magical about this time of year after all. "Ho ho ho," she murmured. Then kissed her very own personal Santa Claus. Best Christmas present ever.

Epilogue

Trevor Hamilton held the door to Gallagher's open for Emma, then followed her in.

"Lovely place," Emma said. "I don't think I ever got over to Willow Creek when I lived up here."

"I haven't been here since I was a lot younger. Pretty cool little Civil War town."

Trevor felt his wife's hand in his and squeezed. He was still a little bit wary about today's meeting, but was admittedly excited to finally have the chance to learn the rest of the story. He'd discovered the secret that Lionel had been hiding all along . . . and it had nothing to do with his personal heritage. He was, in fact, a Hamilton, through and through. He'd yet to really decide if that changed anything inside of him. It didn't feel that way. When he'd decided, four years ago, almost to the day, when he'd met Emma out at Lionel's big mountain mansion, that he really didn't need to know where he'd come from, that it was where he was going that was important . . . that hadn't changed in the years that had passed.

But he'd loved his great-aunt Tru more than anything, and if she truly had a descendant . . . Hamilton or Haversham, well, that mattered to him. He might have decided he didn't want the burden and expectations that went along with taking on any aspect of his family's empire, including all the wealth attached to it . . . but that didn't mean someone else, someone who rightfully had claim to some part of it, would do the same. So, for Trudy's sake, and that of her possible heir, he'd do whatever was necessary to see that person had the chance to make that decision.

A big man with thick dark hair, a ready smile, and twinkling blue eyes met them as they entered the dining area. It was early, before hours, so they were the only ones inside the restaurant.

"Sean Gallagher," the man said, extending his big hand for a quick shake. "I'm really glad you two could make the time for this."

Trevor smiled. "I would have made time, but it worked out well."

"How is your great-uncle?" This came from a tiny brunette, who appeared out from behind the restaurant's owner. "Hi, I'm Holly Bennett."

Trevor shook her hand. "He's not doing all that well, but at his age, it's to be expected. Thank you for asking."

Sean gestured to a table where coffee was waiting, along with a few loaves of homemade bread, along with butter and a variety of jams. "Why don't we have a seat, make ourselves comfortable."

It was hard not to be. Sean had created a warm, very inviting atmosphere here. He pulled out Emma's chair, then seated himself next to her. "Actually, I wanted to talk to you about Lionel," he said once they were all settled. "I've been doing a lot of thinking about all of this. And I'm not sure how he'd take the news. On the one hand, he cherished his wife, and I'd like to think that he'd want to know that she'd had a son. That she'd left something of herself behind. On the other hand, I won't lie. He's a greedy, selfish, controlling old man. Was even as a young man. And I'm not entirely sure he'd like knowing that anyone else had a claim on her, on him, or anything else. No matter why or how they'd come to be on this earth."

"What are you proposing then?" Sean asked.

Trevor sighed and raked his hand through his hair. Emma rubbed his knee and he took the comfort he always did in her steady reassurance. "I saw him yesterday. He's still of sound mind, at least as sound as it's always been, but his patience for things, for people, for life in general, has deteriorated badly. He's . . . never been an easy man. But now—"

"He's almost impossible," Emma put in. She squeezed his knee. "Sorry," she said to him, then looked at Sean and Holly. "But it's true. He's a miserable, crotchety old man, who is very frustrated by the limitations his age and illness have placed on him. It's not dignified and he's all about retaining his dignity. I think . . ." She trailed off, glanced at Trevor, then back at them and said, "To be honest, the only thing that has ever made him feel vulnerable in his life, I think, was his wife. Trudy. And maybe now that he is where he is . . . I think he's ready to be done with this, to . . . I guess, join her again, if you know what I mean. I think he's scared, too, at least a little."

"So . . . do we tell him?" Holly asked.

Trevor and Emma looked at each other for a long moment, then clasped hands on top of the table. "We think he's quite capable of being punitive and punishing to your relative. To Trudy's great-grandson," Trevor said. "Who knows what he'd do."

"But we really don't think it's our place to make that decision for him. We think he should know."

"And . . . if he decides to pull some legal maneuver,

denying Thomas his rightful due, whatever that might be?"

Another glance between them, then, "Then I'll make it right with my own slice of the pie. I haven't touched my trust fund. My own personal thing, but other than provide for the security of any children Emma and I might have . . . I have no plans to use it to further my own goals. So . . . if Lionel doesn't do right, I will."

Sean and Holly looked a bit stunned at the announcement, and he couldn't blame them. It hadn't taken the four of them very long to track down Trudy's heir. So this was all rather an emotional whirlwind, still. In fact, a Gallagher had adopted Trudy's son. Tess and Frank Gallagher were aunt and uncle to Sean's own grandmother. Neither were still alive, and neither was Trudy's son, having died of a heart attack over a decade before. But he'd married and had a son himself. Thomas. Who'd grown up in Willow Creek but had gone back to Ireland, to work for the family over there, overseeing some of the farmlands. He was in his midthirties now, single, with no heirs of his own.

Sean had opted not to contact him until he'd spoken to Trevor and worked out exactly how things would proceed. He wasn't going to drag Thomas halfway around the world until he had a better idea of what he'd be dragging him into. Trevor seconded that plan.

"I'll be happy to meet with him myself, go with him to see Lionel, if that's what he wants to do."

"If Lionel will see him," Emma put in.

"He'll see him," Trevor put in. He and his great-uncle had never had a smooth relationship, but he was at a point in his own life where he wasn't so easily pushed around. "He doesn't have to like it, and he might reject it, but if Thomas wants to meet him, we'll make it happen."

Sean put his hand out and Trevor took it, shook it, then nodded. "I'll talk with Lionel. You talk with Thomas."

"Ultimately, it will be up to him what he wants to do with all this," Sean said. "He might reject the whole thing. I don't know him, but the family here who does says he's definitely his own man, with his own ideas about how things should be."

Holly grinned. "Gee, I can't imagine where he gets that from."

Trevor laughed. "Yeah, well, he's got it from the Haversham side, too, don't be fooled."

"Poor lad, then," Sean said with a laugh. "And here I was, envying him a wee bit."

"I wouldn't be so fast with that. But this could definitely change his life."

They finished their meeting, enjoyed coffee and a bit more chat, then Trevor and Emma finally said their goodbyes. "We'll have to come back as customers," Emma said. "It all smells delicious in here."

Trevor nodded. "I'll be in touch after talking with Lionel."

After a few more pleasantries, the couple left and Sean pulled Holly next to his side. "So many changes. Quite the holiday season."

"I wonder how Thomas will take the news," Holly said.

Sean shrugged. "It'll be interesting, that's for sure."

Holly leaned in to him. "What would you do with life-changing news like that?"

He turned and pulled her into his arms. "I'd grab it and make it my own."

"You do that pretty well, come to think of it," she said, giggling a little when he lifted her off her feet and planted one on her.

"There's something else I hope I've done well," he

said. "Come here." He took her hand and led her through the restaurant toward the kitchen.

"Sean, don't you have like a million things to do? All this stuff with Thomas has taken so much time and I know tomorrow is Christmas Eve and you all have a full house, so "

"So, none of that means anything right this very second. Come here." He paused outside the doors to the kitchen "I really wanted to do this tomorrow, but I didn't want to share it with anyone but family. And you are family now, Holly, you know that."

"I . . . you're all like a miracle to me," she said, never more sincere. "I can't believe how easily you all have accepted me and pulled me in. I thought I'd be more freaked out . . . but it's like—"

"Home?"

She nodded. "Getting that way."

"I'm really glad you think so." He leaned in and kissed her long, and slow, and deep, then lifted his head and whispered, "Happy birthday." Then he pushed the kitchen door open, and every single member of the Gallagher clan shouted, "Happy birthday!" and launched into the rowdiest version of the song Holly had ever heard.

She stood there, stunned. "But—"

"It's your birthday," he said. "It's your day. We're just starting a little early."

He ushered her into the kitchen and she was immediately enveloped by Gallaghers young and old, all smiling and welcoming her with laughs, smiles, and open arms. Sean was right, it wasn't about blood lines and where you thought you fit in . . . it was about creating your own family, your own right place.

She'd definitely, finally, done that.

Bah, Handsome!

JILL
SHALVIS

1

Outside the weather was as the song went—frightful. Inside, Hope O'Brien looked down at the huge box of Christmas decorations she'd dug out of the cellar of her bed-and-breakfast inn and thought maybe *this* would be the year that Santa brought her something she needed. Money to meet her bills for the month would be nice, or lacking that, maybe an orgasm.

Yeah, now that would be *real* nice.

Smiling at the thought, she pulled out some brightly colored balls and ribbons and—

"Mistletoe!" Lori snatched up the dried sprig, and held it to her chest like it was a bar of gold.

Hope slid her best friend a look as wind continued to batter the small B&B around them. "You've been married six months and still drag Ben into the closet whenever you see him. What could you possibly need with mistletoe?"

Lori, also the support staff for the inn, waggled a brow. "It's for you."

"You want to kiss me? Well, why didn't you just say

so." Hope leaned in and puckered up. "Give me your best shot."

Laughing, Lori shoved her away. *"I* don't want to kiss you. I want someone *else* to kiss you. A penis-carrying someone."

"Yeah." Hope sighed. "I think that ship's sailed."

"Honey, you're twenty-nine. That ship has not sailed. You're just being a pansy-ass because your last boyfriend stole all your money and ruined your credit before going to jail, forcing you to go begging from your asshole rich stepbrother."

"Gee, thanks for the recap."

"And you're probably also still feeling the effects from your boyfriend before that, the one who stole your self-confidence. What was his name? *Dickwad?"*

"Derek," she murmured. *Derek the Dickwad.* "And you wonder why I say my ship has sailed. Clearly I can't trust my own judgment."

Lori's eyes softened, and she leaned over to squeeze Hope's hand. "That's because you don't trust your heart. Look, you're pragmatic and tough—you've had to be. But let's face facts. You have a type, and that's the badasses. Joey, Dickwad . . ."

True. Hope had always been a sucker for the bad boy. Someone had once told her it was from growing up without a father figure, but she didn't believe in letting circumstance mold her. She was a "be responsible for your own destiny" sort of woman.

Lori twirled the mistletoe in her fingers. "Did you know if you wish on this stuff, it'll come true."

"Yes, and maybe Santa's reindeers will sprinkle magic dust over all the land and make us rich."

Lori gave her the puppy dog eyes. "Are you really going to suck all the spirit out of the holiday?"

Hope rolled her eyes, but then shook her head. "No."

"Then *wish*, dammit."

"Fine." Hope snatched the mistletoe and closed her eyes. "I wish that the DA would shake my money out of Joey so I can pay back my brother before he calls the loan that's due on January first, which is in . . ." She mentally calculated. *Oh, God.* "Twenty-one days."

"Oh, Hope," Lori said sadly, making Hope realize she was doing it, she *was* sucking the spirit out of the holiday.

"Okay, you're right. Let's try this." Hope paused, the only sound being the vicious storm currently rattling the windows. "I wish for someone to hang up all the Christmas decorations for me. And . . . clear them up after Christmas."

Lori's eyes were censoring. "Stop thinking of the B&B first; think of you. *You*, Hope. Wish for . . . *sex*. Yeah, now *there's* something you could use. How long has it been anyway, six months?"

Six months sounded pathetic, but the truth was even more so. She lifted a shoulder.

"*Eight* months?"

Fourteen, but who was counting? Oh, wait. She was. She was counting.

"Give me that." Lori grabbed the sprig back, once again pressing it to her heart and closing her eyes. In sweet earnest, she said, "Hope's too busy and stressed to think of herself so I'm doing it for her. I wish for a penis for her. One that's attached to a man who knows how to use it."

"It's no use." Hope shook her head even as she laughed. "I'm done with badasses, penises and all."

"A really *good* man," Lori went on, eyes still closed. "Not a badass, but a kind, gentle soul—but good in bed. I can't stress that enough."

"That's funny."

Lori opened her eyes and reached into her pocket,

from which she pulled out a string of four condoms. "Merry early Christmas."

"You are not serious."

Lori merely stuffed them into Hope's jean pocket.

Hope laughed again, then raised a brow when someone knocked on the front door of the B&B. Though it was only six in the evening, it was pitch-black, with the snowstorm still raging out there. "Huh."

"Maybe it's him," Lori whispered.

"Him who?"

"The man I just wished for you, the one with the kind, gentle soul. And the penis he knows how to use."

Hope rose from the dining room table where they'd been sitting. She supposed it could be an unexpected guest. She had six guest rooms, and only two were filled at the moment; her guests either in their rooms or in front of the fire she had roaring in the living room. She'd be happier with more paying guests, but what with the B&B being out in the boondocks two hours north of Denver, and the economy in the toilet, things were slow.

Of course now was the worst possible time for her to be slow, what with her bank accounts emptied and all. She was hanging on by a thread—a thread that had come from her stepbrother Edward, a guy who made Scrooge look like Santa Claus.

It was killing her, knowing she'd been forced to borrow from him, but it was also temporary.

As in a lump payment was due to him in LA by January 1 . . .

Twenty-one days . . .

She'd e-mailed Edward—he didn't do personal contact—to ask for a little teeny tiny extension, but she hadn't heard back yet.

Don't go there now, she told herself, and moved toward

the foyer, followed by Lori. She opened the front door and was immediately assaulted by the wind and snow. She squinted past it to take in the tall, dark stranger who was dressed as if he'd just walked off the cover of a glossy man's magazine.

"Does it always snow like this?" he asked, stomping the snow from his boots, his voice low and husky as if he was half frozen.

Tall, dark and *irritated*, she corrected. "In December, yes. Can I help you?"

He squinted through his glasses past snowflakes the size of dinner plates. "My car got stuck about a half mile back."

Behind her, Lori gave her a little nudge. *See? There he is, the penis I wished for.*

Hope ignored her as she eyed the guy on her step. He had his hood up. Sure his voice sounded fine, even attractive, but that didn't make him a good guy. Until she saw his face, she wasn't letting her guard down. "Four-wheel drive?" she asked him.

"No, it's a rental. I have chains on it, though."

So he wasn't a local. "Yeah, not good enough, not on a night like this one." His clothes screamed big city, from his fancy coat down to his fancy boots. Maybe New York, maybe Los Angeles—either way he was definitely *not* used to Colorado winter driving. "If you'd like to rent a room for the night, I can get you help digging out your car in the morning."

"Yeah, okay. Thanks."

When she moved back and opened the door wider, he stepped inside, giving her a brief impression of a lanky lean build, but not much else. He smelled good, though. Woodsy, citrusy . . . masculine.

He turned to her then and let his hood fall back as he

opened his coat, looking at her with a hint of wariness as if he was waiting for something, which came immediately.

Recognition.

As it hit her, she went still. Danny Shaw, her stepbrother's CPA. He had a striking face, she'd give him that. High cheekbones, rich mahogany eyes slightly magnified by the sophisticated wire-rimmed glasses on his nose. His hair matched his eyes and was trimmed short. With his coat open, she could see his tailored pants and shirt, both undoubtedly as expensive as his glasses. If she hadn't known him, she'd have taken another minute to fully appreciate his fine form.

But she did know him, and all the friendly drained from her, replaced by tension. "Did you come to give me an extension?"

"Unfortunately, no."

She felt the air leave her lungs as if he'd hit her. "Then get out."

"We need to talk, Hope."

"No." She hauled open the door again, ignoring the snow that pelted her. *"Get out."*

"Hope," Lori murmured. "Who is this, another ex-boyfriend?"

"No. Worse. Meet Danny Shaw, my brother's lackey. And I still have three weeks left." She jerked her head toward outside. "Good-bye, Danny."

"You just offered me a room." His voice was very distinctive with its low, husky timber, and she kicked herself for not recognizing it sooner. After all, she'd met with him when negotiating the loan from Edward, because heaven forbid Edward get his hands dirty with the details.

And the details *had* been dirty. Edward hadn't exactly given her a favorable loan. Nope, he'd been less than one step from a loan shark, but she'd figured go with the devil she knew . . . "I've just unoffered the room," she said, once again gesturing for him to go. "You're letting out all my bought air."

"We really need to talk first, Hope."

"Sorry, but I don't talk to rat bastards."

He raised a brow. "Rat bastard is what you call your brother."

"Yes, and as Edward's representative, you get the same consideration. Get out, Danny. Go home. Tell him I'll get him his money on time." Since he didn't budge, she grabbed his hand and pulled him to the door. He stepped over the threshold, then turned back to face her to say something.

But she shut the door in his face.

Danny let out a shuddery breath. Shuddery because he was a minute away from freezing his nuts off. When he'd flown out of Los Angeles that morning, it'd been sunny and a slightly chilly sixty-eight degrees.

Ha. He hadn't known chilly. He hadn't known a lot of things, such as how bad the rental car would be, or the depths of Hope's worry and fear. He wrapped his coat tighter around him and pulled his hood back up before once again knocking on the door.

She didn't answer, but he would have sworn he could hear her breathing through the wood. Hope, of the pretty strawberry blond hair that was slipping out of its ponytail and into her eyes, which were so blue he could have drowned in them. Hope, of the petite, willowy frame that hid an inner strength of steel. That strength shouldn't have surprised him; after all she was an O'Brien. "Come on, Hope. Let me in."

More of her loaded nothing, and he sighed, shoving his hands in his pockets and hunching his shoulders against the wind as if that would help. Christ, why would anyone choose to live here? "Look, I should have called first, okay? But if I had, you wouldn't have agreed to see me."

As proven by the loaded silence.

"I realize you'd like me to just leave," he said. And he'd love to do that. Hell, he missed LA already. He was wet and cold and hungry, and as far as he could tell there was no food in his immediate future. No four-star hotels, either. Nothing but wide open spaces and the utter lack of civilization.

He was on a whole other planet. "I'll freeze to death out here, Hope, you know that. You don't want my death on your hands, do you?" Okay, stupid question. She'd welcome his death and stomp on his grave.

He'd met her for the first time two years ago when she was leaving Los Angeles. She'd come to Edward's office to say good-bye, but Edward had been in a meeting and hadn't bothered to come out—the guy wasn't big on family.

The last time Danny had seen Hope was three months ago when she'd needed money. Once again, it'd been Danny to deal with her, and he'd laid out the terms that Eddie had insisted on—the terms *not* in her favor.

Danny had looked into Hope's eyes as he'd done Edward's dirty work and felt like a complete jerk offering her such a crappy deal. Knowing he could lose his job, he'd shut the file, gone against his duties, and advised her not to sign.

But she'd signed anyway.

"Letting me die out here will only make things worse," he said now. "Come on, Hope. Open up."

"Just leave."

He wished he could. But he had a job to do and that was to protect Edward's investment. Didn't matter that

Edward was a miserly ass who got his jollies over lording it over people, one of those people being his own sister. What mattered, unfortunately for Hope, was that Edward now held the loan on both the land and the B&B itself, and after her extension request, now wanted the situation assessed.

Which is where Danny came in.

Not the most comfortable situation, given that his rental car was truly stuck. Turning away from the front door, he stared out into the nasty storm knowing he had two choices: beg some more, or strike out on foot back to his car where he could run the motor for heat until he ran out of gas. Neither option appealed, but he had a feeling that no amount of begging would work, so he stepped off the top step and into the snow.

Shit, it was cold.

Behind him the door whipped open. "Are you crazy?" Hope demanded to know. "You really will freeze to death if you walk back to your car."

"So you're going to let me in?"

She seemed to gnash on her teeth over that one. She was wearing snug hip-hugging jeans that were frayed at the waist and hem, and torn over one knee. Her long-sleeved v-necked tee revealed sweet curves, and proof that she was chilled. "It's going to cost you," she finally said.

Yeah, he was getting that. "I'm willing to pay your rate."

"For rat bastards, it's double."

He looked into her stubborn, beautiful face and saw that she meant it. "Fine. Double."

"Did I say double? I meant triple."

Her eyes were intense, protective, and dammit.

Hurt.

And wasn't that just the crux. Edward was such an ass. So determined to rise from the gutter from which he'd been born, he was perfectly willing to walk over his own family. Even worse was the knowledge that Hope was trying to do the same, trying to change her life and circumstances, and was getting a bad deal.

But she wasn't his job. Good-damn, he really hated when his morals bumped up against the source of his income. "Just name the price, Hope."

She shoved her long bangs off her face and thought about it.

How any woman could look so sweet and soft, and yet be so fierce, was beyond him, but somehow she pulled it off.

"You might want to consider that I'm standing here with my wallet open and you need the money," he pointed out.

Okay, not his smartest move, reminding her that she was in trouble; he knew it even before her eyes chilled and her mouth tightened.

She had a pretty mouth.

Not that he was noticing. "Look," he said quickly. "The roads are bad, there's no other hotel nearby, and I'm stuck. Whatever you want."

"I want a better termed loan."

"Except that."

She looked at him, proud and desperate, and he felt a crack in his armor.

Not good.

"I'd do it if I could," he said quietly.

"Would you?"

"In a heartbeat." He shifted and lowered his voice. "I asked you not to sign—"

"Don't." She pushed him back a step and pointed at him. "Don't. I'm well aware that *I* screwed this up, and no one else." A sigh escaped her, and once again, she shoved her hair back. "You can have a damn room."

"Thank you."

"Just get inside." She shut the door, behind him this time, still looking deceptively soft and sweet. "You're shivering like a pansy-assed little girl."

2

Hope easily kept busy for the next hour, meaning she paid no attention whatsoever to her unwelcome houseguest.

Or pretended to pay no attention . . .

The only meal she served at the B&B was breakfast, but she did offer drinks in the evenings. Tonight they served eggnog to go with the festive decorations she was still working on, and in the living room people intermingled, having a good time.

Hope was making sure of it.

She considered that a part of her job, and she enjoyed it. She enjoyed the camaraderie, the easy alliances of perfect strangers brought together for short periods of time. She enjoyed hearing people's stories and tonight should have been no exception.

Except she was so painfully, acutely aware of the tall, lanky man leaning against the mantel. She eyed him critically, prepared to toss him out on his bony ass if he tried to stir up trouble, but he didn't. He stood there in his sophisticated clothes and those wire-rimmed glasses, looking as if he could walk into a board room, or an elegant dinner.

Or a casual B&B with a bunch of strangers.

He smiled easily, talked just as easily, effortlessly infusing himself into the conversation with her guests as if he belonged. When asked, he said he was there on business but hoped to take some time for fun, freely admitting he wasn't much of an outdoors person but that he was open to new experiences.

She wondered what new experiences exactly he referred to, and how it sounded vaguely sexual to her, even as she wondered how he'd like the experience of her foot up his ass if he so much as hinted that he was here because she'd screwed up financially.

But he didn't.

After the guests went up to their rooms, she was in the kitchen cleaning up when Danny came in carrying dirty glasses, setting them into the sink.

"Guests don't do the dishes," she informed him.

He merely shoved up his sleeves and dug in. "We both know I'm not a real guest." He turned his head to look at her. *Really* look at her. As if maybe he could see in past the brick wall she'd so carefully built around her emotions and private feelings over the years.

That was new.

And not in any way welcome.

"I pull my weight," he said. "Always."

Now *that* she understood, and she put a hand over his in the sink, surprised to find his warm   she'd imagined they'd be as cold as his heart. Except she was beginning to doubt that was true. "You didn't have to come, you know. I'll get the money."

One way or another . . .

He was close. Close enough that she could have

bumped his body with hers as she tipped her head up and looked past his lenses and into his eyes, which weren't just a solid light brown, but had gold swirling in the mix and were as surprisingly warm as his hands.

"I'm glad to hear it," he said.

"Are you?"

There was a beat of silence, and in it, much of the good-natured humor drained from him, which she found oddly unsettling. He was more sincere than she'd given him credit for.

And tougher.

And something else, too, something that surprised her. He was kind of sexy with that intense, intellectual gaze behind those glasses.

"You think I want you to fail," he finally said with a hint of disbelief.

"I think that would suit Edward, taking this place from me even though he could care less about it. He could probably sell the property in a blink, and, poof, make condos appear, or something else with lots of concrete."

Danny opened his mouth, then slowly shut it again. Hard to argue the truth, apparently. After a moment he shook his head and flashed her a rather grim smile, full of no amusement at all and maybe even some hurt. "The fact is, Hope, I'm here only because your brother wants to make sure the terms of the loan are going to be met, nothing personal. It's just the job. It's business," he said with soft steel. "That's it."

"The terms will be met," she said with equal soft steel. "So you can go home and report just that."

"As I'm snowed in, we appear to be stuck with each other for now. And since we are, maybe I can help. If you showed me your financials—"

"No." She shook her head. "Nothing personal," she

said, sending his own words back at him. "But I don't need your help."

He looked at her, and she'd have sworn she saw a brief flash of empathy, even respect. And also frustration with some caring mixed in.

Which was impossible, she told herself, since he was a rat bastard, and rat bastards didn't care.

As always, Hope woke up at the crack of dawn. It was a lifelong habit. When she was little, her father died from a heart attack, and she'd get up early to make toast and tea for her stricken mother.

Later, after her mother remarried and divorced two more times, Hope still got up early to work at a resort, where she'd cook from dawn until the start of high school since Edward had gone off to college without looking back. Mother had never really recovered from her losses.

Hope had always kept up the early-morning habit because she liked getting things done during those hours when everyone else was snoozing away, but this morning, she suddenly wished she'd developed a different habit.

Like flying south for the winter.

Because this morning, lying in bed in the dark dawn, she kept thinking about the unwelcome guest she had upstairs.

Danny Shaw. He was Clark Kent on the outside and sheer, determined Superman steel on the inside.

And he didn't think she could do this.

Facing that fact made her feel better. Because facing it, she could fight it, do something about it.

Kicking off her covers, she got out of bed and shivered. Holy smokes, it was a cold one. The thermometer on her window said five.

As in five degrees.

And it was still snowing like a mother. She needed to stack some more wood today. She also needed to clear snow and put up the rest of the decorations.

But it wasn't until she stood in her bathroom that she realized her biggest problem. She had her toothbrush in one hand and a mouthful of toothpaste as she stared into the bathroom sink; the handle cranked to full blast, no water coming through.

The pipes were frozen.

"Oh no, no, no, no . . ." Not today, not when she needed to make a *great* impression. Not when she needed Danny to think everything was perfect.

Dammit.

Obviously, the place wasn't perfect. It was built in the 1940s by a wealthy mine owner as a vacation home, then renovated in the '80s by the family of the original owner. Currently the place was in some fairly desperate need of more updates and renovations, which she was getting to on an as-needed basis.

Like the plumbing problems.

And unfortunately, there were other problems as well. Upstairs were the guest bedrooms, which needed paint. Downstairs were the kitchen, dining room, living room, and social area, and a small but quaint servants' quarters off the kitchen where Hope lived.

All of which also needed paint.

And more.

Lori and her new husband Ben, a local handyman, lived about a mile down the road in their own place. Hope could call Ben about the pipes. He'd snowmobile here in a heartbeat, but if she'd learned anything in her twenty-nine and three-quarters years of life, it was to do for herself whenever possible.

Even when it seemed impossible.

The bottom line was that the B&B was everything to her. She'd certainly put everything she had in it, and not just money, but her heart and soul. It was the first thing that had been entirely hers, and having people come and stay and enjoy the Colorado mountains — the hiking, biking, skiing, or whatever they'd come to the wilderness for—never failed to thrill.

It was a world away from where she'd grown up in Los Angeles, in the heart of the city, and a world away from the rat race that had once threatened to consume her when she'd lived and worked there as a chef. Now, here, in the silent magnitude of the magnificent Rocky Mountains, she'd found tranquility and peace.

And frozen pipes. She spit out her toothpaste and looked down at her thin, loose cotton pj bottoms and cami. She added on a pair of thick sweats, a scarf, a knit hat, her down jacket, and her imitation Ugg boots.

She caught sight of herself in the mirror—the Pillsbury Dough Woman—and laughed. Good thing she didn't have a man in her life, she thought as she grabbed her blow-dryer and headed into the kitchen, where she added an extension cord to her arsenal. She plugged the cord into an outlet on the counter, then carefully propped open the cellar door with a large can of beans because it had a tendency to shut and lock.

The stairs made a heck of a racket, which oddly enough had always comforted her. She figured if the boogey man was ever going to climb the stairs to get to her, she'd at least hear him coming.

In the cellar, she eyed the pipes, indeed frozen solid. "Please work," she said, and stretched out on the ground underneath the pipes and turned the blow-dryer on high.

Two minutes later the pipes were still frozen solid, but *she* was warming up nicely, and she blew her out-of-control bangs out of her face to see better. If she'd had a pair of scissors with her, she'd have cut them off right then and there.

She heard someone come down the stairs, and then a set of shoes appeared at her shoulder.

Nikes, brand-new. Size—at least twelve.

"Your pipes are frozen," the Nikes said.

She didn't look up. Maybe if she didn't, Mr. Big City Know It All Rat Bastard would go away. Far away. "I'm on it." She readjusted the heat coming from the blow-dryer and concentrated, picturing the pipes melting because, hey, you had to dream it to live it—

Danny crouched at her side, his legs at least a damn mile long. She'd always thought of him as a little on the skinny side, but with his pants stretched taut against him, she could see that those legs actually had quite the definition of muscle to them. She glanced up the length of them.

And up.

Yep, those pants were expensive. Probably worth more than all the clothes in her closet. Which, as she tended to live in jeans and tees, wasn't saying that much.

"Need any help?" he asked.

"I can handle it." She made the mistake of turning her head and meeting his gaze. First of all, it was barely the crack of dawn and yet there he was, dressed as if he was going into the office, with a button-down shirt and pullover sweater in a deep royal blue that seemed so soft and yummy she almost forgot he was not only Nerd Central but also capable of siccing Edward on her.

And he smelled good, *again*. How that was even possible when she knew he couldn't have possibly had a hot shower, she had no idea. But he looked fresh and clean and neat, his every hair in place, his glasses revealing those warm eyes.

He'd even shaved, with what must have been an electric razor.

And she? With her multiple layers, disastrous hair and no makeup—and she was pretty sure she hadn't shaved her legs this week—she felt extremely out of place. Way to go, Hope. Way to be hot and irresistible.

Not that she cared what he thought about her appearance, but she did care very much about what he thought about how she was running this place. "Go on up," she said. "I'll handle this."

He didn't move.

She swiped her arm over her forehead. Yeah, it was getting hot in here. With one arm still holding the blow-dryer in place on the frozen pipe, she pulled off her scarf and hat, trying not to picture what her hair must look like.

His face appeared next to hers as he, without regard for those expensive clothes and the dirty floor, stretched out on his back at her side and peered at the pipe, an icon of grace and physical power.

"You're making progress," he said. "You have another blow-dryer?"

He was polished, where she was not. He was smooth and knew what to do in any social situation, where she most definitely did not. *He was her mortal enemy*.

So she had no idea why she looked at his mouth and felt an odd pang of excitement. She'd simply gone too long without a man's touch; that was what was causing this ridiculous and untimely sense of loneliness that was clearly making her lose her mind.

"Hope?"

She was still looking at his mouth. It was a really nice mouth. Probably all the better to pull his prey into his web.

He caught her staring at him and skimmed his hand up her arm. "You okay?"

Was she? His fingers were warm and sure, and his body was lying so close to hers that she could almost taste the testosterone coming off him. Tiny prickles of desire raced up her spine to the back of her neck.

Huh.

"Hope? You with me?"

"Yeah." She cleared her throat as he ran his thumb over her knuckles.

He stared down at her hand as he slowly traced her skin. "Blow-dryer?" he murmured.

Right. "Upstairs. Second bathroom beneath the sink."

She didn't have a spare blow-dryer upstairs in the second bathroom beneath the sink, but it would get him out of her hair, because clearly his closeness was killing off her brain cells one by one.

When he left, she let out a long, careful breath. *Whew.* How in the hell she'd managed to both hate him and lust after him at the same time, she had not a single clue. . . .

3

Alone in the cellar, Hope felt the vibration of Danny's footsteps going up the two flights of stairs. Since she was sweating, she pulled off her jacket and sweatpants and went back to blow-drying the frozen pipes. When she heard Danny coming back down, she yelled, "Don't let the cellar door shut!" just as he did exactly that.

Shit! She sat straight up and bashed her head on the now semi-frozen pipe. Stars exploded behind her eyeballs. Damn, shit, *fuck.* Rolling to her hands and knees, she crawled out from beneath the pipe, but before she could get to her feet, Danny was there on his knees, pulling her up against him.

"Are you okay?" he demanded.

"No, I'm not. You locked us in here, Genius Boy." She sucked in a breath and pressed her hands to her forehead. "And you nearly killed me."

"Didn't have to." He pulled her hands down and put his face within an inch of hers as he studied her forehead. "You almost did it on your own." He probed the spot, making her hiss in a breath. "Miraculously, you're going to live. You know your name? Mine? Where you are?"

"Hope O'Brien, Idiot, in my damn cellar."

His lips twitched. "I thought I was Genius Boy. You didn't break the skin, but you have a good-size lump. You need ice."

"Ouch," she breathed when he kept touching it.

"Aw." Lips still slightly curved, he leaned down and pressed them to her forehead.

She jerked back in shock. "What are you doing?"

"Kissing it all better." His eyes were hot silk and sweetness, one hell of an intoxicating combination, quite lethal to her resistance effort. "Did it work?"

Well, her forehead was tingling now instead of aching. And in fact, her entire body was tingling. Good Lord.

"Did it, Hope?"

Yes. "No!"

His slight smile told her he read the lie quite easily.

"We're locked in," she said through gritted teeth. "Let's worry about that."

"Are you sure?" He craned his neck to look up at the door. "Maybe—"

"Locked. In."

"Okay. So we have lots of time for you to tell me why you sent me on a wild goose chase."

She didn't respond. Couldn't. Because he had taken her face in his hands and was staring into her eyes. "Stop that." She tried to pull back. "I'm fine. So don't even think about kissing me again." Because *she* was thinking about it enough for the two of them.

"Damn, you foiled my evil plan." But for all his joking, there was concern in his eyes and his voice, and there was something in her that reacted to that, something she didn't trust. She didn't need worry or concern, she took care of herself. Always had. "You should know, I'm only attracted to the bad boys. You don't come even close."

"I knew I should have worn my leather pants."

She heard the laugh huff out of her and shook her head at herself. Not going to be charmed by him . . . Still way too hot, she yanked off her sweatshirt and tossed it aside. She got to her feet and stalked the length of the cellar. When she whirled back, she stumbled to a halt.

Genius Boy had pulled off his sweater as well, unbuttoned a few buttons on his shirt, and shoved up his sleeves to his elbows, revealing forearms that weren't scrawny but looked surprisingly strong. "What are you doing now?"

"Your radiator kicked on. It's hot in here."

Yes. Yes, it was, and when his gaze dipped from her face to take in her pj's, the worn camisole and cotton pants that somehow she'd actually thought were a good idea, it got even hotter.

His gaze snagged on her breasts. The soft, silky material had been washed a thousand times. The pale blue was most likely a tad bit see-through. With an inward wince, she looked down at herself.

Not sheer, but thin enough to clearly see the outline of her nipples, which for some annoying reason were hard. *Bad nipples.*

"Maybe if we pound on the door and call for help . . . ?" he murmured, his voice husky and low.

She crossed her arms over her chest and shook her head. "There's no one else here."

"Lori?"

"Doesn't come on until eight."

His jaw dropped. "You're by yourself running the entire inn from evening until morning?"

She heard the disbelief, which put her back up. "It's not a big deal." She frowned. "Normally."

"It could be dangerous, Hope. You should have someone here with you at all times."

"The only danger to me is you."

"Me?" He looked horrified at the thought. "You're not afraid of me."

She didn't want to go there. "Look, my point is that I'm selective about my guests, and besides, it's not like this is the big city. Muggings are nonexistent."

"Still," he said, looking worried.

For her, she realized, and stared at him in surprise. He was worried about her.

How long had it been since someone had worried about her?

"And that plumbing should be wrapped in insulation," he pointed out. "If it was, the pipes wouldn't freeze."

"I agree. I have some renovations ahead of me."

"Do they include fixing the drain in the upstairs bathroom—which by the way, doesn't have a blow-dryer. It doesn't even have towels."

"They're in the laundry." She was well aware of the failings of this place. Ben had offered to fix the problems, but she refused to let him work ahead of what she could pay him. Things were getting done as she could afford them.

"Look," he said softly. "This place is great. It's got history and character and charm, but it needs work. You need to get better control of—"

"Control?" she choked out. "I realize I need some things done, and I'm getting to them, but don't you dare stand there and talk to me about control when you don't even have any over your life. You're nothing more than a lackey for a man who likes to torture the less fortunate, and—"

"Hope." He shook his head and dissolved her temper when he stepped close again. "We both know why I'm here, and that's because you're in financial trouble."

"So I've had a bad year—" She broke off when he

lifted a hand to touch the bump on her forehead, which didn't hurt nearly as much as the taste of her possible failure.

His touch was so gentle that she felt thrown, as she did by his nearness. "I really thought I'd have the money back from Joey by now," she whispered.

"Have you looked into alternative financing?"

Yes. And as she was mortgaged to the teeth, she'd been laughed out of three banking institutions to date. She was working on a fourth. "Look, all I did was e-mail Edward and ask for an extension. No big deal. Instead of bothering to answer, he sent you."

"Because he doesn't give extensions," he said softly, his finger still on her.

She slapped it away. "Fine. So now I know. So just go ahead and get out of here and I'll figure something else out."

"Door's locked," he pointed out calmly. "But after we get out, I'll—"

"Damn-A-straight you'll go."

"—help you, however you need," he said with infuriating patience.

"I already told you, I don't need your help."

"Maybe I could—"

"I said no."

He merely looked at her in that quiet and steady way he had, except . . .

Except not. They were toe to toe, standing just a little too close, and suddenly she realized she was breathing just a little too hard. But so was he.

Why did he have to be so . . . sexy? Because that really wasn't a fair distribution of the goods. And what the hell was he thinking about when he looked at her like that, with his eyes so heated behind those glasses? She didn't know, but he leaned in a little, and she did the same, letting out a soft, anticipatory breath as—

At the top of the stairs, the door opened. Lori stuck her head in and peered down at them. "Hey, did you guys know you were locked in?"

4

Danny climbed the stairs back to his room, not thinking about his job or what he was here for or the snow, but how Hope had looked in her pj's, all hot and sweaty and so sexy he'd nearly swallowed his own tongue.

They'd bickered.

Gotten hot.

Bickered some more.

And gotten hotter. Not cold, which would have been the logical response to being locked in a cellar in the freezing alien turf he'd landed in.

But hot.

With a grim sigh, he pulled out his cell phone and called Edward.

"You get a check?" his boss asked.

That was Edward—always on a hell-bent wave to take over the planet. That had been attractive to Danny when he'd first hired on three years back, but was growing old. "Have you been out here at all? Your sister's really done something with the place."

"Did you get a check?"

Danny sighed. "She's your sister, Ed."

"Fine. Renegotiate."

"Really?" Danny asked, surprised. Relieved. "Because she's got the money coming from the lawsuit, or so she believes. A little more time would really help her out. What terms?"

"One year, triple the interest."

"What?" Danny laughed. "Come on, man. She can't afford that. No one could afford that."

"Those are the terms."

Danny's smile faded and he scrubbed a hand over his face. "You can't do this."

"Then make sure she pays on time."

"Yeah." Danny slid his phone in his pocket and shook his head. He loved handling money. Specifically, loved handling *other* people's money. Eddie's had been a challenge and a lot of fun.

But the fun had definitely gone.

Plus there was something else. He needed something more. More fun, certainly. He also needed . . . well, he wasn't sure exactly, but he was beginning to understand that he was going to have to make a change to get it.

He stripped and showered, which didn't cool him off. He'd rather still be locked in the cellar, stuck there with Hope so they could get past their differences.

And their clothes.

Yeah, and now he had that fantasy playing in his head, her naked and gorgeous and—

The thundering sound echoed around him without warning, making the entire house shudder.

Earthquake.

He grabbed a towel, threw it around his hips, and barreled out of his room, taking the stairs so fast he nearly flew, but all he could think was that those rickety old stairs in the cellar were going to collapse and trap Hope, who was still down there with Lori.

Hitting the bottom step, he pivoted toward the kitchen and crashed into Hope. The collision sent them both skidding across the tile entrance hall, and he lost his towel.

"Are you okay?" she asked.

He would be if he wasn't butt-ass naked. He grabbed his towel and resecured it, hoping she hadn't seen.

She was sitting on the floor, staring up at the ceiling in the awkward silence.

She'd seen.

"Well," she finally said. "I guess it's true what they say about a guy with big feet."

Danny felt himself blush. "That was an accident."

"Not a bad one, really. You perked the morning right up."

He closed his eyes, grateful he'd left his glasses on the counter in the bathroom so that he couldn't see worth shit.

Hope shoved her hair out of her face and let out a long breath.

"I'm sorry," he managed.

"For nearly killing me, or for flashing me?"

"There was an earthquake. Probably only a four, but I thought of the cellar stairs, and—"

"There wasn't an earthquake. It was just snow unloading off the roof and eaves."

He stared at her as she burst into laughter. "Not used to being wrong in your world, huh Genius Boy?"

He turned his head and looked out the wall of windows of the living room, which revealed . . .

Snow.

And more snow.

It was piled high in berms along the roof line now that the roof had unloaded. *Shit*. With a sigh, he pushed to his feet, gripping his towel like it was a lifeline. He offered her a hand and she popped up so quickly that she had to put a hand out for balance, which happened to land on his chest.

A simple touch.

An accidental touch.

And yet somehow, it rocked his world. He looked into her face, braced for a mocking smile, but she appeared to be as shocked as he as she stared down at her hand on his bare skin, almost as if it were touching him against her will.

He wasn't touched a lot in his world. He had friends, some of the female persuasion, and he dated.

But it'd been a while.

So Hope's hand had a bolt of heat shooting straight through him. It weakened his knees and left a knot of anticipation in his gut.

Possibly feeling the same, but probably not, Hope shoved free of him and headed for the hallway that led to her rooms. Her pj bottoms were low on her hips, her cami not quite meeting them, revealing a strip of smooth, creamy skin low on her back. Her shoulders were bare, too, and he stood there in his towel, feeling extremely naked. "Where are you going?"

"To watch *Oprah* and eat bonbons," she said over her shoulder. "Because that's what I do, lay around all day and let this place fall apart."

"I never said that."

"I'm going to get dressed. I advise you to do the same. There's enough cracks in this old house. Oh, and I wouldn't bother with the fancy clothes." She stared back at him. "Wouldn't want you to get dirty."

The clothes he'd brought were his work clothes, but she had a point. They were good for his office, but certainly not hers. "I don't mind getting dirty."

"Hmm," was all she said, and kept moving, those thin cotton pants sagging even lower on her hips, making him wonder if she wore anything beneath. He didn't see how, which didn't help, and he gripped his towel tighter. Not that it mattered, she'd seen everything he had to see.

Plus she was already gone.

The storm had dumped four feet of fresh snow overnight, rendering Danny's car completely useless and also temporarily closing the roads.

Since Hope had made it clear what she thought of him being around, he decided to get some work done while she cooked up a breakfast for her guests. Problem was, the Internet connection was shoddy. The only place to get a steady connection was at the kitchen table, which apparently put him in Hope's way because every time she passed by, he felt her boring holes into him with her eyes.

"The roads are closed," he told her lightly, not looking up from his laptop. "I can't leave."

"Which apparently is karma's idea of a joke." With a sigh, she moved through.

"Don't worry about her."

Danny turned to Lori, who came in the back room door taking out the trash. She was taller than Hope, darker skinned and brunette. Beautiful, and simply dressed in jeans and a hoodie sweater. "She's all bark and no bite. Well, mostly." Lori held out a mug of coffee, which he gratefully took.

And then moaned in sheer pleasure. "That's good."

"Better than Starbucks." It wasn't a question, and Lori smiled confidently when she said it. "It's Hope's home-made blend."

"She's amazing in the kitchen."

"She is. She wants her guests to go back to their life and wax poetic about their time spent here."

"You just need more of them."

"True," Lori said on a laugh. "She's working on that. Working her ass off, actually. We're having a big paint party next week—a bunch of friends are coming out, painting for her by night, skiing by day. And she's placed a bunch of strategic ads for after the first of the year, which should be just about when we get the plumbing up-grade finished." She nodded confidently. "She's going to make it, Danny."

"She's had all this time."

"Yeah, well, it's been a rough year."

"Rough how?"

"None of your business." This from Hope herself as she came into the room and gifted Lori with a frosty look.

Lori didn't back down or apologize, just smiled sweetly and handed over the second mug in her hands. "Have some caffeine, honey. You need it."

Hope rolled her eyes, but sipped the brew, then sighed in what could only be deep pleasure. Her eyes were slightly less chilly as she turned to Danny, who was still quite certain her next words would be "get out if you have to fly out." Except Lori subtly intervened, crossing di-rectly between the two of them to walk up to a guy who'd appeared in the doorway.

"Ben," she murmured warmly, sliding her arms up around his neck and kissing him.

And kissing him.

"Ah, man. Get a room." Hope set her mug down on the counter before sighing and looking at Danny. "They're saying the roads might be cleared by four. But honestly? Probably not. Might have to stay another night."

"Let me guess. For quadruple the going rate?"

She shrugged. "Depends on how big a pain in my ass you are."

"I'll try to control myself," he said dryly. "How about we go over your books and—"

"Sorry. I have other things to do."

Lori came up for air and smiled into Hope's eyes. "It's a snow day, honey. Take a day off."

"You're the boss now?"

Ben headed directly to the refrigerator. "Lori likes to be the boss. Hey, baby, you can be the boss of me."

Lori laughed. "Already am, big guy." And she gave him another kiss.

"Oh, good God," Hope said.

Lori leaned into her husband with a silly laugh that somehow warmed Danny. Watching them banter was like watching a really great old movie. It gave him both an odd sense of comfort—they were a family, one who cared about each other—and also an even odder sense of longing.

This. This was what was missing from his life. His family lived back East and there weren't a lot of visits. His friends were nice, but they weren't a replacement for family, not like these guys clearly were.

Ben took a big bite of the bagel he'd taken from the refrigerator, squeezed his wife's ass, and sighed. "I've got to run. The gas station's electricity's on the blink." That said, he leaned in and kissed Lori again. And then, grinning, turned to Hope, who rolled her eyes but gave him a smacking kiss.

"Hey," Lori said to her. "You never kiss *me*."

"Maybe Ben kisses better than you do."

"Kiss," Lori demanded.

With another laugh—God, she was beautiful when she laughed—Hope leaned in and kissed Lori right on the grinning lips. "There. Now can we all get to work?"

Ben's mouth had fallen open. "I'll be able to work all day on that alone."

Yeah. Danny, too.

Hope took in the dazed expression on both men's faces and shook her head. "Men."

"Oh, yeah," Ben said, and headed out.

Lori grabbed her bin of cleaning supplies and followed him.

Danny walked toward Hope, who was dumping left-over breakfast dishes into the sink. "I've already proven that I can do dishes," he said. "Let me do those for you." He gave her a nudge but she didn't move out of the way. "What's the matter, you can't give up the control enough to even let me help with dishes?"

"Hey, I'm not *that* much of a control freak."

"No?"

"No." She turned to the sink and turned on the water. "Give me some room, Genius Boy. Or should I say Runs Naked Genius Boy?"

"I thought there'd been an earthquake," he repeated on a sigh as she laughed.

"Yes, and you were trying to save me."

"Yes," he said as she once again tried to nudge him away. "You could just go do something else." He reached for the dish soap.

"I could," she agreed, but didn't move.

"Maybe you want to be this close to me."

"I don't do close."

"Because you've been burned." He met her surprised gaze. "Right?"

"Right," she admitted.

"How?"

"Two exes, both assholes if you must know."

"They hurt you?"

"Not physically, no. One stole my heart, the other my money. There's nothing left of either."

"I'm sorry. About both."

"Truthfully? The money thing hurts a lot more than the heart thing."

"Which means maybe it was never really available for him to steal in the first place."

She stared at him. "Huh?"

"Maybe he didn't steal your heart at all. Maybe he just bruised it."

She thought about that as she dug into the dishes at his side, him washing, her rinsing and drying, and when she didn't say anything more, he figured that was the end of that conversation.

"Okay, you might be right," she finally said. "No one's stolen my heart, it just got run over a few times. I can't tell you how much better that makes me feel."

He laughed softly at her sarcasm. "Hey, unless you've been screwed over, you can't appreciate the good stuff. Consider it a rite of passage."

She cocked her head at him. "Have you been screwed over?"

He thought of all the girls in high school and college who'd dismissed him as a nerd. And the women since, none of whom had stuck. "I *invented* being screwed over."

She shook her head. "Are you trying to tell me you're a player, Danny?"

He laughed. "The only thing I play with any skill is Guitar Hero. All I'm saying is that we've all been hurt. Everyone has baggage. You getting ripped off by your ex is a crime, but it happens. It's how you move on with what you know now."

She arched a brow. "And what do I know now?"

"Admit your taste in men sucks."

She laughed, as he'd hoped she would. "So you're suggesting a change in men?" she asked.

"Most definitely."

"Any ideas?"

"As a matter of fact . . ."

Her laughing gaze met his. "Let me guess, I should try a nerdy brainiac who's attempting to ruin my world?"

"More like a nerdy brainiac—a very sexy one, by the way—who's going to do his best to help you stay in control of your world."

"Funny, but I've never considered nerdy brainiacs all that sexy."

"Maybe you haven't met the right ones." He waggled a brow, stood up a little straighter, and flexed.

Which cracked her up as she slid another dish into the sink. The angle of the plate caught the stream of water and sprayed him in the chest. At first, he thought it was an accident, but then she did it again.

"Sorry," she murmured.

Sorry, his ass. He pulled the wet plate from the sink and set it on the counter. "You don't want to take me on, Hope."

"No?" She grabbed another plate, but he was quick, reaching his arms around her and bracketing her wrists with his hands.

"Okay, you're good," she admitted. "But so am I."

"Are you?" He shifted as she wriggled, pressing her between the counter and his body so that her back was plastered up against his front, her very sweet ass solid to his crotch.

At the realization, she went still.

So did he. Well every part of him except one certain part.

"Danny?"

"Yeah?" His voice sounded like his vocal cords had been roughed up with sandpaper.

The moment stretched out, humming with tension that

was no longer temper or good humor, but something far more dangerous, and Hope let out a low breath. "What are we doing?"

No clue.

He turned her to face him. She looked up at him, her face quiet and solemn, but there inside the watchfulness was something else, something he'd needed to see.

Desire.

Hunger.

And her conflict over feeling those things.

Slowly he reached out for her, and just as slowly, lifted her up against him.

Her hands went to his shoulders, but she didn't push him away. Instead, she sank her fingers into him.

Letting out a breath, his mouth brushed her jaw, and he closed his eyes to better absorb the feel of her in his arms. Then she turned her head, and somehow their lips met.

At the kiss, a soft sigh escaped her, a sound of both excitement and pleasure, and he opened his mouth on hers.

God, yeah. He deepened the connection, and she met him halfway, sliding her tongue to his in a rhythm that took him from zero to full speed ahead, and only when they were both breathless and panting, did she pull away.

Eyes wide, she lifted a finger and pointed at him. But though her mouth opened, words apparently failed her. "That was . . ."

Amazing?

Perfect?

Both?

"Unexpected," she finally managed, shaking her head as if to clear it. "Clearly a fluke."

Hell if it was. "Care to test that theory?"

"No." She stepped clear when he reached for her again, and pointed at him. "You. With the amazing mouth." She gestured him away from her. "You just stay over there, since obviously, when it comes right down to it, I'm the only one with any control around here."

And with that, she left the kitchen.

5

"Okay, here's the plan," Hope said to Lori and Ben just before noon. Ben was back from his electrical job, helping with snow removal. They all stood outside in their heavy weather gear, being dumped on by more snow as they shoveled the front walk. "We make Danny's stay miserable."

Lori stopped shoveling and leaned on her shovel, watching Ben's butt as he worked. "Why miserable?"

"Because she likes him," Ben said, still shoveling at a steady pace.

"Because he's here," Hope corrected, shooting Ben a dirty look. "Even though I've not done anything to warrant being watched over like an errant teenager."

Lori shook her head. "You're mad at your asshole brother. Which is understandable, but you can't take it out on Danny."

"Hello, he works for said asshole brother."

"If he wanted to hurt you, he'd have done so by now. Give him a chance, Hope."

"A chance for what?"

"To be the guy I wished for you."

Hope put her hands on her hips. "Are you kidding me?"

"Well, I did wish on that mistletoe, remember? I asked for a penis for you."

"I remember," she muttered in tune to Ben's laugh.

"Which should be the next logical step, given that you've already kissed him."

When Hope choked, Ben finally stopped shoveling to stare at her. "You kissed him?"

Hope looked at Lori, brow raised.

"Sorry," Lori said. "But you two were right in the middle of the kitchen. That you never even saw me tells me how good of a kisser he is." She turned to Ben with a dreamy smile. "He's a face holder."

"Easy," Ben said, and resumed shoveling.

Lori looked at Hope. "Come on, admit he's hot. In a glasses-wearing, intellectual, sexy professor sort of way."

"I could be the sexy professor," Ben said gamefully. "I'll dress up and put on some glasses." He grinned when Lori considered that with a cocked head.

"Can we *please* put aside sex for a minute?" Hope demanded. "This isn't high school."

"Hey, you're the one wanting to play high school games," Ben said. "Making his stay miserable and all."

"That's not even high school," Lori said. "That's *middle* school." She reached around behind Ben and patted his butt. "Love those jeans on you, big guy."

Ben's eyes heated. "Yeah? Or is it what's beneath the jeans?"

"Oh, my God." Hope groaned out loud. "Didn't you already knock it out today?"

"I think it's time for our midmorning quickie."

Hope drew in a sharp breath and shook her head. "You two have a serious problem." She stuck her shovel in the snow and put her hands on her hips. "I just want him gone, okay? I'm this close to making the whole thing work, all I need is some more time with no watch dogs."

"Let him help. He said he wants to." Lori tossed up her hands when Hope glared at her. "So I eavesdropped a little."

"I don't need his help. Just keep him out of my hair until the roads are clear and if you can make him miserable while you're at it," she said, only half kidding. "Just to ensure he leaves ASAP."

"Hope," Lori admonished.

"I'm kidding. Sort of. Hey, I know! Get him to help you clean. And you." She looked at Ben. "Keep him busy doing whatever you're doing today. He's a desk jockey, though, so he's probably worthless out here. Fair warning."

"I don't think so," Ben said slowly. "I think he's made of sturdier stock than you think."

"Face it, honey," Lori said. "Fate brought him. You can't mess with Fate."

"Watch me," Hope said grimly, and struck out for the house to begin *Operation: Make Danny's Stay Miserable.*

Lori watched her go, and Ben watched Lori. "I know that look," he said. "It says you have a plan. An evil plan."

"Not evil. Not exactly."

"We're on Hope's side, Lori," he said gently.

"Of course we are. Which is why we're going to help her."

"By doing as she asked."

"By doing the opposite," she corrected. "You know, the old double switcheroo."

He blinked. "Huh?"

"We're going to pretend to do as she asked, while doing the opposite."

"Let me repeat myself. Huh?"

She patted her husband on his big, beefy shoulder. "Trust me, honey. There are some wild sparks between those two."

"Yes. It's called temper."

"No, it's sexual tension. They're attracted. And more than that, he's a good guy in a shitty situation. Same with her."

"Doesn't mean they should hook up."

"She hasn't had sex in a year."

"Can't imagine going more than one day . . ."

She laughed. "I've spoiled you. Listen, all we're going to do is play Santa and give Hope a man, even if it's a temporary one."

"Lori."

"Trust me."

He laughed softly and pulled her close. "Now that's the one thing I can promise you." He pressed his jaw to hers. "For now and always."

"For now and always," she said on a sweet sigh. "That still makes my knees weak, you know that? You make my knees weak. That's all I want for Hope, Ben."

"Weak knees?"

She slid her hand up his chest and smiled. "We can pull it off. She'll thank us."

"If you say so. But if you could pull it off with your job still intact, that would be great."

After an hour of chopping wood, Hope turned and eyed the wood pile she'd made. It was shrinking instead of growing. Then she looked at the deep grooves from the wood pile to the side of the building. Someone had been doing the stacking for her without saying a word. Since

that was extremely unlike Ben, and extremely unlike Lori—
both of whom would do any chore needed at any time, but
with their mouths working overtime—she set down her ax
and leaned on the handle.

And waited.

Sure enough, within a minute, a hooded figure came
from around the back of the house where the stack of
wood was, brushing off his gloved hands. He was as tall
as Ben, but leaner.

And wearing glasses.

She watched Danny walk toward the stack of wood
without even looking at her. Back and forth he went,
working with a steadiness that told her maybe he wasn't
quite the desk nerd she'd convinced herself.

And since that gave her a funny little tingle in places
she'd nearly forgotten she possessed, she turned to head
back inside. She appreciated the help, but that didn't
change the fact that he was here to assess whether she
was going to be able to pay back her loan. No way around
it, Danny was going to cause her trouble.

And heartache.

Because dammit, she loved this place. Loved it like it
was her family, which was ridiculous. It was just a place.
But it was *hers*.

The back door was locked, which was odd. Cupping
her hands, she peered into the window of the kitchen. No
one there. She pounded on the door, but Lori didn't appear and neither did Ben.

Which meant that they'd found themselves a closet or
God knew where and were acting like bunnies again.

Terrific.

She could wade through the snow around to the other
side of the building and let herself in the front door, but
they hadn't cleared the snow from the side yards, and

without snow shoes she'd sink up to her thighs. Not fun. Instead, she whipped out her cell phone and texted Lori.

Let me in pls.

Lori immediately texted back:

Sorry. On a supply run.

"Bullshit," Hope muttered and shoved her phone back in her pocket. No one was on a supply run, the roads were complete muck. Nope, her chef and her fix-it guy were definitely going at it.

Again.

It should have irritated the hell out of her, but instead she found herself sighing. She was happy for them, very happy, but something deep inside her wished . . . what? That she had that same thing? She'd never been one to daydream about the white wedding, white picket fence, and kid-friendly SUV.

And yet . . . She turned and leaned against the door. As far as the eye could see was nothing but a white blanket of snow and gorgeous tall pines masquerading as three-hundred-foot-tall ghosts swaying in the light breeze.

And one hardworking guy stacking wood.

Okay, so a small part of her suddenly wanted the dream, she admitted to herself as Danny dropped his last load on the stack against the house.

He took a moment to eye the job he'd just finished, then came toward her, stride determined, expression inscrutable, forcibly reminding her that the guy was capable of melting her bones.

Oh, and that he could kiss.

That thought snaked in unwelcome, and stuck. Lori

had been correct, he *was* a face holder, and in possession of a very talented tongue, and—

And she wanted him. God, so much. She straightened a bit, her belly quivering in tune to her knees. His expression didn't soften as he came toward her, but it did heat. *He was going to kiss her again,* and in spite of herself, her eyes drifted shut in anticipation.

His booted feet crunched closer in the snow. A steady gait. A sure gait.

Slowing . . .

Stopping.

But the touch of his hands pulling her up to him never came. Nor did the feel of his mouth taking hers.

"See, you're not the only one who can control yourself," came his rough whisper in her ear.

Her eyes whipped open in time to catch a view of the back of him as he vanished around the corner of the building.

And it was a very nice back.

She let out a low, shaky breath. City rat bastard had a sharp wit, she'd give him that. And a good ass.

And far too much of that control she suddenly wished he didn't possess at all.

Danny thought he'd be chomping at the bit to get back to LA, but there was a certain charm to the wilds of Colorado, a sort of . . . quiet calm that he liked.

Truthfully? If it wasn't for the unfairness of Hope's situation, he might have really enjoyed himself out here.

The thing was Hope was a smart woman. She'd updated all the parts of the building that she'd had to for the place to run. And according to the business plan she'd outlined for Edward, she had a clear order of what she wanted to do with the place as the money came in.

Except the money wasn't coming in.

And like most of the other problems she had, it wasn't her fault. She was paying too much on the loan to her brother. She could get a better deal, she *needed* a better deal.

He got online and downloaded her brochure. As he'd clearly told her, she wasn't charging enough. Plain and simple. She needed to up her prices and needed to tout herself as exclusive and luxurious, both of which she had the means to be within her disposal with only a minimal amount of work on her part. She already had the first-class chef—herself—and the gorgeous setting. All she needed were those cosmetic changes: some paint, some six-hundred-count silk sheets and down comforters to go with . . . His fingers worked the keyboard, bringing up new research on successfully run B&Bs . . .

His cell rang.

"So," Edward said without preamble. "Did she agree to the new loan?"

In that moment, Danny had never hated his job more. He really needed that change. "I was hoping you'd rethought things."

"I don't rethink."

"Yeah. Right." Danny shook his head. "Okay, you know what? That was me. *I've* rethought things. I'm not going to do this for you, Edward."

"You handle my money. Doing so is your job."

"Not anymore, it's not."

There was a sharp pause. "Are you quitting?"

Danny drew a deep breath. "Yes."

"Because of this loan?" Edward asked in disbelief.

"She's your sister."

"Step," Edward said. "*Step*sister. And I'd recall on my own mother, you know that."

It was true. Edward had never made a secret about the kind of man he was. But if Danny stayed, he'd become the same. "I'm done, Edward."

"What the hell is going on up there anyway?"

"A lot of thinking."

"Sounds like it. What are you going to do that's better than this job?"

"I'm going to start an accounting firm." A small one, for small businesses, where he could help and maybe even make a difference instead of ruin people. "Accounting and financial services."

"Come on," Edward said on a laugh. "You love big money as much as I do, you big CPA geek."

Yeah, he did. Or had. But big money meant dealing with people he didn't always like or respect, and in return, he would turn into someone he didn't like or respect, either, he felt it.

"If you walk away," Edward warned, "we're done. No crawling back when you decide you miss my millions."

"I won't miss it."

"Is this Hope's doing? Because she has that effect on people. Trust me, she drives them crazy. Just come back, and—"

"I'm snowed in. And she's not driving me crazy." Well, she was. She really, really was, but in a good way. "Goodbye, Edward."

"Hey, you tell her she still has to pay. I'll come up and get that money myself if I have to. You tell her that."

Danny hung up and looked at himself in the mirror over his dresser. Hair neat. Glasses in place. Shirt pressed and tucked in.

Jesus. He really was a fucking CPA geek.

Well, he'd just made a huge life change, he could certainly make a few more. He untucked his shirt, then laughed at himself. Wow, what a rebel. Shaking his head, he made his way downstairs. Lori had asked him to come back down, promising him a surprise in the living room, a surprise he sincerely hoped had something to do with the smell of something *delicious* baking. Stacking wood for two hours had made him as hungry as he'd ever been. Or maybe it was quitting his job.

Or maybe it was a certain stubborn, proud B&B owner who stirred him up in both a very good, and very bad, way.

He heard the banging, then turned the corner into the living room.

Hope stood on a six-foot ladder, wielding a staple gun and hanging a string of Christmas lights. She wore her usual, a long-sleeved tee and hip-hugging jeans. This time she'd added a tool belt to the mix, which was strapped around her waist and immediately made him hot for some reason. She had an iPod strapped through one of her belt loops, earphones in her ears, a Santa cap on her head.

And she was singing at the top of her considerably tone-deaf lungs, which had him grinning. The woman could do anything, which made her quite possibly the sexiest thing he'd ever seen.

Yeah, he'd made the right decision to quit, because there was no way he'd ever pull out the rug from beneath her.

She deserved more.

Knowing she couldn't possibly hear him through the music blasting in her ears, he walked into the room, getting in her line of sight just as she executed a little ass shimmy that made him laugh.

When she saw him, she jumped. "Sorry," he said as she pulled out one of the earplugs. "Didn't mean to scare you."

"You didn't." Couldn't. That was the underlying message she wordlessly imparted. "Lori's bugging me to finish decorating."

"She told me to come to the living room."

Hope's eyes narrowed as she gripped the top rung of the ladder. "She did, did she?"

"Yes."

"Well, you'll have to excuse her. She got married and her brain turned to mush." She stretched out some more lights to hang.

He reached up to help hold the lights for her. "Weather forecast is looking pretty nasty," he noted.

"Hopefully it'll hold." She used the staple gun on the lights, then looked down at him. "I'm sure you have other people to gouge the soul from."

"Is that what I've done, gouge your soul?"

"No." She sighed. "I do realize you're just the messenger."

"Was. I *was* the messenger."

"What does that mean?"

"It means I quit my job."

"What?"

"Yeah. I've known for some time that I've been needing a change."

She stared at him. "You quit your job."

"I'm thinking of starting my own business, where I get to pick my clients." He was looking forward to that. "A small accounting and financial service—right up my alley." And under those circumstances, he could see himself on the *other* side. The good side. Fighting for this woman. This smart, sexy, stubborn, gorgeous woman whose only crime had been to trust a member of her family.

"Are you crazy?" she asked, backing down the ladder. "Have you seen the news? We're in a thing called a recession. Now's not a good time to be without a job."

"I'll be okay. Hope, about your loan."

"I'll be able to pay it."

"How?" he asked frankly, worried that Edward would do exactly as he'd just promised and come here himself. He slid a hand on her arm. "I saw the For Sale sign on the adjacent lot to this one, which you also own."

"Well technically, the bank owns it. But if it sells before I get my money back, then everything's good."

Except that properties weren't moving, not in this market. "What if you got investors to buy your lot?"

"Look, I realize that you no longer work for Edward, and frankly, that says a lot about you, but I'm not about to blindly trust you. I'll do this. *My* way." She reached into a bag for a fistful of greenery and looked around for a place to hang it. "Now if you'll excuse me, Lori insisted on this stuff going up." She headed for the huge, tall mantel.

"It's mistletoe."

"I think I'd know mistletoe." She stretched up to hold the stuff in place while she nailed it with the gun.

He waited until she'd reholstered the staple gun, until she'd turned to face him before putting a hand on the mantel on either side of her. Leaning in close, until their lips were only an inch apart, he waited for a reaction.

Her gaze dropped to his mouth and went to half mast.

He loved how she put herself out there, no façade, no hidden agenda. It was one of the most attractive things about her, and he shifted even closer. His mouth brushed her cheek now, then the corner of her lips, and when her hands came up to grip his shirt, he kissed her.

She immediately leaned into him, making that same soft sigh of pleasure she'd made last time, the one that made him instantly hard. She tasted like warm, sweet, giving female, like forgotten hopes and dreams, and when she moved against him and slid her tongue to his, he thought he might die of the pleasure.

"Okay," she murmured, pulling back, eyes still closed. "Maybe it's mistletoe."

He ran his thumb over a smudge of dirt on her jaw and let out a rough breath. "Yeah."

"That stuff should come with a warning." She turned, and with her tool belt slapping against her hips with every step she took, she walked out of the room.

Hope strode into the kitchen and headed straight for the sink, where she downed a full glass of cold water. It didn't help.

She stared out the window at the still falling snow and put a hand on her heart to keep it from leaping right out of her chest, because holy smokes. *Holy smokes* could that guy kiss. She set down the empty glass and found Lori standing in the doorway grinning at her.

Hope sighed. "Saw that, did you?"

"Seriously. You ever hear of behind closed doors?"

"I know. God." At least no guests had been roaming about. *Real professional, Hope.*

"Look at it this way." Lori gave her a thumbs up. "You're doing a helluva job with that evil plan to make his visit miserable. I bet he hated that torturous tongue lashing you just gave him."

Hope thunked her head on the cabinets. "My evil plan is kaput."

"Good. Why?"

"Because he quit. He's going to start his own business, one where he doesn't have to suck the soul out of people."

"Wow. Good for him. You got to him."

Yeah. And damn if he wasn't getting to her . . .

She shoved away from the counter and headed toward her office.

"Where are you going?"

"To bury myself in paperwork." Anything to avoid reliving the past few minutes, which had been fantasy-worthy, and definitely worth reliving—neither of which she wanted to face. "And like you were helping me make him miserable. You were too busy manufacturing ways to get us together."

"I don't know what you're talking about," Lori said innocently.

"You locked me out of the house earlier. You sent him to the living room where you knew I'd be. You—"

"Wow, you've got quite the imagination."

Hope rolled her eyes. "Okay, fine. Play innocent. Just stop playing me." She hit her office, where she spent the next few hours trying to rob Paul to pay Peter, and unable to do that, did her best to handle the money situation so as to make every creditor happy.

An impossible feat.

With a sigh, she closed her eyes and tried something she hadn't tried since she'd been four and in church with her mother. She clasped her hands together and bowed her head. "God? Do you think you could do me a favor? If you help me, I promise I'll . . ." She hesitated, wracking her brain for a worthy offering. "I'll stop fantasizing about Edward's speedy death." She opened her eyes, peeked at her bank balance, and sighed in disappointment.

As usual, she was on her own.

She turned to the window, where she saw not just the snow, falling much more lightly now, but Danny, walking the perimeter of her property while simultaneously looking down at a large piece of paper in his hands.

What was he up to now?

She should just ignore him. But she could no more do that than stop thinking about how he'd kissed her. How he'd held her face and looked into her eyes before and after as if . . .

As if she meant something to him.

The thought brought a lump to her throat, which pissed her off. Pushing up from her desk, she shoved on her knit cap and grabbed her coat. Because he might have kissed her as if she was the most important thing to him at that moment, but right now he had something else on his mind.

And she wanted to know what.

And . . . and maybe, just maybe, she wanted to see if he meant something to her, too.

So she headed outside, but the cold slap of air on the porch knocked some sense into her and she hesitated.

What was she doing?

She didn't need to talk to him, she needed to ignore him. And repeating that like a mantra, she turned back to the door.

Which was locked.

"Dammit, Lori!" But the door remained locked. With a sigh, she headed toward him.

Danny walked through the snow, squinting behind his fogged-up glasses as he checked the plot map in his hands to the lot Hope had up for sale. It ran adjacent to the B&B, most of it a hill overlooking the valley far below.

A stunning view.

He knew from Hope's business plan that she wanted to

build a sledding and tubing area here. She'd need equipment for the tow lift, maybe some lights to operate at night, and the sleds. Cheap—relatively speaking—and it would give her a nighttime activity for guests. Plus, she could charge for the activity and bring in additional income. He liked it, he liked all of it, and could now see the draw, see what kept her here.

The potential was amazing.

He'd always loved the city life, everything about it; the traffic, the noise, the availability of fast food . . . but he could admit, there was something to this, too. Something wild and almost savage, and incredibly soothing at the same time.

Through the falling snow he caught sight of someone standing on the back porch. Jeans, a white down jacket, snow boots . . . that frown.

Hope.

She was walking toward him with purposeful steps, and at the sight of her a mix of heat and wariness hit him. He couldn't remember ever feeling this way about a woman before; the intense need, mixed with a deep, abiding affection.

As he dealt with the onslaught of emotions over that, he caught yet another movement. Something small, brown . . . a dog. A brown Lab, he thought, bounding up to play with him. Danny crouched low, encouraging it to come up to him—

Whoa. It wasn't a dog.

It was a *bear cub.*

He straightened and stared in shock down at the cub, now frolicking and rolling in the snow at his boots looking like the cutest thing he'd ever seen. But even he, a certified city rat, knew baby bears didn't travel alone.

And sure enough, as he looked up at Hope still coming toward them, he saw the momma bear behind her, heading for the equipment shed and trash box between him and the B&B. Even as he registered that, Hope came to a stop and slowly turned.

And came nose to nose with the momma bear. "Oh, shit."

In answer, the bear puffed itself up and let out a low but unmistakable growl.

Danny leaped forward and let out a primal yell born of sheer terror, accompanying that with waving his arms like an idiot; that's what he'd read one was supposed to do with bears in the wild. Be big and strong and intimidating.

God, he hoped he was looking big and strong and intimidating.

He frightened the baby bear, who cried out and leaped forward to the closet tree, which it scaled in a matter of two seconds all the while whimpering for its momma—

Who turned to the new threat and looked at Danny as if maybe he was a twelve-course meal and she was suddenly starving.

Danny grabbed Hope and tugged her behind him.

Oddly enough, his life didn't flash across his eyes. Probably because Hope shoved free of him and clapped her hands loudly. At the sound, the momma bear let out a low chugging noise in her throat, along with two long lines of drool from either side of her throat as she eyed Danny. *My, but you look delicious*—

"Sorry, but he's mine," Hope told her and clapped again. With one more growl, the bear lumbered slowly off, stopping at the tree for her baby.

"Damn," Hope said. "I must give good trash. That's the fourth time this week she's been by."

Danny would have answered but he couldn't. His legs were masquerading as overcooked noodles, and he sat so abruptly on the steps of the equipment shed that his glasses half slid off.

"Danny? You okay?"

Since he wasn't at all sure, he lay back and stared up at the gorgeous sky. Snowflakes fell on him. One hit him on the nose.

"Danny?"

"Yeah."

He heard her swear softly and drop to her knees at his side, her gloved hands running over him as she tried to figure out if he was hurt.

"I'm not injured," he said. But was he okay? Maybe, if he discounted the fact that he was out in the middle of nowhere, no Thai takeout within sixty miles, actually enjoying the feel of the snow at his back soaking into his clothes. . . . And let's not forget the biggee—that he was in all likelihood falling for a woman who was right now patting him down and making him wish they weren't outside in the cold snow but somewhere warm.

And naked.

A woman he realized he wanted to fall for.

But other than that, yeah, he was just great.

7

Adrenaline flowing, Hope leaned over Danny. She couldn't see any injuries, but the light was low and the snow falling pretty thickly.

Dammit.

Reaching behind him, she shoved open the equipment shed. "Scoot in," she demanded.

"I'm fine."

"Yeah? Well, I'm cold and wet. Scoot in."

"City girl."

Something about the roughness of his voice, with the slight—very slight—edge of humor got to her.

He got to her. "I thought you were hurt," she said as they landed on the floor of the shed.

"Told you I'm not." He pulled off his fogged glasses and cleaned them on the hem of his shirt sticking out from his jacket. "I'm tougher than you think."

Yeah. Yeah, he was. And something else she was discovering . . . she wasn't. She wasn't nearly as tough as she'd thought, or she wouldn't be so worked up right now, heart drumming, pulse racing, even as she rolled to face him. "Why did you try to get between me and that bear?"

He put on his glasses and stared at her. "I don't know, it was instinctive."

"What did you think you were going to do, save me?"

"Well . . . yeah."

Now *she* stared at *him*. "Are you crazy?"

"You can face down a bear, but I can't?"

"You don't even like me, why would you take on a damn bear for me?"

He let out a low laugh and a shake of his head. "And here I thought you were such an observant woman."

She narrowed her eyes. "What is that supposed to mean?"

"It means . . ." He reached up and touched her face, ran a finger over the small bruise she had on her forehead from when she'd managed to nearly knock herself out with the pipe in the cellar. "You're not paying attention."

"I'm paying attention." It was why her heart was pounding in her ears. "Maybe . . . maybe you're just trying to play me."

"Maybe same goes," he said evenly.

She choked on a mirthless laugh as her emotions got the best of her. Never a good thing, but she went into a flurry of motion to get as far away from him as fast as possible, except he anticipated and caught her.

She tried to twist away, but he completely negated her temper, turning into something else entirely when he pulled her down to him and pressed his mouth to hers in a long, deep, wet kiss full of such heat she nearly imploded. By the time he pulled back, she could barely speak. "I'm not a player."

"Good. Neither am I." His eyes verified that fact, and also what he felt for her. That knowledge, combined with the heat they were generating between them, nearly took her breath. But what he did next *did* take her breath. He covered her hand in his and pressed it to his chest. "I like you, Hope." His heart was drumming, steady and just a little too fast. "That's how much."

"Maybe that's adrenaline from the bear."

Eyes on her, his fingers tightened on her hand, sliding it down his chest to the zipper of his pants. Behind it, he was hard as steel. "Is that adrenaline from the bear, too?"

"Huh." Her voice wasn't too steady. "Probably not." She let her fingers play over him, loving the way that had the breath rushing from his lungs. "Some people react to adrenaline in . . . interesting ways," she said.

"No doubt. And while that bear was beautiful, my tastes in females tend toward the furless, not to mention of the human variety."

When she snorted, his hands slid beneath her coat and up her back. "Are we going to wrestle some more, Hope? Or—"

"Or," she said definitively, and fisting her hands in the front of his jacket, she covered his mouth with hers. And right there, on the hard wooden floor, with Danny on his back and the snow blowing in behind her, she straddled him.

No slouch, he slid one hand into her hair to hold her mouth to his while the other gripped her thighs, pulling her tighter against him, and when that apparently wasn't enough, he cupped her bottom and urged her to rock against him. With a helpless moan at the feel of a most impressive bulge between her legs, she had to admit—he was no lightweight. As his mouth worked its feverish way over her jaw to her ear, she pressed her face to the crook of his neck and let her eyes cross with lust. "Danny—"

"Yeah. Right." A low breath escaped her, and he let his hands fall from her to the floor at his sides. "You've come to your senses."

His pragmatic words uttered in such a desire-roughened voice only made her want him more, and she stared down into his face, into those light, warm eyes that always drew her in, and absorbed his easy acceptance of her. *Her*. For exactly who she was. "Yes," she said softly. "I've come to my senses." And still holding his gaze in hers, she pushed him farther into the shed to protect them from the show and any prying eyes, and then went for the button on his pants.

He closed his eyes and groaned when she lowered his zipper and stroked a finger down the length of him. His hips rocked up and her name tumbled from his throat in a low, rough, strangled voice.

Her knees were digging into the hard floor and she didn't care. Her own hands were rough as she shoved up his shirt to reveal a rather impressive set of abs, and with a low, muttered "thank God," his were just as rough as he wrestled with her jacket.

She tore her gloves off with her teeth because she had to touch skin to skin, then waved her arms like a bat trying to throw off the jacket— "Holy shit," she wheezed out when his icy fingers slid up her shirt.

"Sorry." But instead of stopping, he unhooked her bra and pushed it up, along with her shirt and her half-removed jacket, then with a hand spread on the small of her back, nudged her down over him.

"Danny —" His name backed up in her throat as his mouth found a breast. God. *God.* It was like the opening of a damn, as their hands fought for purchase.

"Hope— I don't have a condom."

She stared at him as reality hit, and then she remembered. "I have four!" She pulled them out of her pocket and held them up like a trophy. "The benefit of having a horny best friend who thinks I need more sex."

"God bless horny best friends," he said fervently.

Feeling the same way, she got his pants down to his thighs and he got hers open, but then they got tangled as he tried to tug the jeans off. He wrestled with the clothes for a minute, swearing when he found she also had on long underwear. "Christ, it's just like my high school dreams, where I can't get the girl naked."

"Here." Laughing, she helped kick off her pants, and then the long underwear, which caught on one of her boots. "Leave it," she gasped as his hands pulled her back over him so that once again she was straddling him, where together they got the condom on.

"God, Hope, look at you." He stroked his hand up her inner thigh, letting his thumb stroke over her very center, carefully spreading her open. "You're wet." He played in that wetness, making her cry out and rock against him. "Is that adrenaline from the bear?" he asked, teasing her with the words she'd given him. "Or for me?"

"Ha," she managed, then choked out a needy little whimper when he pushed up inside her, the sound meshing with the low, sexy rumble that came from deep in his throat.

His fingers held her still when she would have rocked, not letting her move. "Not yet," he whispered thickly, and stroked his thumb over her again, and then again, slowly increasing in rhythm and pressure, taking his cues from her reactions, which were shockingly earthy and base. "If you move," he managed in a low growl that she found sexy as hell, "I'm done."

She didn't care, in that moment she only cared about the way his fingers were moving on her, taking her places she hadn't been in so damn long, and then there was how he felt, thick and hot and big, God so big, inside of her. His hands were gentle and tender but there was something so raw about his every movement, so uncalculated, as if it had been as long for him as it had been for her. It had her nerves on high alert, leaving her so pleasure-taut, so unbearably sensitive, she was already on the very edge.

She heard the whimper escape her throat, a horrifyingly embarrassing sound, but she couldn't stop or control herself.

With him, she could never control herself.

So she gave up trying. For this moment, she let herself go, just gave in to it, in to him, and her hands slapped on the hard floor on either side of his head. "Danny, now . . ."

Releasing her hips, he rose up to meet her, his hands sliding into her hair to bring her mouth to his.

Her permission to move.

So she moved. She rocked her hips, then again when he guided her into a rhythm that had her bursting wildly. Even more startling, he came with her. Simultaneous orgasm. It was amazing, soul-shaking, and revealing, almost too much so, and she tried to bury her nose into his throat, but he held her face, letting her see every single emotion as it hit him—the sheer, unadulterated desire, the hunger, the heat such as she'd never known, and perhaps the most devastatingly intimate emotion of all . . .

Affection.

And with his arms banded tight around her, holding on to her as if she was the most precious thing in his world, she stared back into his eyes and gave him the same.

$\mathscr{E}$

Well, holy shit, Danny thought as Hope flopped off him, gasping for breath.

From flat on his back on the floor of the shed, Danny did his own gasping for breath as he stared up at the ceiling. He couldn't have been more stunned if he'd just been hit head-on by a moving freight train. He'd just had the best sex of his entire life. On the ground. In the great outdoors. In the wilds of Colorado.

In the snow.

God, what he'd give to be able to shout it from the rooftops of all the assholes who'd ever given him a hard time in his school days for being the nerd.

Nerds unite.

Smiling helplessly, he rolled toward Hope. She had her pants on one leg, hanging off the other, her jacket half on and her top shoved up to her chin.

God, she was hot. And gorgeous. And sweet. And blurry. Where the hell were his glasses?

She'd flung an arm over her eyes, and was still breathing like she'd just run a marathon, which gave him a ridiculously dopey grin.

And the urge to nuzzle. Yeah, he wanted to draw things out, snuggle, cuddle, the whole bit. Maybe even go for round two. To that end, he scooted closer and slid a hand up her bare leg to her hip—

Sitting straight up, she pushed his hand away and began to right her clothing.

"Hey," he murmured, softly. "Are you—"

His shirt, the one she'd ripped off him only a few minutes before, hit him square in the face.

"Hurry," she said.

He pulled the shirt down "Before the bear comes back?"

"Before someone decides to take a stroll and see us."

"In four feet of snow?"

"We're out here, aren't we?" She jammed her foot back into the one boot she'd managed to tear off. To hurry him along, she tossed his jacket over as well. "Why aren't you moving?"

"My bones dissolved. Hope, that was—"

"Fun," she agreed, not looking at him as she laced up her boot. "Thanks for that, I feel much better now. More relaxed."

"Okay, good, but—"

And while he was still stuttering, she stood up and walked off, her boots crunching in the snow as she went, muttering something about how that back door to the kitchen had better no longer be locked.

He lay back to resume his staring up at the ceiling, but something was under his ass.

His glasses.

He put them on his nose and sighed. They were bent to hell. "Thanks for that," he said, repeating Hope's words, then laughed at himself.

Something brushed his foot then, and picturing the bear, he leaped up, his pants still at his thighs—

And met the surprised gaze of one very curious deer, peering into the shed with huge doe eyes.

"Jesus," Danny said shakily.

Which was apparently too much for Bambi, and she took off, leaping like the picture of grace through the snow across the open yard.

Danny let out a breath and yanked up his pants—a guy needed balls of steel for this place. Giving himself a pep talk, including one about not letting himself think too hard about what he and Hope had just done—or how fast she'd run from it—he managed to get back to the B&B. He let himself in the kitchen door and came face to face with yet another audience.

Lori and Ben.

They were sitting on the counters sipping steaming coffee, but what he noticed most was their matching grins.

"Hey," Lori said sweetly.

"Hey." Danny looked out the window and saw to his relief that the shed was not visible from here. He turned and divided a look between husband and wife as he shrugged out of his jacket. "So I suppose neither of you know how Hope got locked out of here a few minutes ago."

"Um, what?"

"The door," he said. "It was locked."

"Huh." Ben lifted a shoulder. "Odd."

Lori nodded. "Odd."

He gave up and headed across the kitchen to the coffee pot. "I'm going to go check on the road conditions."

"Sure," Lori said. "But you might want to tie your left boot and rebutton your shirt."

He'd buttoned his shirt wrong. Perfect. He fixed that and bent to work on the boot.

"Must be a helluva wind out there."

Danny straightened and met Ben's steady, even gaze. Yeah. It'd been a helluva wind all right, and its name had been Hope. "Do you happen to know if the roads have been cleared?"

"Yes, but it's going to be dark soon. You really going to head out?"

"Yeah." He needed to. Hope was a big girl, she'd made that clear. She didn't need nor want his help. And though she couldn't possibly deny the fact that she'd enjoyed their little outside tussle, he knew she was also over it.

Over him.

She'd be okay. She knew what she had to do to keep this place out of the clutches of her brother. He looked out the windows again. He told himself he was tired of wide open skies and no skyline. Tired of the lack of Starbucks and no New York pizzeria.

But the truth was, the place had grown on him.

And so had Hope.

"Roads might be icy," Lori said gently. "And it's going to snow some more. We're awfully shorthanded. . . ."

"Well," he heard himself say. "If you're shorthanded . . ."

When Hope needed to avoid thinking about something, she'd found that nothing beat manual labor. To that end, she stood on the roof of the shed as the sun sank behind the mountains, shoveling the thick snow off the flat roof so it wouldn't collapse. She had the back floodlights on to see, and brain blessedly blank, was happy in her own little world, where there were no sexy nerds, no evil stepbrothers. . . .

Someone climbed up the ladder. A knit cap-covered head popped up.

Danny.

He tossed up a second shovel. "I know, you don't want

my help. Too bad." With that, he climbed the rest of the way up, straightening with slow caution as he looked down at the ground. "Huh."

She raised a brow as he lost some of his color. "Afraid of heights?"

"No, of course not."

"Of course not," she repeated wryly when he sank to his knees and closed his eyes. "Okay, big guy. You just stay there, I'm nearly done here anyway."

"No. I'm going to help." Resolutely, he used the shovel to pull himself back upright.

Hope stared at him, feeling some more of those unwanted emotions clogging her throat. He was so different from any man she'd ever known. Loyal, intellectual, sharp-witted . . . and strong. So damn strong, from the inside out; strong of mind and character, strong of heart and soul, and that . . .

That was new for her.

He didn't care what people thought, didn't care about anything except doing the right thing, and damn if that wasn't the sexiest thing about him.

It was also more than just a little terrifying given what had happened the last few times she'd opened up and let someone in.

And in any case, she was strong, too. She reminded herself of this very fact as she resumed shoveling snow off the roof. She ran this place on her own and she'd find her own answers, without spending every single breathing moment thinking about what she'd done with Danny in this very shed.

But oh, good sweet Jesus. *What they'd done in this shed.* She couldn't help but think about it. Relive it. And think some more. Because . . .

Wow.

Genius Boy really had had the moves.

She tried to shake it off, tried to go back to the blessedly blank state, but she couldn't. The truth was, she'd managed to avoid thinking too much about her financial situation. She'd avoided thinking about the possibility of something happening to her perfect world out here in the Colorado boonies she loved so much.

But she couldn't keep that up. Things had to change.

Danny had gotten to his feet and was back to back with her, shoveling snow as steadily as she.

He was a rock.

A solid rock.

And if she followed his business ideas as well as her own, she knew she could make it. "Danny?"

Turning his head, he looked at her. Smiled. "Yeah?"

"You were right."

A slow smile curved his mouth. "Much as I like hearing that . . ." He straightened, stretched his back, then leaned on his shovel. "What am I right about—" He broke off when the shovel slid out from beneath him.

"Danny!" she cried as he slipped and the ice layered beneath the snow on the roof propelled him toward the edge of the roof.

"No!" Her heart leaped into her throat as she jumped forward to catch him, but the ice caught her, too.

And she went over with him.

For the second time that day, Danny braced for his life to flash across his eyes.

It didn't.

That's because thanks to the sheer amount of snow they'd shoveled off the sides of the shed, he had a nice, cushy fall.

When he hit the huge berm of snow, he slowly sank in up to his nose. He spit out a mouthful of snow and was trying to figure out how to actually swim out when he was hit in the chest by . . .

Hope. He stared down at the bundle that had landed on him, his amusement at himself vanishing instantly. Heart in his throat, he pulled her in. "Are you—"

"Did I hurt you?" she demanded, getting herself out of the snow pile much faster and surer that he did. She ran her hands up his neck to cup his face. "Danny?"

Maybe it was evil of him but the sheer concern and worry in her eyes alleviated his fear, and in fact warmed him to his very frozen toes. As did the way they kept trying to rescue each other. He had no idea why that struck him so funny, but he loved it.

He'd never in a million years imagined getting stuck in Colorado. Or liking it. But there was real life out here, adventure in every single moment. Not the drudge of an office, or any office politics, but warmth and affection from the people he was coming to know, and an easy, simple joy in the chores to run the place, which were anything but simple—

"Danny," Hope said tightly, running her hands down his body, clearly checking him for broken bones.

It seemed certain things were becoming habit with him—a habit he could get used to.

"Talk to me," she demanded.

"If I told you where it hurt, would you "

"Oh, God. Can you make it inside?" Without waiting for an answer, she slipped her arm around his waist and tried to take all his weight as she led him to the back door. "Almost there—"

"Hope, I was only kidding—"

She took him through the kitchen, down the hallway into her bedroom. She pulled him past her bed and into her bathroom. "You're icing up. Gotta get you out of those clothes."

"Hope—"

"Hold on." She cranked on the hot water and then turning back to him, tugged off his jacket, knit cap, gloves. But it wasn't until she dropped to her knees in front of him that his breath backed up in his throat.

"Lift up," she said, and he realized she'd untied his boots. Before he could say a word, she leaned past him to check the water temp. "Good," she said to herself.

Shaking his head on a low laugh, he reached down and pulled her up.

She immediately went to work on unbuttoning his shirt, but because the feel of her hands on him set him back about thirty IQ points, it took him a minute to say her name again.

By then she had his shirt off and her hands were at the zipper of his pants, except if she got them off, she wasn't going to find an injured man, but a hot, aroused one—

She shoved down his pants, then stared at his erection. "Well, hello there."

"Yeah. I'm not hurt, Hope."

"I'm beginning to get that," she murmured, still looking at the part of him that was the happiest to be naked, which pretty much waved hello at her. "Did you fall off that roof so I'd sleep with you again?"

"Ha— *Jesus*," he managed when she wrapped her hand around him and slowly stroked. "I—"

"Get in the shower, Danny." Letting go of him, Hope put a hand to his chest and pushed him toward the steaming shower. Then she pulled off her shirt.

Never one to argue with a woman who was stripping, he took a step back into the water, not taking his eyes off her as she discarded her boots, unzipped her jeans, and shimmied out of them.

Gaze locked on his, she unhooked her bra, wriggled out of her panties, and then stepped into the shower.

"Look at you," he whispered against her mouth, pleasure suffusing him as their now wet bodies slid up against each other. "You're so beautiful, Hope."

"So are you. Who'd have thought it, but I can't keep my hands off you, Genius Boy."

With the hot water raining over them, Hope moved her hands to his face, so close he could feel her gentle breath on his skin. "This is nice," she whispered.

Nice. It was, but he hoped to hell he could do better than *nice*. Hope's breasts were against his chest, her belly and thighs flush to his, pressing her back against the wall to free up his hands, which he skimmed up her body.

Her breath came out in a whoosh, and she melted against him. "I like it when you take charge," she murmured.

"Yeah?"

"Oh, yeah."

"Then turn around."

"Um . . . what?"

Hands on her hips, he twisted her around so that she was now facing the wall.

"Danny—"

"Shh." He pressed his lips to the nape of her neck, loving how she shivered as he took his mouth on a cruise downward, over the slim arch of her spine, to the sweetest ass known to man. He kissed the backs of her thighs, and then in between, urging her legs open so he could take her over the edge, which she let him do with ego-stroking ease. God. *God,* he thought as she came for him with some more of those sexy helpless little whimpers she made in the throes. He didn't want this to be just a hot weekend affair.

Not when for him it was already so, *so* much more.

Still breathing heavily, she turned around to face him again, pulling him up to kiss his jaw, his throat, whatever she could reach, her mouth telling him that he was the best thing to happen to her since sliced bread, and he could have told her that it was the same for him. This, with her, was the rightest thing in his life. Her arms were wrapped tightly around him, so tightly he could scarcely breathe, and he didn't care. Closing his eyes, he bent closer and tried to breathe her in as he lost himself in her. "Hope . . ."

"This is crazy, right? How much we want each other."

"I know something even crazier." He cupped her face. "How I feel about you. Hope, I—"

She yanked his mouth back to hers, kissing him deaf,

blind, and dumb. Waaaay back in some dim recess of his mind he understood that she wasn't ready to hear his feelings, but then she wrapped her legs around his waist so that he could enter her. "I have three condoms left," she whispered in his ear just before she lightly sank her teeth into his earlobe.

Jesus. Three condoms sounded about right, but damn if he'd rush through this, even for her. Gripping her hips, he pressed her hard to the wall as he kissed his way down her body. The under curve of a breast. A rib. Her belly. A thigh.

Between.

"Again?" she murmured shakily, trembling with excitement.

Oh, yeah, again. "Open for me," he murmured against her, and when she spread her legs, he stroked his thumb over her. With a soft cry, she slid her fingers into his hair to hold on, so gorgeous standing there on quivering legs, the steaming water running down her tight, toned curves. Her nipples were hard, her chest rising and falling with her quickened breathing. She shifted restlessly, opening her legs even more, and he took her in, all pink and glistening for him. He nearly came from that alone as he leaned in—

"Danny," she choked out, tightening her fingers in his hair as his tongue made a slow, torturous pass over her flesh. *"Please."*

Yeah. He'd most definitely please. He'd please her, and then himself, and then hopefully start all over again until neither of them could move. Opening her a little more, he gently sucked her into his mouth and kept sucking in tune to her breathy sighs, the sounds of which drove him a little crazy as he slid a finger into her and drove her to the very edge, then straight off it.

The sight of her coming again was one he knew would

highlight his fantasies for the rest of his life, and as her knees gave out, he caught her against him. Reaching out the shower for her jeans, he found the condoms, then using the wall as leverage, thrust into her.

She revved up fast to join him, which was a good thing because with her mouth racing over his face, his jaw, with his name tumbling from her lips in that sexy breathless little pant of hers, with her fingers embedded into his ass cheeks trying to urge him on faster, harder, more, more, more, he wasn't going to last. "Hope—"

She burst again. Or still. He didn't know, but it cata-pulted him right into an orgasm so intense his toes curled. He completely lost himself as he spent into her, slapping a hand to the wall behind her so that they wouldn't fall. Instead they sank together in a slow, tangled heap right there on the shower floor, with the now tepid water rain-ing down on them.

"Wow." That was all she said, in a dazed, dreamy voice that made him smile. "Wow . . ."

They toweled off. Hope bent for the pile of clothes, and several folded up papers fell out of his jacket pocket, papers he'd meant to show her after they shoveled off the roof. She gathered them up for him, going still as her eyes took in his research and the tentative offer he'd drawn up. He'd hoped to try to buy the lot from her, but that hadn't felt right. This place was hers. So instead he'd planned to lend her the money she needed to pay off Edward.

"What's this?" she asked, a veil coming down over her face.

"A way out of your problem."

"I've already told you I can handle this."

"You're going to lose the B&B, Hope. And it's wrong. You don't need to—"

"Did you have this planned all along?" she asked in a very quiet voice. "You and Edward?"

"Of course not."

"I think you did." She slapped the papers to his chest. "I think you planned this all along. Maybe you didn't really quit."

He stared at her as what she said sank in. "I did quit, Hope. Do you really think I'd—"

"Yes! God, I'm so stupid!" She slapped her own forehead. "Of course you didn't really give up what must have been a solid six-figure salary to start over."

"Careful," he said softly. "You're sounding a lot like that rat bastard you hate so much."

"Is that right? And how exactly does Edward sound?"

"Honestly? A bit pig-headed."

"Pig-headed," she repeated on a mirthless laugh. "Oh, honey. I haven't even gotten started." Buck-ass naked, she walked to the door.

"Where are you going?"

"To call Ben so he can snowmobile you out to your car."

"Hope—"

"Don't." And still buck-ass naked, she walked right out of his life.

10

"You're a stubborn-ass fool, Hope."

Hope stared in disbelief at Lori. They stood in the kitchen, squared off at the island. "Um, excuse me," she said very carefully. "But I don't think you heard me correctly."

"Oh, I heard you. Danny came here to—"

"—take my business."

"To check on his boss's investment," Lori corrected. "And instead of being a stubborn-ass fool—like a *certain* person I know—he adapted. He worked his tail off for us, even going over and beyond to help you research alternatives, including offering you a personal loan to buy you both time and financial freedom. You know what, Hope? You're right. He's a bastard."

Hope let out a breath and turned to Ben, who was suited up in his snow gear, with his snowmobile just out the door ready to take Danny back to his car.

As she'd asked. "Maybe you could talk some sense into your wife, Ben."

And Ben, sweet, kind, wonderful Ben who *always* had

Hope's back, shook his head. "Not this time, baby. I'm sorry. But my wife has a point."

"Goddammit. You're just saying that because you sleep with her."

He smiled, warm and sure. "Well, there is that. But face it, the guy hasn't done a thing except try to help you, Hope."

"He came here—"

"Because of his job. And yet once he arrived, in fact from the *moment* he arrived, he did nothing but try to help. Problem is, you don't do help, do you?"

He didn't mean it as a jab. She knew that, but it felt like a red hot stab of poker in her gut just the same because *dammit*. Was she really that person? Was she that much like Edward? Since she didn't like the answer to that question, she closed her eyes, and when she opened them again, Danny had come into the room, jacket on, duffle bag over his shoulder. He moved to hug and kiss Lori good-bye, then turned to Hope. "January first," he said solemnly. "And don't mistake my softness for his. He won't be soft if you don't pay. You know that."

"You're not soft," she whispered.

He looked at her for a long moment but said nothing, and then turned and nodded to Ben. They both went out into the dark, stormy night, where the wind and snow battled to come in until the kitchen door shut.

Closing them out.

The cold didn't leave Hope, though, and she wrapped her arms around herself. She felt her eyes swim, and knew the truth. Danny was right. Lori and Ben were right. "Okay, fine. I'm a stubborn ass who's far too much like the family I resent with all my heart."

"Yes," Lori agreed mercilessly. "You are."

Hope choked out a laugh as outside she heard the snowmobile rev and take off. Her heart did the exact same. "No!" She went running out the door to stop Danny from leaving, and—

Plowed him over into the snow.

They landed hard with him on the bottom.

"Oh, my God, I'm sorry!" she cried. "Did I hurt you?"

"No—" He hissed out a breath when she cupped his face with her snowy hands. "Your hands are cold."

"I'm sorry." But she didn't take her hands off him. She couldn't. She didn't want to take her eyes off him, either. "You aren't even gone, Danny, and I miss you."

His eyes seemed to glow behind his glasses. "You . . . miss me?"

"Yeah."

"But . . . you asked me to leave."

She sat up and pulled him up with her, keeping her hands on him, noticing with a heavy heart that he didn't do the same. "You didn't."

"No."

"Why?"

He looked at her, his glasses fogged and wet with snow. "First tell me why you came running out of the kitchen like a bat out of hell when you thought I'd left."

Heart pounding in her ears, she gently pulled off his glasses and cleaned them on her sweatshirt, then replaced them, relieved to see his warm eyes were still warm.

And on her.

"I was wrong," she whispered, glad Ben was gone and that Lori hadn't followed her out. She wanted to be alone, no audience for this one. "Really wrong."

He nodded agreeably. "About anything in particular?"

She stared at him and had to laugh. Wasn't that just like him to sit there in the snowstorm patiently waiting for her to get her words together? "About getting scared and sending you away."

"So . . . now you're not scared?"

"I've taken my time letting a guy in before, and gotten *royally* screwed. Maybe the answer is in trying something different this time. *Someone* different." She shook her head at his silence. "Okay, I'm not making sense. Look, the important thing to note here is . . . I'm over myself."

"Good. So when were you under yourself?"

She looked into his smiling eyes and felt her own help-less smile curve her lips. "I've never been good with ask-ing for help, Danny."

"You didn't ask. I offered."

"Turning it down was instinctive," she admitted. "I wanted to handle things on my own."

"Understandable." He reached for her hand, and just like that, the fist around her heart, the one that had been there so long she'd forgotten what it was like to take a full breath, released. "So back to my change in tactic," she whispered, her voice rough with emotion. "I want your help—not your money. I can't take your money, but—"

"Hope—"

"I mean, I want you, Danny. Your brain, your sense of humor, your incredible roof-shoveling skills . . ."

His next smile came slow and sure, and he pulled her in for a hug that warmed her from the inside out. "Seems fitting," he said. "Since I want you, too, temperamental stubbornness and all."

She pulled back to look into his face, feeling her relieved-smile face. "So . . . I don't suppose you get to Colorado often."

"There's no CPA in town, did you know that?"

"I guess I never noticed." She found that her throat was tight, almost too tight to talk. "You'd really be happy here?"

"I think it's the company," he said with a serious nod. "Though it might be the bears and frozen pipes."

God, his smile. "Danny."

"It's you, Hope. It's all you." He squeezed her hand, running his thumb over her knuckles. "But there's something you should know." He brought her hand up to his mouth. "I'm falling for you. Hard and fast."

"You—" She let out a breath and touched his jaw. "Really?"

"Yeah. So what do you say, are you going to go out with me when I move here?"

A bone-deep warmth filled her. "I think I could clear my schedule now and again."

"Good." He slid a strand of hair behind her ear and smiled into her eyes. "You asked why I didn't leave. It's because I asked you to accept my help, without first telling you how much you've helped me."

"Come on. I didn't help you with anything."

"Yes, you did. You made me remember to feel for something other than just work, to feel something with my entire heart and soul."

Emotion welled up and threatened her air supply. "That's convenient," she managed. "Because my heart and soul seem to want to be with yours."

His eyes were shiny, so damn shiny she couldn't look away. "The best Christmas present I've ever had," he murmured, and leaned in and kissed her, giving *her* the best Christmas present *she'd* ever had—him.

It's Hotter
at Christmas

HelenKay
Dimon

1

Ted Greene passed a uniformed valet and jogged up the four steps to the open-air lobby of exclusive Kalihiwai Beach Resort. In keeping with Hawaiian tradition, the main hotel area lacked walls, letting the trade winds breeze through from one side to the other.

All the easier for Ted to get in and out. At least he hoped that was true.

"You're late," Nicki Albright said. Her high heels clicked against the shiny white marble floor as she made her way from the registration desk to stand in front of him, fancy clipboard in hand.

"Be happy I showed up at all." Ted glanced at the fourteen-foot Christmas tree wrapped in wide red ribbon and sitting in the middle of the room. "That thing touches the ceiling."

She followed his gaze. "Looks good, doesn't it?"

More than good. He knew Nicki arranged the hotel's holiday decorations, right down to the twenty-foot–square gingerbread village and gumdrop train set running through it, with a precision usually reserved for a military offensive. Last year's efforts gained the attention of a big travel magazine that named the hotel the "it" place to visit for Christmas this year. From the number of people walking around, Ted guessed a lot of folks checked out travel magazines for vacation advice.

"At least you don't have to wear a Santa suit," he said, thinking back to her previous job at a discount hotel chain.

She glanced down at her navy dress pants and Hawaiian print shirt. "That is the only good thing about this uniform."

"You'd think the assistant hotel manager could wear whatever the hell she wants."

She shrugged. "The tourists like this look."

"I find that hard to believe."

"You're a fashion expert now?"

He excelled at many things. Picking clothes for females wasn't one of them. He preferred them in as little clothing as possible. A bikini. Better yet, nothing.

Yeah, mostly that last one.

"I'll skip the clothing advice and stick to law enforcement," he said.

"Which is why I called you."

"Yeah, the question is why I bothered to show up."

Nicki flashed one of her "too big to be real" smiles. "Because I asked so nicely."

"Uh-huh."

The corners of her mouth fell. "How about because you're the deputy police chief of Kauai?"

"Which means I should leave stuff like this to someone else. Hell, your security folks should be able to handle this situation."

She rolled her eyes. "Fine. Then how about because you're my big lug of a brother and you owe me."

She finally hit on the one argument guaranteed to get

his attention. If his sister or brother called, Ted came running. Had nothing to do with obligation. Had everything to do with a pact the three of them made long ago. When a guy lost almost everything, he grabbed on to whatever was left and held on.

"One of these days that guilt thing isn't going to work, you know," he said even though he knew the statement was a damn lie.

"Sure it will."

He laughed. "You win."

" 'Bout time you bent to my superior will."

"Dream on." He abandoned the brother–sister jabs in favor of a strategy sure to change the subject. "Really, though, the place does look good."

He knew the floor-to-ceiling tapestry hanging behind the registration desk cost more than his house. The thing had that antique Hawaiian royalty look. It was probably worth more than he'd earn in a decade of working for the Kauai police department. It should be in a museum, but tourists liked authentic Hawaiian art, so someone shoved it behind glass and put it up on a wall.

From the carved koa wood furniture to the huge hand-blown glass sculptures and elaborate red and green holiday floral arrangements set around the large room, the place reeked of wealth. So did the guests. The couple walking past him talked on matching cell phones as they dragged brown luggage with little symbols all over it behind them. Some called that designer. Ted called it a waste of money. Not to mention damn ugly.

If you could ignore the floors of annoying visitors, which he tried to do since Kauai needed the tourist trade to survive, the place did have an ass-kicking ocean view. The boutique hotel sat high on the rock lava cliffs on the North Shore of Kauai overlooking the Pacific. From the middle of the lobby, he could see the infinity edge pool down in front of the outside eating area and the bright blue ocean water beyond.

The scene made him want to go surfing. Go anywhere else but there, actually. But he had a job to do. He showed up for one reason—a conversation with Ms. Marissa Brandt. Make that *another* conversation with Marissa Brandt.

"I guess we need to get to it," he said.

Nicki's smile brightened. "I wondered how long you planned on stalling."

As long as possible. "Where is she?"

"Marissa Brandt?"

"Who else?"

"Just checking." Nicki nodded toward a door marked PRIVATE on the far side of the lobby and started walking toward it. "My office."

His frustration gave way to a brief window of concern. After all, the woman in question was a victim. Of what he wasn't really sure, but something was going on with her. Something that kept dumping her right in his path.

"She okay?" he asked.

"This time." Nicki fiddled with the cap of her pen. "I'm starting to worry about next time."

"I'm sort of hoping there won't be a next time."

"With Ms. Brandt?" Nicki snorted. "Oh, there will be a next time. Count on it."

"You know something about her I don't?"

"Let's just say trouble seems to follow the woman."

As if he needed a reminder of that fact. In two days he had seen the Brandt woman three times. Most tourists came and left Kauai without ever meeting the police. This lady had been interviewed by three officers plus a federal agent. And without his intervention, she would have been fingerprinted and interrogated by an overzealous newbie

FBI agent in connection with a little airport confrontation that went on to make the news.

"I knew I should've gone away for Christmas," Ted mumbled.

"Too late, big boy." Nicki pushed open the door to a long hallway leading to several offices and motioned for Ted to take the lead.

This wasn't exactly how he planned to spend the Monday before Christmas. The holiday would arrive in four days, which meant long hours on call in order to let the other officers take a few days off. That was the deal he and the police chief, Kane Travers, had struck to keep everyone happy despite budget cuts.

Now Ted seriously considered getting back into his car and leaving. Instead, he rapped twice on Nicki's door before entering. "Hello?"

If his presence shocked Marissa, she sure didn't show it. She sat in the chair across from Nicki's big desk and stared out the window looking out over the water in the distance. At the sound of his voice, she glanced up at him, but that was about it.

With or without a warm welcome, he'd recognize Marissa anywhere. There was something about her smell, a mix of flowers and East Coast money. Straight brown shoulder-length hair and wide chocolate brown eyes, five-foot-six and slim with a round face and small upturned nose. She was one good-looking woman under all of that bad luck.

Her pink complexion suggested she spent little time in the sun. Her firm body made it clear she spent most of it in a gym.

Which brought his mental wanderings to her ass. That translated just fine no matter the geography. He couldn't appreciate it at the moment since she was sitting on it, but he remembered. Ah, yes. Hard to forget something so round and perfect.

The pretty face and smoking body worked for him just fine. Her uncanny ability to get into trouble on his watch was the problem.

"I'll stay here," Nicki said.

He left his sister, smirk and all, lounging by the door and stepped in front of Marissa. The move forced her to lift her chin to meet his eyes.

"Officer Greene," Marissa said in a husky tone that vibrated right down to his feet.

"I thought you were leaving Hawaii today," he said, going with the least offensive small talk kicking around his brain.

"Believe me, I tried."

He slid his thigh on the edge of Nicki's desk. The move brought him even closer to Marissa but still far enough to be able to read her actions and assess her mood.

"Your identification paperwork came in?" he asked.

"Yes."

He couldn't blame her for the curt response. Last time she tried to leave the state, TSA officials at airport security detained her. The memories couldn't be good ones. "I take it you never even made it out of the hotel this time."

"Obviously not." She rubbed her hands together on her lap. "And I still say that incident yesterday wasn't my fault."

Incident. Such a little word for such a big mess. Ted suspected he'd be answering questions and filling out paperwork over Marissa's TSA run-in for months. Sure as hell would take that long for Kane and everyone else at the station to stop laughing over Ted's attempts to keep Marissa from getting an armed escort to jail.

"You threatened the TSA agent," Ted pointed out for what felt like the tenth time.

"He wouldn't let me past security."

"Because you didn't have a license or other form of photo identification."

"It was stolen along with my purse earlier that afternoon," she said.

He noticed she kept missing the point. "True, but—"

"And before you say my attitude was the problem, we both know that guy with the big neck and little brains could have let me through security after a secondary search." Her face flushed redder with each word. "He chose not to. He decided to be difficult and then acted all surprised when I got ticked off."

"Probably had something to do with the fact you kicked him."

From what Ted could tell the agent had asked Marissa a few questions, she got frustrated, then insulted, and then started yelling. Stolen wallet or not, that was never a good idea at airport security.

But that was only Marissa's first robbery of her trip. He was at the resort today to talk about the second one . . . or what Marissa claimed was another one. He was starting to wonder. Kauai had its share of petty crime, but for some reason this woman was the only victim these days. Seemed like an awful big case of bad karma. An unbelievable one.

"What exactly happened this time around?" he asked.

She frowned, her big eyes growing darker with each breath. "Are you blaming me for this, Officer Greene? If so, your good cop routine could use some work."

"I'll try to remember that." He folded his arms in front of him. "Suppose you tell me what the issue is." He fought the urge to say "this time" but he could tell from his sister's dramatic eye roll that he got the point across.

Marissa sat back in her chair. "Someone broke into my room this morning."

Marissa. Bed. An interesting combination. "And you were . . . ?"

"Excuse me?" Marissa didn't even try to control the rise in her tone.

The little lady was pissed. *Yeah, well, she could get over it.*

"Were you in the room or somewhere else?" he asked.

"I was in the gym."

"But you were supposed to fly home today."

Her hands froze in mid-wring. "So?"

Nicki made a noise somewhere between a wheeze and a chuckle, but Ted ignored her.

"You're dedicated to fitness. Got it." He forced his gaze to stay right on Marissa's face. He wanted to let it wander, see if he could make out her body under her baggy sweatshirt, but he refrained. For now Marissa seemed calm. He had seen her wound up and trembling with fury at the airport. He preferred her current quiet seething.

"When I got back to my room it was evident someone had been in there. The comforter was on the floor. My suitcase had been turned over." Marissa sighed. "You get the idea."

What he was getting was a headache. "Are you sure it wasn't the maid?"

Marissa's mouth opened and shut twice before she spit out an answer. "Maids don't throw everything on the floor and then leave."

"We do frown on that sort of thing," Nicki said.

Ted didn't need to see his sister's face to know she wore a smirk. "Don't help."

"Sorry," Nicki said in the least apologetic voice possible.

He eased his grip on the edge of the desk. It was either

that or crush the wood in his fists. "Was anything missing?"

"No," Marissa said.

"Yet you're sure someone came in."

In that second, a strange calm washed over her. The tension eased from her shoulders and a small smile played on her lips. Ted knew enough to see the newly relaxed position as a sign of verbal war.

"I'm not an idiot," Marissa said in a tight voice that stood in sharp contrast to the carefree way she brushed her hair off her shoulder.

"Never said you were."

"Maybe not in so many words but I sensed it."

The woman sure was touchy, so he used his best soothing cop voice. "You've had a rough time."

"I've been in Kauai for five days and robbed twice."

Like he said, tough. "Technically nothing was missing this time, so—"

Marissa shot him a frown severe enough to crack teeth. "Your point is?"

That she was either the unluckiest woman ever or, well, nuts. He hoped for the former. "Is it possible you have an enemy on Kauai?"

"You're the person I've spent the most time with at this point."

"No wonder she hates Hawaii," Nicki mumbled under her breath.

Marissa didn't lower her voice in return. The husky sound boomed through the room. "I like Kauai just fine. I just want to go home and spend Christmas in the snow as it should be."

To Ted snow could never be considered a good thing. Christmas meant time off to surf and hang out at the beach. Maybe fit in some sailing and a short trip to Oahu to watch the fireworks over Waikiki Beach. Why anyone would want to bundle up in a thick jacket just to go outside was beyond him. He had tried it and hated it.

"Where is home, exactly?" he asked even though he knew. He'd checked on her age—twenty-nine—address, driver's license number, and a bunch of other useless information as part of the investigation into the altercation with TSA.

"Philadelphia."

"If it helps, the city got about eight inches of snow this morning," he said.

When both women stared at him he guessed a man couldn't give the weather report without drawing unwanted attention.

"This isn't funny," Marissa said, pointing out the obvious.

"You're right." No matter how odd the situation seemed with the double robberies, the woman deserved respect. And his sister looked pissed, so Ted grew more serious. "I'll have some of my men dust your room for prints and look into the break-in."

Nicki stepped up and touched the other woman's shoulder with a gentle hand. "And I'll move you to a suite. You'll be more comfortable there."

That sounded suspiciously like Marissa was sticking around. Ted couldn't think of a worse idea. "When is your flight home?"

She blew out a long, slow breath. "I've missed both of my flights. The original and the rescheduled one."

A tumbling sensation took off in his stomach. For some reason he knew he had to get rid of this woman as fast as possible. "We have more than one flight a day out of Kauai. I'm sure you can find another."

Marissa did that head flip thing again. The way her brown hair fanned over her shoulder mesmerized him.

"Ted." That one word carried Nicki's usual "are you dense?" tone.

He guessed he was because he didn't see the problem.

Marissa took pity on him. "With the holidays, I'm having trouble finding an alternate flight. Right now I have a guaranteed flight out on Christmas Eve, but I might be able to fly standby before then. The airline said the twenty-third is the best bet for that."

"Oh." That's all he had. No solutions. No comeback. Just a mind racing with the possibilities of the kind of trouble this woman could get into in the two days until the standby flight. Forty-eight hours could last forever in the life of an unlucky person . . . or to the poor police officer assigned to keeping her breathing.

"You don't need to worry," Nicki said, still patting Marissa's shoulder in comfort.

Marissa frowned. "I don't?"

"She doesn't?" Ted asked at the same time.

"I'm sure Ted will solve all of this long before the twenty-third."

2

Marissa thought Ted looked a bit green around the mouth as he ran from the room. Okay, he didn't run but he didn't exactly walk either. While Nicki sang his praises, he excused himself to make a call to the office.

The by-play between Ted and Nicki made Marissa smile. Also made her a bit envious. Despite the humiliation the day before of being dragged out of the airport terminal to a little back room for questioning then on to the police station by several government agents, she had managed to hold her emotions together. A mix of anger and frustration had bubbled up inside of her when she realized she had zero control over what was happening to her. The rest of it, including the threats of being hauled off to jail, turned her fury to terror.

Then she saw him. About six-one with a muscular build and black hair. A square jaw and coloring that hinted at Asian heritage mixed with something else. And those grass-green eyes. She had never seen such a crystal-clear color.

Ted Greene walked in wearing a blue uniform and a gun strapped to his side and demanded attention. He had taken control and escorted her back to the hotel she had left for good only hours before. Seeing him now, so comfortable with Nicki, supported Marissa's first impression of Ted as a man who dominated his environment with a knowing hand.

And then there was the fact he qualified as handsome in a "that can't be good for you" sort of way. Marissa wanted to spend Christmas back home in Philadelphia, to take a few days off from her never-ending work schedule, but having the chance to stare at Ted Greene for a few more minutes sure wasn't a hardship.

"How long have you two been together?" Marissa asked Nicki.

"What?"

Marissa nodded toward Nicki's wedding ring. "Married?"

Nicki coughed until her eyes watered. After a few seconds she stood up straight again and gulped in air. "To Ted?"

"You mean you two aren't . . . ?"

"Siblings?" The hacking subsided but Nicki's bug-eyed look of shock remained.

Now it was Marissa's turn to be confused. "What?"

"Ted's my brother." Nicki slipped into the red leather chair behind the desk.

Marissa stopped dwelling on her travel disasters and took a nice, long look at the other woman. The coal black hair. The perfect figure and matching perfect face. Yep, Marissa saw the resemblance now. Perfect, perfect, and perfect. Of course Ted and Marissa were siblings. Their parents probably sold their collective souls to the devil to give birth to kids who looked that good.

In case that devil thing turned out to be true, Marissa rushed to clear up any insult. "I just figured . . ."

Nicki waved her off. "No problem."

Actually, Marissa had a big problem. The huge wave of relief that washed through her over the sibling talk was not exactly welcome. Ted Greene was a distraction she didn't need or want. Chalk it up to the uniform or that sweet smile, but the guy was a plan-killer and she was a woman who always had a plan.

She'd be gone soon. With the way her last few days had gone, a one-night stand was out of the question. Not her thing anyway. Her relationships tended to be quick and intense, but still relationships. With her work hours, romance was delegated to the position of afterthought. That was the only explanation she had for why she was alone and six thousand miles from home right before the holidays.

She had planned to work right up to Christmas Eve and then head to her mom's house outside of the city for the day. Then her boss got in his head that sending two of his creative directors to the Kalihiwai Beach Resort to start working on competing advertising campaign ideas would be the perfect way to figure out which one of them should land the open Executive Creative Director job at work. That put Marissa and Hank Fischer on a plane to the tropics instead of at home in the Philadelphia snow.

As usual, work sucked up her private life. This time, it had almost landed her in jail. That would teach her to abandon her usual "sweet talk people in power" way of life. If she hadn't been so exhausted from her schedule, figuring out her wallet was missing and the sidelined flight wouldn't have amounted to a big deal. Maybe she did need a real vacation, because Hank had to pull her off the TSA guy. Ted handled the rest.

She knew she should hate the idea of being rescued by two males in the span of a day, but she sort of enjoyed it. She spent most of her time running a team of males and juggling their egos all while answering to another idiotic one who ranked above her. All that man-pleasing at work got old. Letting someone else take the lead and blowing off some steam felt right.

So did sitting in a room with Ted Greene, which was exactly why she should stay out of any room containing this guy. With the badge and that face, she knew he could win over even the most strident woman. She didn't need to get her groove back and wasn't looking to test out men in the tropics, so she needed to pass on whatever non-law enforcement skills he might possess.

It was a good plan until the man in question walked back into Nicki's small office. There was something about him. Maybe it was the confident swagger, but something appealed to her on a very fundamental, your-bed-or-mine way.

"My officers are coming over," Ted said.

Marissa figured that was Ted's way of telegraphing that he was in charge. She had bigger problems than his ego at the moment, including the fact she had stepped right into the path of a burglar not once but twice. "What's being done for security at the hotel?"

Ted and Nicki stared at each other. Then they took turns staring at her. The looks they were shooting at her suggested they didn't understand public relations all that well.

Marissa turned to Nicki. "Have you decided on a strategy to handle this?"

The question only earned her more staring from matching sets of green eyes. Did these two really not know how to run the press on a story like this?

To break up the dead silence, Marissa tried a different tack. "Have the other guests been warned about the robbery spree?"

"This is hardly an epidemic," Nicki snapped out.

Marissa saw Nicki's clenched jaw and figured she was

appalled by the idea of an intruder loose in the hotel. Marissa didn't blame her, but Nicki needed to be reasonable. This was the sort of incident that could kill an up-and-coming exclusive resort. They needed to come up with a marketing angle to spin the story the right way. Having a serial theft problem on the premises was not the best way to lure in rich tourists.

"From what I can tell, this is a targeted scheme," Ted said.

Finally someone had a theory they could use. Marissa worked better with information. She could assess the situation and come up with the best way to handle the issue once she knew what Ted knew.

"How does the scheme work?" she asked.

"Basically?" He leaned against the doorjamb with one ankle crossed over the other. "It appears people see you and then try to steal your stuff."

Okay, maybe he didn't get the marketing problem after all. "But who are the other victims?"

"Well, there's you and . . ." He closed one eye and stared at the ceiling as if contemplating the question. "No one else. Just you."

"What are you saying?"

"I already said it."

She was the sole target of some big theft ring? "But, that's ridiculous."

"My thoughts exactly," he said.

The edge in his tone caught her attention. There, under all of the smooth talk and the flip remarks lurked something else. Something a little ugly that she didn't appreciate one bit. "Are you suggesting I'm making this up?"

"I can't figure out why you'd do that."

Talk about your non-denial denial. "That's something at least."

He held up a hand. "I didn't say you weren't concoct- •

ing all of this. I just said I can't understand why you would."

She wondered if she was supposed to be grateful for his halfhearted support of the theory that she wasn't a total whackjob out there seeking attention by causing trouble.

"I'm not involved," Marissa said even though she couldn't believe she had to state that obvious fact.

Ted nodded. "If you say so, I guess that settles it."

He suddenly didn't seem so cute. "Are you always this obtuse?"

"Since I don't know what you mean by that, I'll say no." He pushed away from the wall and came over to stand next to his sister. "Here's what we're going to do—"

As if she wanted to deal with him now. "Is there another officer I could talk to?" Marissa asked.

"No." He didn't take even a second to deal with the request. "Nicki is going to get you settled in your new room. Only the three of us are going to know what that room number is."

There was one little problem with that plan. Well, not so little. The problem was more like five-eight, two hundred pounds. "What about Hank?"

Ted's eyes narrowed until she couldn't see their vibrant green color. "Who the hell is Hank?"

Ted had shouted the question loud enough to bring security. Of course, at this point Marissa wondered if the resort even had security. If so, where were they every time she ran into trouble? Someone stole her purse right off of the patio when she was having lunch. Someone else broke into her room during the short time she wasn't there this morning. As far as she could tell, the security staff took off early for Christmas.

"Hank Fischer. He's my co-worker," Marissa explained.

"Does he know about the newest theft?"

Everything Ted said offended her on some level. It was as if he thought she were the center of all trouble on the island. "No. He's off sightseeing."

Ted waved off her concerns "Then we'll keep him in the dark about the latest."

That was a bit cloak-and-dagger for her taste. "Don't you think that will be a bit odd?"

"Not unless you're dating him."

She was not talking about that subject with Ted. Not when she'd spent part of the time she'd known him fighting off a fantasy about hitting the sheets and the other part thinking about strangling him with them. "Tell me the rest of this plan of yours."

"I want you to stay in the room and out of trouble. I'll come up in a few hours so we can go over who might have a grudge against you." Ted hesitated for a few beats. "And anything else you want to discuss."

What was that supposed to mean? "There isn't anything else."

"We'll see."

Sitting alone in a bedroom with Ted. Yeah, not a good idea. "Are you sure there isn't another officer I can talk to?"

"It's the holidays and we're short staffed, so you get me."

"I'll go grab my bag from the main desk," Marissa said as she stood up.

"Go from here to the reception desk and stay there." He barked out the orders as if talking like that was normal for him.

As far as Marissa was concerned that bossy attitude of his sure did cut into his hotness factor. "Excuse me? And by that I *mean what the hell is wrong with you*?"

He didn't back down even an inch. "Someone on this

island is determined to make your stay here miserable. So, for now, I don't want you alone."

"I don't want a bodyguard."

"Would you prefer to get robbed again?"

He clearly had the easier argument here and that ticked her off. Rather than back down, she tried changing the subject "I'd rather go home."

"That makes two of us."

"Fine." Marissa let him win this round. Besides, she hadn't had a post-workout shower. And a day or two in a suite didn't sound so bad. She could get a lot of work done in all that privacy. "I'll be in the hall."

Ted nodded. "We'll be out in a minute."

Marissa didn't wait for him to change his mind or issue new orders. She walked out wondering if free room service came with the deal.

Nicki waited until Marissa left to turn on her brother. "You were a little hard on her."

It was the only way Ted could think of to stay focused on her as a victim and a case. "Something's wrong here."

Nicki eased back into her chair and crossed her legs. "Other than the fact she keeps getting robbed?"

"Either someone is going after her, and if that's true I want to know why and stop it."

"Or what?"

He wasn't ready to deal with the alternative. "Nothing."

Nicki frowned. "You think she's crazy."

"I've seen plenty of crazy on this job. This is something else."

Nicki's foot bounced around as she swung it back and forth. "Something as in you're attracted to her?"

Now there was a subject he refused to discuss. Pretty or not, Marissa screamed trouble. He'd had his fill of problem women to last him a lifetime. He kept the bills from his former divorce lawyer in a box under his bed to remind him whenever he was tempted to forget.

"This is my job," Ted said, hoping it would end the conversation.

"I have eyes, you know." Nicki pointed from her face to his to prove her point.

He was beginning to think nothing would stop the discussion. "But yet it's your mouth that refuses to stop."

"We'll see how you feel on Christmas when it's time for Marissa to go home."

"She can fly standby on the twenty-third." Unless he could unload her before then.

A smile lit Nicki's face. "Something tells me she's not going to make that flight."

Ted refused to back down. He knew his sister would pounce if she sensed weakness. "I'll escort her to the plane myself to make sure she gets out of here."

"This should be good."

Yeah, that's what he was afraid of.

3

Marissa spent the next two hours enjoying every inch of the two-room suite. From the king-size bed with the fluffy white comforter to the full family room and flat screen television, the place was both bigger and nicer than her condo at home. The nightly rate posted on the back of the door came close to the amount of her mortgage payment.

Well, if she had to be stuck in paradise, at least she was stuck in style. She already set up her laptop and took care of the wireless connection. The room had a fax machine. Between her cell and the room phone, she could get a lot of work done without much interruption.

To make the most of the scenery, she unpacked and showered then sat out on the patio and surveyed the four floors below and the impressive ocean stretching out in front of her. Turned out talking on the phone wasn't so bad from this view. The whole eighty-five degrees in December thing didn't make sense to her, but there was something special in listening to the boss complain about shoveling snow in Philadelphia while she sat in Hawaii getting a tan.

Then there was the little matter of telling her boss she needed another day in Kauai to finalize the campaign. Funny how she didn't feel bad for even one second for having lied. But with the string of bad luck she'd experienced she didn't think she had a choice. No way would she get the promotion if her boss decided she was cursed. Since he fired one guy for refusing to play on the office softball team, she was sure being a beacon for disaster would result in a pink slip.

She had more pressing things on her mind at the moment anyway. Namely one deputy police chief Ted Greene. She expected him to show up any minute, which had nothing to do with why she applied lipstick or brushed her teeth three times. Also completely unrelated to the black lace panties she put on and the reason she changed into her best ass jeans and snug T-shirt from her sweats.

Pure coincidence. No hidden sexual message there at all.

When the doorbell chimed a minute later she abandoned the mirror and her hairbrush in favor of the peephole. And what a sight awaited her. The man somehow managed to look good through a tiny slit in the door that distorted most people into fat round globs.

The fact Ted had changed into faded jeans and a long-sleeved white oxford shirt that highlighted his tanned skin didn't hurt either. In or out of uniform this guy could make a woman's thoughts stray right from the boardroom to the bedroom.

"Officer Greene," she said as she opened the door and motioned for him to step inside.

"You can call me Ted." He walked through the small foyer and into the family room. Kept right on walking until he hit the glass doors to the patio.

"Is that appropriate?" she asked more to fill the silence than anything.

He glanced over his shoulder at her. "Would you rather call me Mike?"

"Is that your real name?"

"No, my name is Ted." He nodded toward the door. "And you might want to close that since we're trying to hide your whereabouts."

She followed his directions without thinking. "Why would I call you something other than your name?"

"No idea. You seemed upset at the idea of calling me Ted, so I thought I'd give you an alternative."

Uh, yeah. Because that made sense. "You're the police."

He dropped down on the couch. A small notebook and pen appeared in his hands out of nowhere. "And we're not supposed to have names?"

She thought about hanging out near the door. Seemed safer than getting close, especially in his current mood, which she could not read at all. But she was not the run-and-hide type, so she moved into the room and took the chair next to the couch. That put a whole glass coffee table between them.

"Are you trying to be difficult?" she asked even though she knew he would never give her a straight answer to that one.

"Actually, yeah."

At least he was honest about it. "Care to tell me why? Is that some sort of police tactic?"

"No."

"Do you just hate people from Philadelphia?"

"Never been there but you seem okay."

"Gee, thanks."

He hesitated before continuing. "My reasons are much more personal."

With those few words he kicked the tension in the room up to unbearable levels and dragged them right into the danger zone. She could feel it as sure as if she walked off a cliff with only air below her for a cushion. "Care to share?"

Something sparked in those sexy green eyes. "I'm going to be dead honest with you."

Her stomach plunged to the floor. "I appreciate that."

"I want you."

If he told her he planned to jump out the window using the sheet as a parachute she would have been less stunned. "Really?"

He smiled. "Does that surprise you?"

"Your honesty does." Even though it shocked her, she found his openness refreshing. After all the hours spent negotiating signals and deciphering comments at the office and on dates she appreciated a more direct approach. Adults should be able to talk about their attraction without all the "does he or doesn't he" stuff.

He leaned back on the couch. "The men back in Philadelphia must be pretty dull if they can't recognize a beautiful woman and then do something about it."

If there were men like him in Philadelphia, she would be there right now with one of them. "I'm sure I should rush to the defense of the hometown men, but I'll pass."

"So, you don't have a boyfriend?"

She thought about making him work for it then realized that would be one of those games she claimed to hate. "No."

"Good."

"Why is that good?" But she knew.

From this wide smile, he knew. "We have some business to discuss but after . . ."

The man jumped from topic to topic and managed to

knock her totally off stride. Part of her wondered if that was the goal.

"After we do what?" She could guess the direction of his thinking but kind of wanted him to say it. Actually, she'd be happy if he did anything other than sit there tapping his pen against his notebook while he grinned in a way that made her resistance melt into a big puddle of goo.

"First business, then we talk about the wanting you part," he said in a voice so low and inviting that she almost jumped on top of him.

Sweaty palms were not a usual problem, but this guy made every part of her body kick into gear. "You're making some pretty big assumptions."

He stretched his arm across the back of the light blue sofa. "You saying the feeling isn't mutual? Come on. Give me some credit. I felt it that first day, even with all of the other stuff going on."

She dug her fingernails into the armrests. "Okay, sure. You're an attractive guy and —"

"Fine."

"Fine?"

"We'll get to that after we do a little work." He flipped his notebook open.

Did he really think they had moved on to the interrogation part of the program? "You can do that?"

He glanced up from his notes. "Talk?"

Oh, the man could definitely talk. He could argue and circle and throw her a glance that made her blood heat until it simmered right under her skin. And while he set off a rocket of confusing feelings inside her, he just sat there nice and calm.

Men. She sometimes wondered if they were human.

"Compartmentalize like that. You talk about work and have that sturdy police stance—"

He coughed. "The what?"

"—and then you mention feelings and shoot me this sexy little smile."

"Sexy, huh?" This time his smile almost blinded her.

"You're missing my point."

"I think we understand each other just fine."

Not if they kept heading down this road. "You're saying there's no conflict of interest for you if we get involved?"

He pretended to think about the question. "That's a mighty big and complicated business term for something pretty simple."

Fine. She would spell it out and then they could deal with the fallout. "You can sleep with people linked to your cases?"

His left eyebrow inched up. "You're the only one talking about sex."

"Don't be obtuse."

"That's the second time you've accused me of that."

"It fits."

"What you see is what you get." Ted held his arms wide to his sides, showing off every inch of his broad chest and trim waist. "I need to talk to you about the break-in. After that, I want to talk to you about that shirt and how nice you look in it."

His words started a tingle at the base of her neck. "And you won't get in trouble at work for that?"

"Are you going to turn me in?"

Not if that meant the flirting tango would stop. "No."

"Then we're fine. Let's get the work out of the way so we can get to the good part."

4

Despite his attempts to stay in control, Ted hadn't been fine since he walked into the fancy hotel room and saw Marissa standing there in an outfit that skimmed her body and showed off every curvy inch. Just looking at her, seeing the way her hair fell over her shoulders and framed her long neck, robbed what was left of his common sense.

Sleeping with her wouldn't exactly be a conflict, at least he didn't think so, but it wouldn't be a good idea, either.

He cleared his throat, hoping that would push out some of his more vivid and x-rated thoughts about her clothes and her not being in them. "So, you're in Kauai on a work assignment."

The faraway look in her eyes cleared a bit. "Yes."

"Who knows you're here?"

"My boss, everyone at my office—"

Before she got wound up and handed over a list of a thousand people, he decided to target the conversation where he wanted to go. "Tell me about this Hank guy."

She smiled. "I told you we weren't boyfriend and girl-friend."

"I get that *you* think so, but why is he here?"

"Word is that your sister's resort is planning to launch a new marketing and advertising plan. My company is interested in the job. Hank and I lead creative teams," Marissa explained.

She lost him ten words back. "Should I know what that means?"

"We're tasked with coming up with separate campaigns for the resort to review. We have to present our preliminary ideas to our boss on December twenty-sixth. The final product is due in January."

Ted officially had no idea what she did for a living or why an assignment was due the day after Christmas. Sure, he understood marketing. It was all this fighting within the same agency thing that didn't make much sense. "Why don't you guys work together to come up with the best campaign possible?"

"It doesn't work that way. My boss thinks competition is good for morale, so he sets us up on separate teams and we work against each other. The company wins because we all work our butts off to get campaigns."

Ted shook his head. Clearly her boss had never heard of the concept of teamwork. "That's the dumbest damn thing I've ever heard."

"The advertising world can be cutthroat and filled with pressure." The flirty lightness had left her voice. She was all business now.

"So why do you do it?"

She shrugged. "I'd prefer to work in my own office with a team all focused on the same goal and without the office politics, but the real world functions differently."

His did. He didn't understand why others' didn't. "Sounds to me like you need a new career."

That back of hers snapped even straighter. "I happen to be good at this one. Besides, I'm in line for a big promotion."

So she could be the dickhead boss? Yeah, didn't make sense to Ted. "Is that a good thing?"

"Of course."

Sounded to him like she was getting her priorities confused. If she hated the game, why play it?

"If Hank wins, he gets a promotion at work. If my idea wins, I get it," she said as if she were talking to a child.

She might think he was slow, but he was catching on just fine. "So Hank would benefit if you had a problem getting home or getting to that December twenty-sixth meeting."

"He volunteered to stay here with me when I had the original flight problems. He didn't know I missed my morning flight. I just left him a message to let him know."

Ted had to admit that part of the story messed up his theory. Still, he would bet Hank was working a scheme at Marissa's expense. She wasn't stupid, but she refused to see the potential problem. That's what happened when a person assumed everyone played by the same rules in the same game.

"When is Hank scheduled to leave?" Ted asked.

"Tomorrow, but you're making all of this into something it isn't." She shook her head as sadness filled her eyes. "We're friends. We've been co-workers for years."

"So there's never been a time when the two of you . . ."

Her mouth twisted in something close to revulsion. "Absolutely not."

"No flirting. No dating. Nothing?"

"Nothing . . ." She glanced around the room. Everywhere but at Ted. "Well, no, nothing."

Uh-huh. Just as Ted suspected. Something. A very big something. "Tell me."

She waved a hand in front of her face. "It wasn't a big deal."

Sure. That's why she kept refusing to talk about it. "I'll decide."

"Hank got drunk and made a pass. It was silly, really. We both laughed about it the next day." She threw in a nervous chuckle as if to prove her point.

"Which day was that?"

"The day I was supposed to leave the first time. We celebrated the night before we were to get on the plane and head home." She shot Ted a level stare. "And the timing doesn't mean anything."

Yeah, it did. It was starting to sound as if the infamous Kauai Robber was really a chubby lovelorn ad executive from Philadelphia with a crush on a co-worker. "What's his room number?"

"Why?"

"Because I thought I'd invite him to dinner." Ted exhaled to let her see his frustration. "Why the hell do you think? I want to talk to him."

She chewed on her lower lip. "The pass was embarrassing to Hank. I don't want you going in there, throwing elbows, and scaring him."

Oh, Ted planned to do more than that. "Hank is a grown man, right?"

"It was nothing."

Ted held up his hand to stop her annoying apologies for her stalking co-worker. "Since you've said that about fifty times, I'm thinking it was something."

"I want to be there."

She said the words so fast that he almost couldn't understand them. But he did and the answer was no. "When?"

"When you talk to him."

"No."

This time she crossed her arms over her stomach. "Then good luck finding him."

Ted exhaled in an attempt to hold on to his anger and keep it from exploding. "My sister runs the place. I can have Hank's room number in ten seconds."

Marissa's breath rushed out. She reached out and laid a hand on his knee. "Ted, please. I don't want you accusing him."

The gentle touch of her fingertips on his pants set off a brushfire in his nerve endings. "You have very little faith in my police abilities."

"Am I wrong? You think it's him and plan to scare him, right?"

Sure but he planned to be subtle about it. He was a trained professional after all. Ted thought about pointing that out but let it drop. "It's against the rules to bring civilians along on interviews."

She moved her hand back. "Now you're making things up."

He was. "Don't you think being there will make Hank more uncomfortable?"

"Doesn't matter because I'm going to be there."

He ended their staring contest with a vow. "I can forbid it."

"Then I guess our discussion is over." She clicked her tongue against the roof of her mouth. "All discussions on any topic, work or not . . . if you know I mean."

Every woman knew how to play this game. Ted wondered if they got a manual in their teens or something. "That's sexual blackmail."

"You can call it whatever you want."

He called it typical. "If I don't give you your way then—"

She nodded. "Yep."

"We both lose in that deal, you know."

She had the nerve to look bored. Even stared at her fingernails for a second. "I was planning to leave the island anyway."

As if he could let her walk out now without tasting her. "You don't play fair."

"The gauntlet has been thrown. It's your move, officer."

It wasn't as if he had a choice. He wanted her. He needed to talk with Hank. There was no real reason that Marissa couldn't be there except that he wanted her away from Hank. Yeah, Ted knew he was going to lose this fight. "You would have to sit there in the same room and be quiet."

A huge smiled spread across her lips. "I can do that."

"I haven't seen any evidence that's true."

"Maybe you would prefer to spend an evening alone." She did that hair flip thing that drove him crazy. "Does your house have a cold shower?"

"Fine," he said through his locked jaw.

"Meaning?"

"Business is over." He threw the notebook down on the coffee table. "Let's get to the non-business part of our meeting."

"Already?"

"I have my officers combing through your old room, checking for fingerprints and looking at the security tapes. I've talked with you. We'll track down Hank in a few minutes."

"Minutes? Man, you work fast."

Did she think he was going to throw her on the bed for a quickie? Because he sure was thinking about it. "I can go whatever speed you want."

"All men say that." That flirty tone moved back into

her voice. Played in the way she held her body. So inviting . . .

He shifted to the front of the couch cushion. The move had their knees touching. "Believe it or not, all men are not the same."

"If you say so."

"Instead of debating that point, we could try a test."

Her body stilled. "With homework and stuff?"

He winked at her. "More of a hands-on experiment."

"You do know that I'm leaving in a few days."

"What does that matter?"

Her face went blank. The smile, the gleam in her eye—all gone. "Right."

The flat tone threw him. "Did I say something wrong?"

She shook her head. Kept shaking it. "No."

He had no idea what the hell was going on with her. But he thought he knew how to bring all that heat rushing back. "Maybe I should skip talking."

"Good idea."

He grabbed her hand and stood up, taking her right along with him. For a second they stood facing each other, her breasts touching his chest and her warm breath puffing against his cheek.

"Are all the women in Philadelphia as pretty as you?" He brushed the back of his hand down her cheek and watched her brown eyes flush darker.

"Thinking of moving there?"

He'd already relocated once for a woman. Learned that lesson the hard and expensive way and had no plans on repeating it. "No."

Her fingertips snaked up his stomach to rest on his chest. "Then I guess you're stuck experimenting with this woman from Philadelphia."

Hell, yeah. "Works for me."

The minute their mouths met he knew every part of her worked for him. Soft lips pressed against his, gentle at first, and then anything but. One minute she leaned into him, and then next she tried to crawl inside him. Her hands rubbed over his shoulders and back as her mouth slanted over his again and again.

And she was not alone in her eagerness. He couldn't get enough of her. Her taste. The feel of her firm body under his hands. The smell of shampoo in her hair. The heat radiating off of her as his fingers learned her shape. That hot, wet mouth pressing and licking against his.

Within seconds his body reacted. It was as if he hadn't held a woman or had sex in years. Like he was starved for her. He wanted to pick her up and take her to bed like in some 1950s movie and carry her away to a place where they could forget about anything and anyone else for a few hours.

Instead he broke off the kiss and gulped in air as he took a small step back. He didn't drop his hands from her waist because his hands refused to let go. They stayed right there, on her, locking her close.

This being on-duty thing sucked.

She smiled up at him, her hands still resting on his forearms and her gaze still cloudy from the mind-blowing kiss. "Your eyes are the prettiest shade of green."

He'd never been called pretty before, but many people commented on the recessive gene that gifted him his eye color. "My Japanese mother and Caucasian father produced two green-eyed children and my brown-eyed brother."

"Good grief. That means there's another one like you out there somewhere?" She sounded a bit in awe of the idea.

"Is that a bad thing?"

"I wouldn't be kissing you if it were." She drew her finger along his jaw line. "Now what?"

Ted had to swallow three times to keep from lowering his head and capturing her mouth again. "We find Hank."

Her smile grew even wider. "That's really what you want to do next?"

What he wanted to do was her, but he had to make sure she was safe first. That he had a handle on the mess swirling around her. "A man's gotta work."

She tapped his nose. "You're compartmentalizing again."

And it was killing him. They were going to sleep together and soon. That fact was the only thing keeping him from losing his mind now. But he had to figure out the reasons behind the robberies first. They had days. Waiting a few more hours wouldn't kill him. At least he hoped that was true.

"Like you, I have a job to do," he said.

She dropped her hands. "And you're going to do it now."

"We are. And then we'll come back and have dinner. I hear the room service here is good." Screw the food. He planned to work his way through a box of condoms before letting anyone else near the room or Marissa.

"So we're not done with this non-work conversation." She toyed with the top button of his shirt.

"Not even close."

She kissed his chin. "Good."

5

"Marissa, there you are." Hank threw open the hotel room door before Marissa finished knocking.

He reached out and dragged her into his room before she could catch her balance. When he tried to close the door on Ted as if he were just an escort or something she figured she better clear up any confusion before Ted unloaded on the guy.

"Hank, wait." The second she saw Hank moving in for a hug, she shoved against his chest and turned back to the hottie in the hallway. "This is Ted Greene."

"Oh, sure. The policeman who helped you earlier." Hank held out his hand. "Thanks for that. We missed each other at the police station because that guy from the FBI wouldn't let me come back and take care of Marissa."

Ted eyed Hank as if the older man were a bug about to be squashed. "It's my job to get in the way of the FBI."

"Really?" she asked, strangely intrigued by the idea of Ted taking on the feds.

"Not really." Ted shook the other man's hand but didn't push to enter. He was too busy looking Hank up and down and glancing into the room behind him.

Seemed the good officer was always on duty. Certainly back in business mode. Marissa appreciated Ted's determination; she just wasn't so sure she liked being relegated to the position of job assignment.

"Did you have some follow-up questions for Marissa?" Hank kept a death grip on the door and positioned his body to block Ted from following her into the room.

If the testosterone move bothered Ted, he sure didn't show it. His voice stayed even. "You could say that."

For some reason Marissa felt obligated to protect Hank. Ted wore a mask of calm, but she guessed he wasn't all that pleased at being treated like the hired help.

"He's here because I had another problem," she explained.

Hank brushed a hand up and down her arm. Funny how he could have done that yesterday and she wouldn't have given it a second thought. Now, thanks to Ted's prodding, she saw warning signs flash before her eyes.

"Your phone message was garbled. You said you had to stay because of the purse snatching?" Hank asked.

"Because of a second attempted theft," Ted said.

Hank grabbed her hands. "What do you mean? Why didn't you call me?"

"I did," she said as she tugged out of his grip.

Hank pushed the door halfway closed right on Ted who just stood there with a half-smile on his face. Rather than allow the slight to escalate into an all out war, Marissa stepped back and out of Hank's touching zone. She also slipped a foot into the open doorway in case Hank got the idea to slam the door on Ted's face. When her foot brushed against Ted's she realized he had the same idea.

"You were out seeing Kauai. You probably didn't have service. Besides, it was your first chance to visit the island," she said.

"Wait. You haven't done any sightseeing?" Ted asked

the question to her instead of to Hank, the surprise in his voice evident.

"I've been working."

The corner of Ted's mouth kicked up. "There are parts of Kauai worth seeing other than the hotel and the airport, you know."

She did. That was one of her many frustrations with her job—the lack of downtime. She loved analyzing a problem and coming up with art and sales concepts, but she missed the quiet moments. She had been working her tail off for years. She watched her father leave and her mother struggle to become independent. Her mother's identity consisted of being a housewife and cook. Nothing else.

With that as a role model, Marissa vowed never to be beholden to a male for financial security and happiness. She could make her own way. If that meant a little less personal time, she had accepted that. But now, being on Kauai and not having a minute to enjoy it, she wondered if her vow of independence had taken her to the extreme.

"Thank you, officer. I can handle it from here," Hank said and then, as expected, tried to shut the door with Ted standing right there in the path.

Ted was faster. He grabbed the edge and shoved back, hitting Hank in the forehead.

"Hey!"

"Sorry about that," Ted mumbled.

From what Marissa heard, the good officer sounded anything but sorry. Looked rather pleased with himself, in fact. Accident, like hell.

"What are you doing?" Hank asked as he rubbed his head.

Ted whipped out his notepad and pen. "I wanted to ask you a few questions."

"I'm not sure I can help, but come in." Hank grumbled

under his breath about civil servants as he walked to the edge of the queen-size bed.

"Subtle," she whispered the word to Ted.

He winked. "Wasn't trying to be."

"I told the FBI and the police officer all I know about the problem at the airport." Hank dropped onto the bed. "The TSA guy really gave Marissa a hard time for no reason. She knew she should be allowed on the plane despite the lack of identification. He refused to listen."

"Which is exactly what I've been saying," she pointed out even though she knew they were there for another reason.

"Did you know about the clearance regulations?" Ted shut the door behind him and walked over to the chest of drawers as he asked Hank the question.

Marissa noticed that Ted talked and scanned the room at the same time. What she initially took for disinterest was anything but. He hid his high-alert status behind a calm, almost bored, demeanor, but he never stopped drinking in his surroundings.

"I looked it up on my computer and took a printout of the procedures with me just in case there was a problem," Hank said.

Ted nodded. "Very enterprising of you."

Hank's chest puffed out under Ted's false praise. "The TSA agent went off on Marissa before I could talk to him and explain that she needed a special screening."

Marissa wanted to roll her eyes. She knew the rules. She had looked them up before leaving for the airport and didn't need Hank riding to her rescue. She told him that in the cab. Said it again before they got in the security line. She had the entire situation under control. Well, everything except the TSA guy's attitude. The moron had something to prove and she became his example.

Without any fanfare Ted picked up the plane ticket sitting on Hank's suitcase, looked at it, and set it back down again. "I'm not here about the TSA problem."

Hank's gaze darted around the room. "You're not?"

"Were you in your room this morning around seven?"

"Of course. I was asleep." Hank started fidgeting. First his hands, then his feet. His body stayed in motion. "Why? Is that when this other issue happened?"

If he meant issue as in break-in, yeah. "Someone got into my room," she said.

Hank came up off the bed. "What?"

Ted motioned for Hank to sit back down. "Your room is across the hall. I need to know if you saw or heard anything."

"Were you hurt?" Hank asked, his voice filled with concern until he turned on Ted again. "And what the hell is wrong with the police on Kauai?"

"Can you be more specific?" Ted asked with a load of sarcasm that seemed to miss Hank.

The more flustered Hank got, the calmer Ted became. Marissa figured it was some top-secret police trick. Whatever it was, it impressed the hell out of her. She wished she knew Ted's secret to self-control.

"You have a crime wave," Hank said.

Ted pretended to think about the comment. "It does seem that way, doesn't it?"

"I'm the only victim," she said before Ted won some sort of acting award.

Hank's mouth dropped open. "You mean that in the entire hotel only your room got hit?"

Ted tapped his pen against his notepad. "Strange, isn't it?"

Hank reached for her hand. Instead of pulling away, she let him take it. After one squeeze she dropped her arm to her side again, relieved he let go before Ted hit him with the television.

"You should move in this room with me," Hank said.

Now there was a terrible idea. "I'm fine in my room."

"She's safe." A sharp tone replaced Ted's usual lazy drawl.

Hank missed the change in mood, but she didn't. Even Ted's stance morphed from relaxed to stiff. From his feet, hip-length apart, to his shoulders he stood perfectly straight. Nothing moved. Loaded and ready to pounce. She would bet Ted just wanted Hank to slip up, give a reason, for a fight to start.

Hank's face turned as red as the throw pillows on the bed. "I'm supposed to believe you?"

Ted smiled. "Most people think I'm trustworthy."

Ted was just playing with Hank now, wanting the older man to react and react poorly. She would bet her life on it. "Uh, maybe we should—"

Hank cut her off by yelling. He was pointing and gesturing and otherwise making a scene. "She's been robbed and now attacked."

Ted's eyebrow inched up. "When was she attacked?"

"Well, she could have been. Thank God she was working out instead of in her room when the robbery happened."

The room fell silent. For a second no one said a thing. Marissa had no idea what just happened, but she was grateful when Ted's shoulders relaxed.

"Yeah. Thank God." Ted folded his notebook and tucked it in his shirt pocket. "I think we're good here."

The man never ceased to surprise her. Here she thought they were getting started on Hank and Ted was done. "Really?"

Hank blew out a long breath. Something that looked like relief flashed across his face as the deep lines in his forehead eased. "Thanks for looking into this. I'll make sure Marissa stays safe until she leaves."

She rolled her eyes. "Marissa can take care of herself."

"Marissa will be fine with me," Ted said.

Hank's defensive shield went right back up again. "What are you talking about?"

Ted shot her an I'm-in-charge look, one that suggested she agree.

"Marissa is under my protection for the remainder of her stay."

Hank's cheeks grew even redder. "That's not necessary."

"I agree," Marissa mumbled.

"I think it is." Ted slipped his hand under her elbow in a gesture that caught Hank's attention and held it. "Can't have some sick wacko taking shots at tourists. It would be bad for Kauai's image. You guys know all about image."

Hank's gaze stayed on Ted's hand. "That's admirable but Marissa will be fine with me."

"Why do I feel like a stuffed doll?" Marissa asked.

Ted ignored her comment and kept holding on. "You have her cell and she has your numbers. We'll be in touch."

Hank started sputtering. "But—"

Ted maneuvered her out the door and closed it behind her before Hank could protest further. She was halfway down the hall before her brain clicked back into functioning mode. "I told you he was innocent."

Ted made a face and not a nice one. "For a smart woman you're being kind of dumb."

She thought about being insulted but went with honest instead. "Okay, maybe Hank does have a little crush."

Ted's mouth dropped open. "Little? That's like saying the ocean is kind of big."

Yeah, she wasn't sure when it happened but Hank seemed jealous. More bossy than she remembered, too.

Great. Getting him to aim his affections somewhere else would be a delicate task since there was a male ego involved, but she'd figure it out.

Ted smacked the elevator button and turned to face her. "He's guilty."

Marissa saw the accusation coming and was ready with a counterargument. "He's overzealous, maybe, but all he did was step up and offer to help. That's hardly a crime. Certainly not the act of someone who would want to hurt me."

Ted slammed his hand against the button a second time. "Are you kidding?"

"No, and don't roll your eyes at me." When the door chimed, they both stepped in the car and faced front.

Ted put his hands on the railing along the back of the elevator, sliding his arm to just behind her back. "Did you notice how Hank knew you were in the gym this morning?"

Uh, no. She'd missed all that through Ted's verbal volleys. "The fact I like to work out isn't a secret."

Ted leaned his head back against the mirrored wall and touched his shoulder to hers. "Did you tell him you were going to the gym?"

"Well, no."

"Did you work out in the gym every morning while you were here?"

This just got worse and worse. Ted's interrogation tactics didn't help, either. "I didn't have time."

"Do you see why I'm skeptical about the guy?" Ted whispered the question into her ear. Even managed to make it sound kind of sexy.

She fought back the shiver that raced from her neck to her knees. "But why? We've known each other for years."

"And now you're vying for the same job. Combine that

with the fact he made a pass and you turned him down, which bruised his ego—and stop shaking your head at me because you know I'm right."

She turned sideways to face Ted. Being this close made a serious conversation tough because all she wanted to do was kiss him, but she tried to stay focused. "Then why would Hank stay on Kauai with me?"

Ted grinned. "I haven't figured that part out yet."

"Then I guess you don't know everything."

His gaze searched her face. "I'm working on it."

"Well, I'm only here for a few more days so think fast."

"Speaking of that," he said as he brushed his fingers through her hair. "I'll be back to your room for dinner in a few hours."

The commanding tone warmed her from the inside out. "Are you asking or telling?"

His finger traced a line down her cheek to her jaw. "I thought we settled this."

"Assuming we're going to have sex is tacky. You should ask. At least try a little foreplay."

He dropped his hand. "Oh. Sorry."

She immediately missed the intimacy of his warm touch. "You're forgiven."

"What should I say?" He brushed his fingertips along her collarbone.

"I doubt this is your first date."

"Hardly, but the clock is ticking." He pointed to his watch and made a clicking sound.

"True but that doesn't mean you can·take me for granted."

"Understood." With his hands on her shoulders, his thumbs kneading her flesh with a soft touch, he leaned in and kissed the space right under her ear. "So, Ms. Brandt, would you like to have dinner with me tonight?"

She almost fell to the floor at the mix of mouth and hands. "Wh-where?"

He planted a line of kisses across her cheek, each one softer than the one before, until he reached her mouth. His lips hovered just above hers. "Wherever you want to go."

"My room is fine." In fact, she thought they should skip the food and the work and head there right now.

"Isn't that what I suggested in the first place?" His lips touched hers in a short, sweet kiss.

"Yes," she whispered on a breath.

"So, you just wanted me to work for it." No accusations. Just a statement.

If this was any indication of how he argued, she planned on fighting with him every minute until she got on that plane for home. "Exactly."

"This should be an interesting night."

"I certainly hope so."

Ted put his feet up on Kane's desk and stared at his friend. "I have a problem."

Kane glanced up and frowned. "You will if you don't move your shoes."

Ted ignored the threat and kept the sneakers right where they were. "I need off the Brandt case."

This time Kane dropped the file he was reading and gave Ted his full attention. "The lady who caused the scene at the airport?"

"The TSA guy didn't help to diffuse the situation, but yeah, that's the one."

Kane leaned back in his big chair and threaded his hands behind his head. "Isn't she off Kauai by now?"

"She tried but had a break-in at the hotel this morning and is now staying on a few extra days until she can get another flight out."

A nerve ticked in Kane's cheek. "Another problem? What the hell is going on?"

"That's what I've been trying to figure out." It wasn't exactly a lie, but it wasn't the truth either. In reality, he wanted her safe but he also just plain wanted her.

Kane sat up straight and dropped his hands. "Is something wrong with her?"

That seemed to be the first question on everyone's mind. Ted almost felt bad for wondering the same thing about Marissa at one point. "I'm thinking it's a co-worker with an agenda."

Kane picked up his stress ball and started squeezing the life out of it. "Any chance she's making it all up?"

"She's not crazy."

Kane's eyebrows shot up. "Interesting."

Aw, shit. "What?"

"You jumped to her defense kind of fast there." Kane whipped the ball at Ted who caught it with ease.

"Which is why I need off the case." Talk about the most uncomfortable conversation ever. Ted set the ball down before he ripped it to pieces. "I'm planning on sleeping with her tonight."

"Huh."

"That's your only comment?"

"You usually don't share your private life, so give me a second to catch up here."

Kane was right. Ted separated his work from his home life on purpose. Sure, everyone knew about his sister and brother. Most knew Ted returned from Southern California a decade ago to help out after his parents died in a freak house fire.

Not many knew he left a broken marriage and angry wife behind. Tessa had wanted him to leave Hawaii and get engaged, so he agreed and they got married. She wanted him to put her before his parents and siblings, so he did and regretted it every day since. She wanted him to become some corporate moneymaker and give her money and status at the country club, and he finally balked at her demands. When he insisted on coming back to Kauai to see Nicki through her senior year of high school and help

Aaron recover and stay on track once their parents were gone, Tessa told him to stay out. It was the only part of their relationship Tessa ever got right.

And Kane knew it all. Kane had lost his first wife in a drunk driving accident. He understood Ted's rage and desire for vengeance at the sudden loss of his family. Kane helped Ted funnel all of that energy into a law enforcement career. When the position for deputy opened up, Kane told Ted it was his.

"So, Ms. Brandt knows you intend to have sex with her?" Kane asked.

Ted knew his friend was trying to hide a smile. Good thing someone was enjoying the conversation because Ted sure as hell wasn't. "Yeah."

Kane laughed. "Damn, Ted. I was kidding."

"I told her. She's on board." Seemed logical and smart in Ted's mind.

Kane's grin grew to shit-eating proportions. "You just out and out informed her? Hell, man, I'm thinking you could use some work in the romance department."

Wrong theory. This was not about candlelight and roses. "It's just sex."

"Let me get this straight." Kane leaned forward on his elbows. "You want me to pull someone off another case so that you can go have sex with an alleged victim without any guilt about a work conflict."

It sounded kind of stupid when Kane said it like that, but . . . "Yeah."

Kane shook his head but his smile stayed in place. "No fucking way. And I mean that literally."

Shit, maybe this was a conflict he couldn't overcome. "You're forbidding me from having sex?"

Kane screwed up his mouth in disgust. "Hey, I'd never deprive a man of sex. I'm just not letting your love life dictate my work assignments."

"I'd do it for you."

Kane pointed at Ted. "Which is why you're not in charge around here yet."

They both laughed and the building tension disappeared. It had always been like that between them. It's part of the reason they functioned so well as a team.

"She's worried our being together will conflict with my job." Ted explained the situation without squirming in his seat, even though he wanted to. Hell, he wasn't a prude by any stretch but talking sex with his boss, friend or not, was unusual.

"Sounds as if you guys talked this through like a business proposal," Kane said, his face blank for the first time since the conversation started.

"Marissa's only here for a few days. I couldn't exactly waste time with foreplay." Ted shifted in his chair. The thing suddenly felt two sizes smaller than his ass. "Am I in trouble here?"

"No, but I think I need to get a look at any woman who would go along with this plan."

Ted wasn't about to let Kane near Marissa. That was a situation Ted couldn't control, so he ruled it out. "Stare at your own woman."

"Which is the only reason I'm not jumping all over your ass about this. Annie was a visitor on Kauai and in trouble when I met her. She'd find this whole weird idea of yours romantic."

Ted remembered the days when Annie and Kane circled each other. Everyone who saw them knew they would end up together. Everyone but Kane. Ted had watched as his usual unshakeable boss lost his fucking mind over Annie. She walked into Kane's life and never left. They'd been married for about a year and every officer in the station thanked Annie for Kane's improved mood.

Ted decided to go there even though he knew it would likely get his ass kicked. "I'm assuming you didn't wait until after Annie's case was solved to—"

Kane's smile disappeared. "No."

"Then we're good." Ted started to get up.

Kane wasn't having it. "Sit."

"But I thought—"

"This is a dangerous game you're playing."

Ted was getting a little tired of making excuses for Marissa's behavior. "I told you she's not nuts."

"That's not what I mean." Kane played with the handle to his coffee mug, shifting in his chair and generally looked as uncomfortable as Ted had ever seen him. "I know what it's like to fall for someone who lives outside of Hawaii, but you need to be smart about this."

Whoa. "You've got this all wrong."

"What, you think you're going to be able to sleep with this woman and then put her on a plane and wave good-bye?" Kane shook his head. "I don't see it happening."

"I've slept with other women and said good-bye."

"Yeah, but you've never asked my permission before."

The comment stopped whatever else Ted was going to say. He wanted to believe Marissa was like the others, but maybe she wasn't. "I'm not doing that now. I was just obeying the chain of command. Wanted to get your take on the situation."

Kane nodded. "Which you plan to ignore."

"Well, yeah."

"Because you want her no matter what I say."

Ted saw where this was going and put on the brakes. "When did you become a girl?"

Kane ignored the insult. "When is she supposed to leave?"

"The twenty-third. Christmas Eve at the latest."

Kane toasted Ted with his coffee mug. "Then we'll talk about this again on Christmas Day."

"It will be over by then. Which reminds me, I need tomorrow off."

"So now your sex life is going to mess up my schedule." Kane yelled the observation.

"That pretty much sums it up."

Kane grabbed for the assignment sheet on the corner of his desk. "You'll owe me."

"And I'm sure you'll collect."

"Damn straight."

7

After an hour with Nicki, Marissa decided she liked the other woman. They sat at the table in her suite's makeshift dining room and looked over Marissa's preliminary notes for the hotel's advertising campaign. Marissa knew she was breaking office protocol, but Nicki had asked for her thoughts and Marissa didn't see a reason to ignore the request.

Besides, Marissa was desperate to find some common ground with Nicki other than Ted. Nicki kept bringing up her brother's name. Really, it was more like twice, but since Marissa had a severe case of Ted-itis, every mention of him only made the situation worse.

"So, you're saying we should underplay the ads." Nicki shuffled the papers.

"Exactly. The concept is to telegraph the idea that the hotel is so exclusive it doesn't even need to advertise. And, honestly, photos would say more about this place than any slogan we could come up with. You show a shot of the view and then have a pithy phrase and the hotel's name. That's it."

"What phrase?"

"I'm still working on that part."

A faraway look moved in to Nicki's eyes. "The spot is amazing, isn't it? I knew the first time I came here."

Marissa jotted down some possible catchphrases that popped into her head and then crossed them off as she found fault with each. "When was that?"

"When I graduated from high school. Ted brought us here to celebrate."

Make that three Ted references this hour. "Us?"

"Me and my brother. Ted wanted it to be a special day."

Nicki's wistful tone caught Marissa's attention. So did a little problem with math. "He doesn't strike me as being that much older than you."

"He's thirty-four. I'm twenty-eight."

"And your parents . . . ?" Marissa let the question hang out there. She was digging, but she did intend to sleep with the man in about an hour, so knowing a little bit about his background wasn't completely unreasonable.

"They died."

Not at all the answer Marissa expected. She could almost feel the waves of sadness coming off Nicki. "I'm sorry."

"It was ten years ago."

Nicki didn't volunteer any more information and Marissa didn't ask. The memory struck her as too intimate. Too personal. Marissa didn't want attachments like that in Hawaii. She wanted to enjoy a few hours with Ted, spend tomorrow checking out some of those tourist sites he thought she should see, and then get on a plane the next day.

"What do you think of Ted?" Nicki asked.

Reference number four and how the hell did she answer this one? Saying he seemed nice sounded silly "He's been helpful."

And that sounded even worse.

Nicki coughed out a laugh. "That's the word you came up with?"

"Yeah, I know. It's just that—"

Nicki nodded. "It's not my business."

"I didn't mean—"

Nicki put up her hands. "Trust me, Ted will kill me if he finds out I'm talking about his love life at all."

"Does he have one?" It was one of those questions that slipped out before Marissa could come up with a better way to phrase it. Or skip asking it at all.

"Now who's fishing?"

Apparently that honesty streak ran through the entire Greene clan. Marissa decided to respond in kind. "I like him. He's attractive. He's honest and trustworthy."

"He's not a puppy."

Marissa sighed knowing she'd been bested. "The reality is that we've known each other for a short time and live six thousand miles apart."

"So?"

"Those are pretty big problems, don't you think?"

"If you let them be. Sure."

Nicki made it sound so simple.

"Life doesn't work that way. You don't go to a beautiful exotic location, find a great guy, and change your whole life." Then why did it suddenly sound not so out there, Marissa wondered.

"You sure about that?"

Marissa didn't want to be right about this, but she was. She knew from experience what happened when a woman poured her entire life into a man only to have him move on and leave her behind. "Absolutely."

"Just do me a favor." Nicki reached across the table and took Marissa's hand. "Give him a chance."

Marissa didn't pretend to misunderstand. "I have."

Neither did Nicki. "That's not what I mean."

"Then what?"

"You'll figure it out." The doorbell chimed in the middle of Nicki's comment. She glanced at her watch. "That will be Ted now."

"How do you know?"

"He's deadly punctual. One of his many talents." Nicki got up and looked through the peephole. "And he's also the only other person who knows you're here."

She opened the door. Marissa couldn't see Nicki's face, but she could see Ted's. His smile fell when he glanced at his sister.

"What the hell are you doing here?" he asked in the roughest voice Marissa had heard from him.

Nicki didn't back down. "Visiting with our guest."

Ted shot a glance in Marissa's direction then looked back at his sister. He hadn't tried to come inside. Didn't move his hand from behind his back, either.

"Are you done?" he asked.

Nicki turned and winked at Marissa. "Should I invite him in or let his head explode in the hallway?"

"Inside will be easier to explain to the other guests." Besides, Marissa had no intention of having sex with him in the hall, and that was exactly what she intended to do with him the second after Nicki left.

"Good choice." He kissed Nicki on the cheek and then brushed past her.

From the harsh lines etched on his face, Marissa wondered if he had other plans for the evening. Something that involved screaming and yelling. "Are you okay?"

"I will be." He glared at his sister. "Shouldn't you go home to your husband?"

"Your delivery lacks a certain subtlety." Nicki waved to Marissa. "Thanks for the information."

"It's the right plan," Marissa said with the utmost confidence.

"I think you may be correct." Nicki closed the door behind her with a click.

"What the hell was that about?" He stopped less than a foot in front of Marissa and his voice hadn't softened one bit.

"The hotel's ad campaign."

"That's it?" He stood stock still as if waiting for a wrong answer.

"Afraid we were talking about you?"

He dropped his keys and a small paper bag on the dining room table. "I know my sister."

"She's a big fan of yours."

"That's interesting since she calls me a jackass at least once a week."

Marissa could almost hear Nicki saying it. "I'm guessing that's normal for siblings."

He put one hand on the top of the chair and leaned. "Do you have any?"

"Just me and my mom."

"Dad?"

"Left long ago."

"Ah, I see." He brought his arm around and stuck a bouquet of purple orchids under her nose. "These are for you."

They were stunning. The sweet smell and vibrant deep color charmed her more than she thought possible. And the gesture, well, that squeezed the area around her heart until she thought it would burst from happiness.

Here she was planning a seduction and he was out there setting up a date. The man just kept right on impressing her.

"You are going to get so lucky tonight."

He didn't crack a smile. "They aren't foreplay. I wanted you to enjoy a piece of Kauai before you left."

Oh, yeah, he was definitely going to get lucky. "Is this part of your routine?"

"What do you mean?"

"You find a woman from the States—"

He tapped the tip of her nose. "I know it's only been fifty years, but Hawaii is a state now."

"Right." She felt the heated blush from the inside out. "I meant from the continental U.S."

"Sure you did."

She decided to ignore that. "Then you lure her in with that face of yours—"

"What's wrong with my face?"

"Not a damn thing. That's my point."

"Go on. This is fascinating." He picked up her hand and placed a small kiss in the center of her palm.

"You're obtuse and you boss her around. Then you swoop in and charm her with your sweetness."

He peeked up at her in mid-kiss. "I'm not sweet."

"But you are sexy." She wrapped her arms around his neck. "Very, very sexy."

"Right back at 'ya, sweetheart."

The endearment sent her heart tumbling. "So what are the plans for the evening?"

"Do you really need to ask?"

The bulge pressing against her leg told her everything she needed to know. "No."

"And for the record, I don't make it a habit of dating non locals."

The way he phrased that confused her. "Are you anti-Philadelphia?"

"Just don't see any purpose in starting something with a woman who's going to leave."

Did he not understand she was leaving? "Now I'm confused."

"I'm making an exception for you."

"Don't I feel special." But she didn't. There was something about the way he said it, almost like a warning. That struck her as odd.

"You are."

The words slipped out before Ted could stop them. Yeah, Marissa was special and, yeah, he was breaking every single one of his dating rules to be there with her. But he didn't have a single regret over the decision. That's the part he couldn't understand.

From the first time he saw her he felt a shot of something move through him. He chalked the experience up to overwhelming lust. Figured he could forget her, but then he walked into his sister's office and saw Marissa sitting there. When he should have been interviewing her he was too busy noticing her stealing a look here and there. He could see the same intensity that churned inside him bubbling inside of her, and he realized the local-tourist fantasy could become a reality.

She wanted him. He wanted her. No big deal.

But it was. That's why he stopped to get the damn flowers. Why he arranged for a surprise later this evening. He didn't want her to think she amounted to nothing more than a convenient booty call on a short layover. If he wanted sex, he could have sex. Truth was he wanted a night with *her*. Not any woman. Her.

His hands traveled down her back to settle on her sweet behind. Cupping her in his palms felt as good as he knew she would. "I'm trying to be somewhat respectful."

"Why?"

He liked the way her mind worked. "Because jumping on top of you and ripping your clothes off seems like a jackass move to me."

Her fingers speared through his hair and massaged the back of his neck. "The one thing you aren't is a jerk. Obtuse, sometimes."

"I'm still not sure what you mean by that, but I'm hoping it's not a bad thing since you keep saying it." He kissed her bare bicep. Then her shoulder through her tee.

"It's all good," she said.

Better than good.

And he couldn't wait one more second.

He took her mouth with his, letting the heat explode and wash down over them. This coming together was just as frenzied as the last. Hands moved and explored. Fingers shaped and caressed. Her soft lips moved beneath his as his tongue licked and tasted.

He kissed her with the pent-up desire that had been simmering between them all day long. Kissed her for all they would share and the wealth of experiences they wouldn't.

He was dying to get his hands on bare skin. To palm her breasts. To explore every inch of her smooth skin. To get inside her that first time.

She must have read his mind because she started pulling on his shirt. He felt a yank and then heard a pop before a button bounced against the floor.

Hell, she could rip the thing to shreds for all he cared.

"What is it about you?" she asked between kisses against his neck.

"I was wondering the same thing about you." She was all he thought about lately. But he didn't want to dwell on what could be or should be. He wanted—no needed—to be with her.

He didn't hesitate another second. His hands went to work dragging her shirt over her head and unbuttoning her jeans. They were a tangle of clothes and arms as they stripped each other down. He didn't stop until she wore only a tiny pair of lacy black panties.

His thumb traced the pattern. Heat and wetness greeted his fingertips. "You have good taste."

"Take them off," she ordered in a voice smoky enough to burn him.

His head snapped up to meet her gaze. It didn't take a genius to see the need burning in her eyes. She didn't attempt to hide her desire and he silently thanked her for not playing games and driving him insane. Not intentionally, anyway.

She reached for his belt. The metal clanked as she opened his jeans and slid the zipper down nice and slow.

"God, yes." He almost didn't recognize his own voice.

Before his pants dropped and his common sense headed for vacation, he reached into the bag and pulled out a box. In two more seconds, he had a handful of condoms spread across the dining room table.

Marissa stood up on her tiptoes and looked over his shoulder at what he was doing. "You're very prepared."

"Comes with the police training."

"I do love a man in uniform."

With his hands on her waist, he lifted her to the table. She sat on the edge, her legs open giving him more than enough space to step up and pull her close.

"Let's see what else you like." With a gentle push, he lowered her to her back.

Seeing her there, spread out and rosy pink from the fever raging inside her, his will broke. He slipped his fingers up and under the elastic to her underwear. When she lifted her hips, he skimmed the tiny scrap of material down her lean legs and threw it on the floor. The move left her bare and open to his gaze.

God, he liked her.

She inched her legs open even farther. "Here?"

"We'll start here."

Pushing her high round breasts even higher, she stretched her arms over her head. "Then?"

The sight mesmerized him. "Keep going until we run out of rooms."

With his hands on her ankles, he spread her legs even wider. This he would savor. Seeing her wet and ready for him, smelling her salty scent, made him want to make every moment last forever.

Then he tasted her. His tongue licked deep inside, flicking against her clit and sending her hips arching off the table.

"Yes," she whispered as her head fell back.

His fingers joined his mouth, opening her until her thighs trembled. His tongue circled and his mouth sucked. Every time he pulled back, her legs flexed and her insides clenched against him. But he didn't stop. He kept up the gentle massage until she grabbed on to the side of the table and her knuckles turned white. When her head started thrashing from side to side he touched the spot he knew would drive her over the edge.

As she screamed and her body bucked, he dropped his pants the rest of the way to the floor and slipped on a condom. Every cell in his body screamed for him to hurry. Marissa's panting only spurred him on.

He pushed her legs back until her thighs touched her flat stomach. Just as he finished rolling the protection on, she reached around and guided him to her opening. That was all he needed. He pressed up inside of her with one smooth push.

Being inside her felt tighter, richer, than he dreamed. Her inner muscles contracted around him, stealing what was left of his breath. Then he moved and kept moving. With her hands on his ass, he plunged in and out. The steady rhythm of their bodies and heavy breathing touched off a second wave inside of her.

The tighter her body pulled, the harder it was for him to hold back. He wanted to milk every last ounce of pleasure out of her, but his body betrayed him. The second her shoulders slammed against the hard wood on a second orgasm, the tension in his body exploded. When Marissa's mouth opened, he bent down to kiss her, drowning out her scream with one of his own.

He yelled her name over and over as the table rocked and creaked beneath them. He jerked and emptied right as her body clenched around him again. And when her body settled and her mouth opened on a sigh, he bent down to kiss her. This time with tenderness.

It took another fifteen minutes for their bodies to cool and for them to scramble to the bedroom. Two hours after that they finally fell asleep.

"What's this?" Marissa asked from the patio doorway behind him.

She wore a big white fluffy robe tied together with a thick belt. Ted hoped that was all she had on because he could be out of his boxer briefs in less than two seconds.

"This is one of the best ways to enjoy Kauai."

"With a half-naked Hawaiian native standing in front of you?"

"From your balcony." He lit the final candle on the small table and held out a chair for her.

The dinner had arrived just as he planned. It helped with the coordination to have a sister who ran the place. All he had to do was call downstairs and have the pre-selected dinner items brought to the room. Marissa napped and he set everything up. For a few minutes he even watched her sleep. So peaceful, so beautiful. Both giving and untouchable.

"Tablecloth. Nice china." She folded her fingers in his and slid into her seat, flashing him a long line of leg as she went. "I'm impressed."

He couldn't resist kissing her, so he didn't try. When he lifted his head again, they both were breathless.

"This is only the start," he whispered against her lips.

"Excellent lovemaking. Now food." She picked up a strawberry and bit into it then offered him a bite.

Hell, this woman even ate sexy.

"There's a great big beautiful ocean out there, but it's too dark to really see it," he said.

"I can hear it." As if on cue a wave crashed against the shore with a giant roar. "I could get used to this."

She could have two days of paradise then she had to give it back. She wanted to go home and he had no intention of following her. He kept repeating that mantra in his head.

"There's a bit more entertainment ahead. The kind you can only get at Christmas in Hawaii."

"Really?"

Her pink skin glowed and brown eyes brightened with each bite she took. From the way her hair slipped out of the ponytail and her robe fell open to treat him to more than a little skin, she intrigued him.

After hours of sex, he still wanted her. Didn't want to be separated from her. Couldn't stop touching her.

"There is one problem," he said.

"There is?" She asked the question over a mouthful of bread.

"We need to share a seat."

She glanced at the open chair across from her then back up at him again. "I can see that we're one short."

The fact she played along only made him more determined to hold her. He lifted her up without any trouble and then took her seat with her on his lap. With one hand, he anchored her legs across his. Even tunneled his fingers up to brush against her silky thigh.

She leaned her head against his shoulder. "We're not going to get much eating done if you keep doing that."

He was counting on that. "Soon, but you have a show to watch first."

Her eyes narrowed. "What do you have planned?"

"I can't take credit for this one." He nodded out to the water. The vast ocean remained dark except for the flashing light connected to a buoy.

"Are you seeing something out there that I don't?"

He rubbed a hand up and down her back. "Wait for it."

"I don't—"

"Be patient. It starts at nine."

She gave him a long, lingering kiss that almost made him forget about anything but dragging her back to bed. Almost.

"So, Officer Greene, what is 'it' exactly?" she asked when she finally lifted her head.

"Look."

She followed his gaze out to the water. There on boats and floating barges was a holiday light show to make even the biggest Scrooge smile. Flashing red, white, and green lights brightened up the dark sky. Outlines of blinking colors in the form of angels and snowmen danced across the water. A tree with wrapped packages underneath moved back and forth in front of the other boats.

Marissa sat up. "Look at the Santa!"

She practically vibrated with excitement. With wide eyes and clapping hands, she watched the parade of lights and listened to the faint sounds of Christmas carols playing from one of the barges.

When he hugged her close, she willingly fell back into his arms. She hummed and smiled. He had seen her in passion and in anger. Seeing her filled with happiness far surpassed anything else.

"They're beautiful." She whispered her thoughts in a reverent tone of the type usually reserved for church.

Not more beautiful than her. "They do it every year during the week for Christmas."

"How did I miss this yesterday?"

"You were probably working."

She turned around and planted a hot, wet lingering kiss right on his lips. "Thank you for sharing this with me."

"My pleasure."

"I almost hate to leave."

But she had to. "I thought you despised Kauai."

"I never said that."

"I thought I heard you scream that very thing in the airport right after we met that first time."

She had the grace to blush. "I wanted to be home for Christmas."

He tried not to tie any significance to her use of the past tense. "You will be."

And for the first time, that sounded like a terrible idea.

The next afternoon Marissa stood at a scenic overlook in the bright sunshine and stared down at the deep purple and brown bands of rock and dirt that ran to the bottom of Waimea Canyon. Ted had disappeared a few minutes ago. She used the rare minutes alone to think.

For the first time in her life she wore shorts at the end of December. But then, this was a week of firsts. First stolen purse. First run-in with a government official. First time in Kauai. First time at Waimea Canyon. First time she cared about something more than the office.

That last one scared the hell out of her.

Instead of planning her schedule and working on her presentation, all she wanted to do was spend time with Ted. The same man who promised to pack her up and put her on a plane tomorrow.

After all that time spent spinning and racing from one place to another, she enjoyed the downtime. The idea of going back to the office politics of saying what needed to be said instead of what should be said nauseated her.

"Told you this was worth it." Ted stepped up beside her

at the railing and handed her a disposable camera. "You should have photos of your time here."

The idea that photos would be all she ever had filled her with an unexpected sadness. "Can I take one of you?"

"Sure. I show up on film."

She lifted the camera and watched him through the small lens. He stood at the edge of the deep cavern wearing jeans and a navy T-shirt. The dark blue highlighted his tan skin. The trim tee showed off his broad chest and muscled arms.

She snapped three photos as he smiled and made silly poses. When he turned around to watch a helicopter fly down the canyon, she took a few more. She already knew the second set of shots would be her favorite. In those silent moments his sexy smile and relaxed stance came through. That was the real Ted. The man who loved the outdoors and smiled up at the warm sun.

Snow didn't seem so great after all.

She slipped the camera into her pocket and stepped up next to him. Without thinking about it, she mimicked the way he leaned on his elbows against the rail and stared out over the scarred earth.

"I have to leave soon," she said more to the wind whipping around them than to him.

"Of course."

Such a quick response. And not the one she expected or wanted. Part of her wanted him to beg her to stay—something. If he did, she had no idea what she would do, but his curt comeback felt like a sucker punch to the gut, harsh and unexpected.

"I don't want to go back," she said, testing him and hating herself for playing that game.

"But you will."

This time his shot ticked her off. "What does that mean?"

He tapped his fingers together. "You have a life in Philadelphia."

She had a job there. She no longer saw what she had as more than that. "True, but everything is so easy here. Well, not everything. I guess I should say everything but the robbery and airport altercation."

"It's compelling now because you're on vacation."

"I'm here for work."

"And that ended. You've hit that time most tourists get to. We call it Polynesian Paralysis. You're relaxed and enjoying the weather. You've been away from work a bit and find that not killing yourself in an office twenty-four hours a day makes you feel better. The tension has eased."

All of that sounded right. "Are those bad things?"

"They're just not real." He tucked her hair behind her ear. "Life isn't vacation. Living here means going to work, getting groceries, and dealing with all of the stuff you deal with in Philadelphia, like mortgage payments and colds. The only difference is that the weather is better and the scenery more impressive."

And him. He would make being here instead of there different. Better. "You always this anti-tourist?"

"I've seen hundreds of people come here for a week and decide this is the perfect place to live. After only a few days, they drop their old lives and move thousands of miles away."

"Isn't that the American dream? To settle by the beach and live out their lives in paradise?"

"That's exactly what it is. An unrealistic fantasy. See, they get here and figure out that Hawaii has crime and traffic. That their old problems followed them here and now they live in a place where everything is more expensive and harder to get."

If he was trying to warn her off, he was doing a good job. Nothing he said was scary or surprising. It was the fact he felt the need to make a life here sound so unappealing for her. That he painted a horrible picture so that she wouldn't want to be with him.

"You might want to turn down any offers from the tourist board. You don't exactly sell the place," she said.

"I don't want to."

His words sliced through her. Somehow, some way, she had given him the power to hurt her.

She was about to lay into him when she noticed his face. He hadn't looked at her. He delivered his keep-out speech without giving her eye contact. "Any chance this theory of yours comes from experience?"

"I told you I've seen it happen."

He was evading as sure as she was standing there. "More personal experience, I mean."

His movement slowed. "Did Nicki tell you about Tessa?"

Another woman. Marissa suddenly felt the need to kick something. Like him. "No."

"She came here and fell in love with the place, or so she said. By the time we were married, she wanted off Kauai and insisted we head for California."

"You moved away?" Marissa could not imagine him anywhere but here. He fit here. The world of Kauai made sense with him in it.

"Not that I wanted to." He looked at her for the first time. "I was trying to make her happy."

"But it didn't work."

"Nope. See, Hawaii wasn't the problem. Tessa was. She wasn't settled. She wanted her life to be something different. For me to be someone different. I couldn't give it to her and came back."

He was trying to draw a parallel. He wanted to stuff her into the role of Tessa and write her off. Make walking away easy. Expected.

Marissa wasn't buying it. She didn't know what she wanted or even if she could open up after all she saw her mother go through, but she knew if she did she wouldn't let a stupid thing like geography scare her off. Hell, even her current situation with Hank and all the bad stuff went away when she was with Ted.

"Your ex-wife sounds like an idiot to me."

The darkness cleared from his eyes as a smile slipped across his lips. "I'm not exactly perfect, either."

"Yeah, no kidding." She glanced down at her hands. "So is all of this your way of telling me Kauai isn't for me?"

"You don't want to stay."

Nothing grated on her nerves like being told what she wanted. "Really? And just what do you think I want?"

"A nap."

That came out of nowhere. "Talk about getting an answer wrong."

He slipped his arm around her shoulders. "I'm just saying I could stand to lie down for a second."

When he wiggled his eyebrows, she got the point. "Oh, that kind of nap."

"Yeah, the naked type."

The abrupt change of conversation made her feel empty, but if this was all he could give her right now she'd take it. She glanced around to make sure they weren't corrupting minors. The only other people braving the high winds were a group of Japanese tourists and a family that was more interested in all of the wild chickens running around the area.

"Then we may as well nap together."

He kissed her. "Now you're talking."

10

The rest of the day raced by followed by a night of the hottest sex Ted had ever had. Marissa's focused determination translated just fine in the bedroom. She knew what she wanted, knew how to please, knew how to enjoy.

But it was time for her to go home. He stood in the middle of the airport holding her bag, watching her talk with the check-in agent, and wondering how he was going to let her go. The past few days had been so damn good. Having someone to come home to, someone to fight with knowing the argument would challenge him and they'd end up in bed. For a man who talked big about the fantasy of Hawaii, he sure was buying into it.

The practical part of him knew that once the fun of vacation wore off, a woman like Marissa would crave the pressures and freedoms of city life. He wasn't living through that again. One divorce and thousands of dollars in legal fees were enough for a lifetime.

"Where is this woman who has you looking like a whipped dog?" Kane appeared out of nowhere, wearing his uniform and his usual stern frown, and stood beside Ted.

"I take it you're ready to make an arrest."

"The dumbass is right there on the security tape breaking into her room."

"How did he get the key?"

"Nicki is working on that. Your little sister is 'throw someone out the window' angry."

Ted smiled. He could just imagine Nicki on a rampage. She'd rip the hotel apart until she found the person who gave Hank the key to Marissa's room. And if it wasn't one of her people and Hank managed it himself, she'd likely rip his arm off and beat him to death with it.

Kane nodded in the direction of Marissa's ass. "Is that her?"

"How did you know?"

"You're staring and drooling."

He was half right. "Shut up."

Kane looked down at his feet for a few seconds. Ted knew what was coming. His friend was winding up for a lecture. Ever since he got married, Kane gave a lot of those. Something about being married and settled made him want all of his officers to know the same.

"You can always ask her to stay, you know," Kane said.

"It's Christmas. She wants to get home." It got harder and harder to parrot back the standard line.

Even as he wanted her to make the decision to stay he knew he would never believe it was a permanent one, or even the right one. People came in and out of Hawaii all of the time. People like her belonged somewhere else. And that part sucked.

Marissa turned around. While Hank walked beside her, almost on top of her, carrying on an animated conversation, Marissa just stared at Ted. The new tan gave her a fresh glow but the sparkle he had seen in her big brown eyes over the last few days had faded.

"Yeah, she looks really excited to get out of here," Kane said with a snort.

"No one ever wants to leave Hawaii. You know that."

"Isn't this the same woman who got so angry about having to stay here that she kicked a TSA agent?"

Hank and Marissa were only a few feet away now. Ted could make out Hank giving a description of some restaurant he liked. Marissa didn't say a word.

Ted tried to signal her about what was to come. Having a guy in a police uniform next to him probably gave her a clue because her eyes grew wide. And Hank kept right on talking until he almost walked into Kane.

"Marissa, this is police chief Kane Travers."

Kane nodded. "Ma'am."

"This isn't about the TSA incident again, is it?" Hank asked, his words rushing together from what Ted assumed was a bad case of nerves. "She has her new identification. We are just going to get on the plane quietly and leave. I'll take care of everything from here."

At that comment Marissa looked at Hank for the first time. Whatever she saw had her frowning.

"No." That was all Kane said, but the word was enough to get Hank squirming.

"Did you really think a hotel like that wouldn't have security cameras in the hallway? That we wouldn't wonder about the eighteen calls a day to her cell phone?" Ted asked.

Marissa edged away from Hank to stand closer to Ted. To be sure she was out of Hank's grabbing range, Ted held on to her elbow. If Hank was going to lose what was left of his mind, he wasn't going to take Marissa with him.

Hank looked around like the trapped weasel he was. Even bent his knees as if he thought he could sprint for the door. Ted guessed Hank thought he could walk right through Kane. Now that would be interesting to see.

"There is an officer behind you, so don't even think about moving." Kane pointed to the policeman standing ten feet away.

"And it's an island. You couldn't get very far anyway." Ted thought that was kind of obvious, but he decided to make the explanation anyway

Marissa was far less calm. She dropped her new purse to the ground and lunged at Hank. Got right up in his face before Ted could stop her.

"You broke into my room? You stole my purse?"

People stopped walking around them and some stopped to see what was happening. Marissa's screaming guaranteed an audience.

Ted pulled her back. "Let's not torment the lovesick crazy person."

"Is that what this was?" Marissa's cheeks turned pink as she locked her hands into fists. "I turned you down, so you decided to harass me?"

Hank sputtered before he got any words out. "Of course not!"

Ted shoved Hank back from Marissa another foot. "I think it had more to do with him wanting to be your savior. *He* would be the one to get you on that plane when your license was lost. He would keep you safe. He wanted to make it so that you needed him. When you left with me and he couldn't get to you, he went nuts. All those calls harassing Nicki for information. Pretty unhealthy shit."

Ted had worked all that out. It was the only answer that made sense. Hank didn't seem to want to hurt her or even scare her. Not yet. But that's how obsession of this sort started. It was when Marissa turned him down again that she would have been in danger. Ted vowed not to let that happen and turned up the heat to settle the case today, before she got the plane and left with Hank.

"That's sick." The sour look on Marissa's face said it all. The idea of being stalked by Hank had been a blow. She wanted to believe a stranger and a case of bad luck were to blame, not someone she knew and trusted.

"It sure isn't a good way to meet women," Kane said.

"Don't listen to them. Don't you see, they can't solve your case so they're blaming it on me."

Hank just wouldn't give up, so Ted spelled it out for him. "You're on the videotape. You knew Marissa would be out. You had access to her purse. I bet when we search your bag, we'll find some of her personal items."

Marissa looked as if she'd been hit with a pan. "What kind of . . ."

Ted guessed underwear and other personal things Marissa had forgotten about. "You don't want to know."

Her eyes widened as she figured it out. "That's disgusting."

Hank lifted his chin and tried to step around Kane. "I'm leaving."

Kane caught him with one hand. Wrenching Hank's arm back stopped him. Before Hank could yell, Kane put the cuffs on him. "You're under arrest."

Hank's eyes grew wild with fear. "Marissa, don't let them do this!"

Ted pulled her back a few more feet. "You don't need to see this."

But everyone could see it and hear it. Hank was yelling up a storm. Passengers loading and unloading stopped to look at him. Others walked in wide circles around him.

"I don't understand why he would do this. We've known each other for years," she said, the mix of disgust and shock evident in her voice.

"And he's probably been harboring feelings for you for

all that time. Throw in a trip to sexy Kauai and his fantasies spun out of control." The fact this guy got close enough to touch her, to almost hurt her, made Ted shake with fury.

When Kane reported back this morning about the security tapes, Ted went into a rage. He needed a new desk chair as a result. He also took himself right off the case. Kane insisted on making the arrest saying he feared Ted would kill Hank and cause a whole lot of paperwork on Christmas.

Kane handed off a screaming Hank to one officer and ordered another to clear away the crowd. By the time he joined Ted, Kane's mouth had flattened into a thin line.

"You okay?" he asked Marissa.

"Stunned." She shook her head. "I just don't get how I didn't see it."

Ted rubbed his hand up and down her arm. She shook from head to foot, but he doubted she even realized it.

"That's not unusual," Kane said. "This kind of thing isn't always rational on the part of the obsessed person. In his mind the two of you were communicating and he was sending out signals that you understood. In reality, you just saw him as you always saw him."

"It's part of the sickness," Ted explained.

"It's like a nightmare."

"Sorry we had to make the arrest in public and that I couldn't warn you." That was the part that got to Ted. He had wanted to bundle her up and keep her far away from the airport as this unfolded. "We'd been watching Hank, waiting to see if he would do anything else."

"You have?"

"And in addition to the manic calls the fingerprints from your room came back. His were all over the place," Kane said.

"I wondered why I couldn't find my phone."

"I took it while you were in the shower. Saw the missed calls." Ted refused to apologize for breaking off Hank's communication with her.

Marissa's hand shook as she brushed her hair back off her shoulder. "To be fair, Hank had been in the room for work while I was there."

The skin on Kane's cheeks pulled tight. "These were in places I don't think you would have let him go."

"Like?"

Kane glanced at Ted who nodded for him to continue. "The bed. The drawers where you kept your clothes."

All that shaking turned into screaming anger. "Bring him back here so I can kick him."

Kane smiled for the first time. "From what I've heard, you've done enough kicking in this airport."

A blush stained her cheeks. "Sorry about that and for all the trouble."

"Ted explained. It's fine." Kane glanced at his watch. "Don't you have a plane to catch?"

Subtle as ever. Ted was surprised Kane didn't go the extra step and ask Marissa to stay.

"Thanks for your help." Ted said the words but shot Kane a "get the hell out of here" look.

Kane took the hint. "I'll let the two of you work this out."

"He's your boss?" she asked the minute Kane walked away.

Kane was much more than that, but Ted thought that description was good enough for now. He had other things to discuss. "Yeah."

She looked at the clock on the wall. Her feet. Everything but him. "I guess I should get to the gate."

"You should stay."

Her head snapped up. "What?"

"Until your scheduled flight," he rushed to say. "You've

had a tough few minutes. There's no need to wait around and see if you can fly standby on a packed flight."

"I don't have anywhere to stay. I gave up my room."

He had ordered Nicki to keep the suite open. "Your room is still there."

"Really?"

"You can catch the early evening flight on Christmas Eve and still be home by Christmas morning."

Her gaze studied his, but her expression was blank. He couldn't read her at all. He tried to sweeten the deal. "The snow will still be there. Besides, I have some more things to show you on Kauai."

This was as close as he would ever get to begging her to stay. He made the suggestion, made it all possible, and now it was up to her.

"You're willing to play tour guide?" she asked.

"Sure, and some of those sights may even be outside the hotel room."

Her mouth broke into a huge grin. "Now you've sold me."

"I knew I should have led with the indoor activities."

11

Christmas Eve. Marissa tried to remember the last time she spent a holiday rolled up in bed with a handsome hottie from the tropics.

Yep. Never.

She folded the sheets down and brushed her fingernails across his bare chest. When she settled her head on his shoulder, his body shifted but his eyes remained closed. Poor baby. Spending hours in bed had worn him out.

In a way she was happy for the quiet. She could watch him sleep. Even relaxed he still looked potent. The dark hair and sleek tanned chest highlighted his sexiness. He could wield a gun and make her laugh then fill her with a driving need like she had never known before. He made her crave balance, to find something outside of the office that would just be for her.

She had called her mom and told her about the delay. Marissa blamed it on the flights. She expected a guilt trip in return. Instead, her mom wished her well and told her to call once she knew her plans. Seemed everyone expected Marissa to cancel holiday plans in favor of work.

Thinking back, she realized she had done just that many times. She didn't want to be that person anymore. Ted had helped her see that.

It was simple. She was falling for him.

She respected him, liked him, and had started to love him. It wasn't all that hard to do. Under the gruffness and bossiness he was good and sweet, romantic and solid. He was everything her father wasn't. Ted wouldn't dump his wife for a younger, prettier model. Ted wouldn't leave his wife and child penniless while he established a new family. Ted wouldn't run when times got hard.

But Ted wouldn't love her back. He saw her as transient. As the Marissa she was just a few days ago, before Kauai changed her. Before she realized the feeling of Christmas didn't have anything to do with a place or snow.

"I can hear you thinking," he mumbled without opening his eyes.

Marissa dragged her foot up his calf. "I thought you were sleeping."

"I was doing some thinking of my own."

Her heart jumped. "About?"

"Food."

So much for romance. "Did you work up an appetite?"

His eye popped open. "I could eat for three days."

"Good thing Christmas is tomorrow."

"Good thing someone other than me does the cooking." He propped his head up on his arm.

"Nicki?"

"Yeah. She puts out a spread. Aaron and I come over."

"Aaron?"

"My brother."

Marissa realized she knew so little about the man who had come to mean so much. Maybe Ted was right and this was all illusory and short term. Maybe she would go back home and go fall right into her routine, forgetting everything she had learned and had come to want.

Both of his eyes were open now and his gaze centered on her. "What's wrong?"

"Nothing."

He lifted up on one elbow. "Something."

Something like how she wanted him to ask her to stay. She picked at the bedspread. "I'm going to miss Kauai."

He hesitated, not rushing to fill the silence. When he finally spoke, he said exactly the wrong thing. "It's always here. You can come back and visit."

His solution deflated her. It amounted to a "come back and we'll sleep together now and then" proposition. No thanks. "Will it ever be as special as this first time?"

"Probably not."

He continued to hold her at a distance. He would shower her with romance and help her discover every lovely spot on the island, but he wouldn't let her inside him. Not in any real way that would break through the protective shell he built up around him after his divorce.

"I'm not Tessa." Marissa blurted out exactly what she had been thinking.

He didn't even flinch. "I didn't say you were."

She sat up, dragging the sheet along with her and holding it against her breasts. "I wouldn't drag you away from Kauai."

"I wouldn't let you."

He refused to bend even a little. He was forcing her to do all of the hard work, to put her heart out there without any promise that he would take care of it or return her feelings.

So, she asked the one question where she dreaded the answer. "Do you want me to leave?"

"Your vacation is over."

The sentence tore into her with the strength of a knife.

She never knew words could hurt that much. "There are other flights. I could leave later."

Or never. The unspoken words hung in the air. She knew he understood what she was saying. She could see it in the stark way his eyes flattened.

"You love Philadelphia. You love your job."

"Those aren't answers." In a way they were, but she wasn't ready to give up on him yet.

"Can you really see yourself here, Marissa? No snow. No cold Christmas night."

No co-workers stalking her, less pressure, and a man who made her insides burst with happiness. Lately, a life in Kauai with him was the only future she could see. The only one she wanted.

"You really think I'll miss the weather?" she asked.

He sat up and leaned against the headboard. His broad shoulders slumped. "I think you'll miss everything about your life there. Eventually."

"What about us?"

"We're inside the fantasy." He rolled his head against the wall. "Don't you see that this is part of the web Kauai spins? Add in Christmas and the decorations and all of the feelings that come with the holiday and you get a false picture."

The more he spoke, the more he seemed to buy into it. "Do you really believe that crap?"

"Yes."

She waited for him to say something else. Hoped he would. When he remained quiet, she threw off the sheet and stood up, naked and proud. Let him see what he was giving up.

"Then I guess we're done here." Everything inside her wanted him to beg her to stay.

He barely looked at her. "Don't do this."

"Leave? I thought that's what you wanted."

"I didn't say that."

Anger rose up in her belly. She went from being hurt and rejected to being pissed off that he could not meet her partway. "Then what did you say, Ted?"

He shook his head in a move so sad and lonely that it broke her heart. "I can't ask you to stay. I won't ask you to give up your life. That happened to me and it was a disaster."

"I'm not Tessa." Marissa practically screamed the words.

"You said that already."

"I thought if I repeated it, you might believe it."

He sighed. "I don't know what you want me to say."

"Nothing." Marissa grabbed the blanket off the bed and wrapped it around her.

"You need your old life."

She didn't know which one of them he was trying to convince, but she needed him to get out before she fell to the floor in a pile. "Merry Christmas, Ted. You know the way out."

Two hours later she had packed and checked out. Waiting for the taxi almost killed her. She stood there outside the lobby with happy families chattering about Christmas and everything they planned to do in Kauai. She saw the tree, the water. If the cab line didn't move any faster, she was going to lose it right there.

"Marissa."

Nicki. The one person she didn't want to see, so she clipped that string too. "Good-bye."

Nicki touched her hand against Marissa's elbow in a move so reminiscent of Ted that the tears threatened to fall. Marissa pushed them back by sheer will.

"Are you really leaving?" Nicki asked.

"It's time."

"Can I talk to you for a second?" Nicki didn't wait for

an answer. She pulled Marissa out of line and into a private corner of the lobby.

"I need—"

"I have a proposition for you," Nicki said before Marissa could get away.

Story of her life. The wrong Greene was making her an offer. "I need to go."

"Work for me."

Not at all what Marissa expected to hear. "What?"

"Be my in-house marketing and public relations person." Nicki focused her attention on Marissa with the force of a laser beam. "I don't need a firm. I need a person who loves Kauai and this hotel and understands what it can be."

"You think that's me?"

Nicki ticked off her reasons. "Your designs. The way your face lights up when you walk in the lobby. Yeah, it's you."

Marissa did love Kauai but that was because of Ted, not some building. "I have a job and it's six thousand miles away."

"I need you here."

Something in Nicki's tone struck Marissa as being off. The usual smooth-talking woman sounded frantic. Her green eyes showed worry and something that looked a little like fear.

"The hotel needs you," Nicki said. "Don't go."

Marissa wished for the first time that she had a sibling. That someone loved her enough to step up like Nicki was doing for Ted. "Are you offering me a job to keep me near Ted? If so, you're wasting your time. He is more than ready for me to leave."

Nicki grabbed on to Marissa's hands, as if willing her to understand. "I'm offering you a job because you're damn good. But, yes, I want you to stay because I love Ted and I know he loves you."

Marissa's heart danced at the thought, but she knew the truth. "You are way off."

"Am I? You know how many days he's taken off in the last three years? Exactly three. You know how many he took off to be with you, the same number. I watched him leave this hotel earlier, Marissa. I haven't seen that brokenhearted look on his face since we lost our parents."

Marissa couldn't believe. She couldn't buy into this after sitting on that bed and watching Ted tell her in a deadpan voice that she needed something else. "He told me to go."

"He doesn't know how to ask you to stay. He's not the guy who asks anyone for anything. He gave up his life to raise Aaron. He walked out on a marriage long after he should have gone because he was desperate to save it. He mourned his parents' death in silence because he thought he had to be strong."

Marissa's heart broke for him. Broke for them. "I can't do it alone, Nicki."

"I am taking away any reason you have to leave. You have a job here. I can give you a place to stay. All I'm asking is that you stay and fight for him."

"I have a life in Philadelphia." One she no longer wanted and dreaded returning to.

"You could have a *future* here."

Marissa had to get out of there before Nicki's pleading wore her down. She wrapped her arms around Nicki in a big hug and whispered into her ear. "Goodbye."

It was not until Marissa was halfway over the Pacific Ocean that her crying stopped. The poor woman sitting next to her looked ready to bolt for the nearest emergency exit. But when Marissa's tears turned to anger, it festered.

Ted thought he knew everything, but he didn't have a clue what she needed.

The idiot.

Here she was afraid she'd end up like her mother because she depended on a man, yet she was depending on a man to make the move and ask her to stay. She had taken charge her entire life except on the most important decision ever.

She didn't need him to ask. She would ask. She'd be stronger and the one in control.

He wanted her in Kauai. She knew that as sure as she knew anything. He was obtuse and dumb as shit because he loved her and couldn't say it. And as soon as she got off the plane and found another one heading back to Kauai, she'd walk right up to him and tell him what he needed. Her.

12

"Tell me again why you're in the office on Christmas Day." Kane sat down on the edge of Ted's desk as he asked the question.

The answer was simple. Because the only person Ted wanted to be with was on a plane taking her thousands of miles away from him. And because he was dumb enough to let her go. He knew she was fishing back in the hotel room when she asked all of those questions. She wanted him to beg her to stay. Every part of him wanted to give in and do it, but he couldn't force the words out. He couldn't stop worrying about what would happen if he did and then it all went to shit.

Instead of telling Kane the truth, Ted went with the short answer. "I said I'd work."

"You're on call. You don't have to be here."

Ted couldn't stand to be anywhere else. Marissa had never even been in his house and still he couldn't go there for fear he would feel her. Without her everything struck him as sterile and dark. "Why are you here?"

"Because I'm in charge."

Ted propped his feet up on his desk. "Well, you can go home. I'll handle whatever happens."

"Annie would kill me."

"She doesn't want to be with you on the holiday?"

"She doesn't want anyone else having to work. She plans to come in a little later to keep me company."

Now that was just about the last thing Ted wanted to see. Happy couples needed to stay out of his sight for a few days. Or forever. As it was, he had to refrain from knocking down the Christmas tree when he walked into the office.

Hell, how could he feel this way after only a few days? His chest actually ached at the thought of not seeing Marissa again. The scent of her shampoo still lingered in his head and refused to get out. The touch of her skin, their lovemaking . . . every memory battered him.

"This wouldn't have anything to do with a certain hot brunette, would it?" Kane asked.

"She's gone."

Kane frowned. "Why the hell did you let her go?"

The same question Ted kept asking himself. He could have given her the words she wanted and put the burden on her to make the decision. Instead, he made it for her. For them. "She doesn't belong here."

"You get to decide that?"

"She was here for a few days, not forever."

"Like Annie."

Ted's head began to spin. Between the drumming up there and the pain slicing through him from neck to gut, he didn't know how much more he could take. "That's different."

"How?"

Ted had no fucking idea, but it was. It had to be or he

was a bigger jackass than he thought he was for letting his woman walk out.

The harsh lines around Kane's eyes eased. "Look, Ted. I've known you for a long time."

"You're not going to give me love-life advice, are you?"

"I'm telling you to take a few days off, get on a plane, and fly to wherever she lives to work this out."

"I kicked her out." It actually hurt to say the words. "I'm the one who did the walking, but I basically kicked her out."

"Then you might want to apologize once you get to her."

Kane was a practical man with practical advice. But nothing about this felt that neat and tidy. Ted had let nights of great sex turn into so much more. He loved Marissa. Tear-your-heart-out loved her.

Ted asked the one question that kept playing in his head. "What if she tries it here and then wants to leave?"

Kane groaned. "Damn it, Ted. What if she wants to stay? Have you thought about that?"

Could it really be that easy? Could everything he ever wanted come in a package from Philadelphia? She'd been gone for less than twenty-four hours and every single minute of that time sucked. He couldn't eat or celebrate the holiday. His favorite time of year had all but passed and all he wanted to do was call back the last few days and relive them.

When Ted lifted his head again, Kane hadn't moved. He was ready with a questiion. "You know you love her, right?"

Why fight it? "Yes."

"Then don't be an—"

The outer reception office went from quiet to pandemonium. Ted heard loud voices but couldn't make out the problem.

"What the hell is going on? It's too early for the New Year's drunk and crazy patrol to start," Kane said.

Ted dropped his feet to the floor. "I'll go check."

"No. You stay here and get your head out of your ass." Kane glanced toward the outer office. "If you hear me yell, come running."

Two seconds after Kane walked into the reception hall everything quieted down. No surprise there. The man had a natural ability to calm even the wildest person.

Ted was just grateful Kane hadn't needed backup because he was too busy playing the game of should-I-or-shouldn't-I with the telephone. Ted stared at it, even thought about picking it up and trying to call an airline.

Just then the door to the back offices burst open. Kane came through with a huge smile on his face and Marissa by his side. Ted blinked three times to convince himself it wasn't a dream come to life.

He stood up nice and slow, careful not to scare the vision away. "Marissa? What are you doing here?"

"You have the gall to tell me that you think you know what I need?" She dumped her purse on the nearest desk. "You think you really know what I need? Right now I need a shovel so I can hit you with it."

The two other officers in the large room dropped their phones and started watching Marissa. Kane just grinned like a stupid fool. "Look who I found out front. She came in and demanded to know where you live."

"Why?" Ted asked.

"Why are you working on Christmas Day?" she shot back.

"Nothing else to do."

"How about coming to the airport to stop me from getting on a plane? Didn't that plan ever occur to you?"

"That was yesterday."

"Did you ever even think about trying to stop me?" She marched right up and stopped in front of him. "I'm not Tessa."

"You told me that already."

"Do you believe me?"

He did. Tessa would not make this scene. She would never have made a public declaration or fought for him like this. Only Marissa would fight for him, and Ted loved it. Loved her. "You're nothing alike."

"Then why do you keep damning me with her actions?"

He did that. He cursed them both by assuming everyone was like Tessa. That a strong, smart woman couldn't know what she wanted or want to find a life with him.

"It's not that simple," he said because he didn't know what else to say.

"Your sister thinks you can't ask for what you want."

"You talked with Nicki?" The idea of the women in his life meeting and talking about him made him sweat.

"Is she right?"

"I'd answer but I think you have a response in mind."

Marissa did. She knew what she needed Ted to say. What she wanted him to say. What he better say or she was dragging him outside and throwing him into traffic.

"What do you want, Ted?"

He didn't hesitate this time. "You."

That was almost too easy. Maybe she lost her hearing with all that flying back and forth between Kauai and Los Angeles. "What?"

He closed the gap between them with one step. "I want you here with me."

She stuttered a few times before getting the words out. "What changed your mind?"

Ted glanced over her head at Kane before looking at her again. "Nothing. I wanted you from the minute I saw you. Loved you about ten seconds after that. Was desperate for you to stay but afraid to ask you to do it."

Definitely had a jet lag problem. "I just flew back-to-back standby flights in middle seats, so let me make sure I understand you."

"Middle seats? That's love," Kane mumbled.

She was too focused on the brightness shining from Ted's green eyes to hear his friend. "Did you just say—"

Ted brushed his hands up her arms and tugged her close. "I love you, Marissa Brandt."

She heard the words. Could see the truth right there on his face. Happiness flowed out of him. "But . . ."

He slipped his arms around her. "I was an idiot to let you go."

"True."

He kissed her. Not a peck. Not deep. Just a touch of his lips against hers in a way that made a silent promise of forever.

"I won't make that mistake again. I will never let you walk out on me or push you away." He leaned his forehead against hers. "Ever."

"You said you love me." The words kept scrambling in her brain. "You actually said the words." The realization made her want to raise her fists toward the sky and shout in victory.

"And I'm assuming from all that nonstop flying that I might not be alone in that feeling."

"Don't be obtuse." She punched his shoulder. "Of course I love you. Why else would I make an idiot out of myself not once but twice to try to tell you?"

"Well, I'm listening now."

He was. Every part of him was open and happy. From

his smile to the way his hands held on to her as if they'd never let go. She said the words. Felt them with every inch of her body. "I love you."

He closed his eyes for a second. When he opened them again she saw wetness in the corners. Somehow, some way, she had brought this strong, silly, loving man to his knees.

And to his senses.

"I take it this means you're not going to send me away," she said.

"I'm going to drag you back to my house and"—he stopped and looked around at his audience—"nap."

The love inside of her grew tenfold. She didn't think it was possible to love him more than she did that moment but she suspected she would. Time would give her that. Give it to them. "I would love a nap."

The officers cheered and Kane clapped. Ted and Marissa took it all in, laughing both at their private joke and from the joy of the moment.

"Some Christmas wishes do come true," he whispered as he buried his face in her neck.

She sifted her fingers through his soft hair. "It will be hard to top this next Christmas, but I'm sure we'll think of something."

He squeezed her even tighter. "Forever."

"Yeah, forever."

Who wants to be good?
THE NAUGHTY LIST is much more fun!
Try this sexy anthology from Donna Kauffman,
Cynthia Eden, and Susan Fox, in stores now.
Turn the page for a sneak peek at Cynthia's story,
"All I Want for Christmas."

The strains of Elvis's Blue Christmas drifted in the air as Christie Tate tried really, *really* hard to disappear inside the women's restroom.

"Did you hear?" The more-than-slightly catty female voice asked from a few feet away.

Christie hunched her shoulders and stared at her heels.

"Charles Donnelley is already seeing Vicki from accounting. I mean . . . what's it been? A week? Two? He and Christie were—"

"I think he was seeing Vicki on the side," another female voice chimed in, oozing sympathy.

Fake sympathy.

Christie stared at the gleaming black door, aware of the heat building in her cheeks. Was this what she'd become? A thirty-year-old woman hiding in a bathroom stall?

She knew those voices. Marsha Chad, a marketing assistant, was the one with the fake sympathy. And the other one—

"I heard Charles thought Christie was just . . . boring," said Lydia Clyde. "I mean the woman's a genius, but when it comes to men and sex, she's . . ."

Enough. Christie's spine shot up at the same instant her hand slammed into the bathroom door. The door flew forward and she caught the sound of two feminine gasps.

Her eyes narrowed as she took in the two women. "Lydia. Marsha." So what if her cheeks were flaming? She wasn't going to hide in the bathroom another second.

Not thirteen anymore. Not the nerdy girl.

"Christie." Lydia's blue eyes bulged. "I didn't realize you were—"

Christie jerked the faucet on and washed her hands. "For the record . . ." she lifted her head and met her own gaze in the mirror. *Backbone, girl, backbone.* How many times had she heard her mother say that over the year? *Don't ever let them see you break.* "Sex with me is never boring."

She saw their jaws drop. Good. Great. She kept her chin up, kept her back straight, and with really fast steps, she was able to escape that hell-hole.

And to trade it for another one.

Christie burst from the women's restroom and walked straight into the full-on madness that was the Tate Toy Company's annual Christmas party. Bright lights. Elaborate bows. Mechanical toys—trains and soldiers—that marched across the floor. And Christmas trees. So many giant, colorful Christmas trees. Normally, she would have loved this site but right then—*just want to escape.*

She sucked in a sharp breath and tasted pine. Christie glanced to her left and found her ex, Charles, arguing with Vicki under a giant piece of mistletoe. The pretty redhead's hair tumbled down her back as she shook her head at Charles, then she jabbed a finger into his chest. Trouble in paradise?

I think he was seeing Vicki on the side.

Jerk.

A waiter sidled by her. She grabbed a glass of champagne and drained it in one gulp. Elvis kept singing.

Can't get much bluer than this, buddy.

She marched forward, putting more needed distance between her and Charles. *Can't attack.* Because, no, that wouldn't be classy. A lady couldn't go up and jump on her ex's back as she started to pound the crap out of him. A good girl wouldn't do that. She'd been raised to be a *good girl.* Good girls became ladies, right?

But she was damn tired of being good. Damn tired of being gossiped about. Damn tired of it all right then.

Even tired of Elvis. And she loved the king.

Christie marched through the crowd, only stopping to pick up a few more glasses of champagne. Oh, but that bubbly went down nice and fast. Some folks tried to talk to her, but if they didn't have a tray of champagne flutes near them, she kept going.

Kept going until . . .

Until she reached the giant black chair that waited in the middle of the room. Santa's chair.

Presents wrapped in red and green paper surrounded the massive chair. Small surprise gifts for all the staff at Tate Toys. Santa would be coming soon. He'd be there to hear all their Christmas wishes. There to make those wishes come true.

Christie's fingers tightened on the champagne flute.

Then she caught a glimpse of Santa, and she spilled the rest of her champagne over the front of her red reindeer shirt.

Wow.

Santa was a stud.

She swallowed as she got a good look at the jolly old elf. Santa stood just inside the doorway of Tate Toys, a thick sack flung over his left shoulder—and what a nice

shoulder it was. Actually, Santa had *two* nice shoulders.
Nice, wide, broad shoulders that stretched the red coat he
wore.

Her gaze tracked slowly down his body. No shaking
like a bowl-full-of-jelly there. Oh, no, that man—*Santa*—
was built. Tall, strong. His muscled thighs stretched the
red pants and his powerful legs disappeared into a pair of
knee-high black boots.

Santa stalked toward her. A fluffy white—and fake—
beard covered his face and a bright red hat hid his hair.
All she could see were sparkling green eyes and high,
tanned cheekbones.

"Have you been a good girl?"